DUST EATERS NORTH

By

Ronan Cray

ABRASAX

Copyright © 2016 by Ronan Cray
Published by Abrasax Press
Edited by David Jones
Cover Art by S. B. Scott
First Edition

Printed in the United States of America

ISBN-13: 978-0-9912555-3-5

To
My father for his inspiration
My wife for her patience
My son for his growth
My family for their encouragement
Mrs. Mooney for the extra credit
And you, dear reader,
These pages are affectionately inscribed.

Dear Reader,

Upon proofing an early copy of Dust Eaters, an intelligent friend asked me, "Is this one of those 'how much ammo do you have' books? If I read the whole thing and it's just a first person shooter, I'll be angry."

Somehow, he uncovered my shallow ploy to profit from a fad. At the time I thought, "I'll jump on the zombie bandwagon, get rich, and use that money to write literary fiction no one will read."

A year passed. Then another. I couldn't finish. The characters wanted to tell their own stories, but I wasn't listening.

I needed to see it for myself: the journey, the battlegrounds, the resting places. Two days on a train took me north to Churchill in the dark of winter. I lived the terrible circumstances I put them through. I walked that frigid emptiness. I met the warm people who, in this history, disappear.

I understood.

This is a story of sadness, of all we have to lose, of a world where even victory is defeat.

Stop reading now. This is the first book of the series. Why read on, knowing this isn't the end of the misery? Why heal only to have those wounds, like eyes once closed, re-open?

Ronan Cray
New York City
October 4, 2016

Even the finest arms are an instrument of evil,
A spread of plague,
And the way for a vital man to go is not the way of a soldier.
But in time of war men civilized in peace
Turn from their higher to their lower nature.
Arms are an instrument of evil,
No measure for thoughtful men
Until there fail all other choice
But sad acceptance of it.
Triumph is not beautiful.
He who thinks triumph beautiful
Is one with a will to kill,
And one with a will to kill
Shall never prevail upon the world.
It is a good sign when man's higher nature comes forward,
A bad sign when his lower nature comes forward,
The death of a multitude is cause for mourning:
Conduct your triumph as a funeral.

The Tao Te Ching
by Lao Tzu
Circa 560 B.C.

夫兵者，不祥之器，
物或惡之，故有道者不處。
君子居則貴左，用兵則貴右。
兵者不祥之器，非君子之器，
不得已而用之，恬淡為上。
勝而不美，而美之者，是樂殺人。
夫樂殺人者，則不可得志於天下矣。
吉事尚左，凶事尚右。
偏將軍居左，上將軍居右，言以喪禮處之。
殺人之眾，以悲哀泣之，戰勝以喪禮處之。

老子《道德經》

PROLOGUE

We are driven by what we leave behind.
A word unsaid.
An opportunity lost.
A love left alone.
In the end, we finish nothing.
If death has a synonym, that word is 'abandon'.

Tara should have been cold, but body and mind did not walk together. She pushed through waist deep snow in clothes poorly chosen in haste. Her boots siphoned melting granules into her socks. Her jeans clung to her legs, dark from the thigh down. They chafed and pulled with each stubborn step. A chunky backpack of canned food and bottled water hung in the small of her back. Both hands, ungloved, curled around her one good idea, a Savage .308 rifle.

The Manitoba woods kept the wind at bay, but the temperature on this morning dipped below twenty, the "minus" assumed. Though her body signaled a warning to take shelter, her mind was not there to receive it.

Her mind lagged behind.

Follow the trough of powder in her wake, back through the unfarmed copse of pine and stunted paper birch, past the humanoid creatures who hunted her scent, over the farmland and buried roads, into the town of Ochre River, across more than one body cradling a bullet from her gun, into the elementary school functioning as a clinic, past a charcoal smear that may have been human once, until you reach the closed door of a classroom turned triage center. There you'd find it, under buntings of stick figure drawings and colored construction paper, above a floor muddy with blood.

But this is not a story about the past. The past is dead. This is a story of that grey period after the past dies, before the future rises from its ashes. This is a wake.

Tara wasn't cold. She was burning up.

She heard a purr, like a panther in the dark. She kneeled in the snow, bringing the Savage to her shoulder. There, behind a tree not thirty meters distant. He must have come upon her trail at an angle.

"Go away," she said, not loud enough for him to hear. She squinted her eyes, emotions conflicted, fear and sadness. She didn't want to shoot him. She never wanted to shoot anyone. She just wanted it to stop. "Don't follow me! Please!"

What could she do? Beg? Cry? No survival tactic she ever learned would stop him. Could she appease him? Tell him she would do better? Ask for forgiveness? Offer her tender affection? What did he need?

This man, this... thing... would never apologize later, never promise not to hunt her, never tell her,

"This is the last time. I'll get into a program. I'll get help."

This thing in front of her, it was pure aggression. She knew that face, knew it since she was a little girl. That face wanted to hurt her, to take from her. It wanted what *it* wanted. She had no value beyond its needs. She felt small and hollow. It was time to run and hide, find a secret place to wait, until he slept it off, until the mood passed.

There was no shelter. There was not sleep. It would not pass.

She placed her finger on the trigger. She knew, though, to hesitate. If she dropped this one, the sound might draw more.

The metal pipe she had found would be quieter, but she didn't have the strength to wield it anymore. It had accumulated gore, sucked it into that iron marrow, condensed it like a dwarf star, until the weight of the carnage made it impossible to lift one more time.

Darkness in March came early, less than an hour away. Bare trees cast long shadows on the snow, shadows that hid her pursuers.

Thinking too long, her finger froze to the bare metal trigger. The rest of her ungloved hand went numb. Her back ached. Her temples pounded. Her brow burned with fever. Despite the danger, her head nodded. She brought it up, but it dipped again. Her eyelids sank.

She forced them open, glared down the scope, sought out the fiend through that bright tunnel. The black creature stood out against the snow, six feet tall, face blackened by frostbite, jacket torn and dirty, hair frozen in place. Thirty steps separated them, but she could smell it, like a freezer three weeks after a power outage.

Shoot or fight.

She had trusted her husband to protect her. *Don't worry. You'll never be alone*, he had told her. All those nights in preparation, the supplies and food and chopped firewood. The reloading equipment in the basement. The arguments and assurances. The ego and the pride. He was ready, he had said.

He wasn't ready.

Even if she made every shot count, did she have enough cartridges? How many followed her from the school? The whole damn town?

Her hands shook with adrenaline and fear. Her breath came ragged, accompanied by a high-pitched wheezing.

Through the scope, the crosshairs shivered. Frosted hair dangling from the skull made it hard to spot the center. She decided against shooting.

She would brain it instead.

It closed the gap, slow and deliberate, time on its side.

She tried to pull her finger off the trigger. The skin stuck, like glue. She hesitated, fearing it would tear. She couldn't afford any wounds. She tried to spit on it to loosen it. Dehydrated, her mouth was dry. Blowing didn't help.

Ten steps. Tara didn't have a choice. The beast's forehead went blurry in the scope.

She fired.

The rifle crack echoed through the forest like a slow avalanche. Black and tan matter dotted the ice encrusted snow.

She grimaced, teeth bared. Sobbed once. Tears squeezed from her eyes. She wiped one away and rubbed it on the trigger.

Her finger slid free.

She willed her legs to move, to run, but couldn't. She hunched in the snow, leaning on the rifle, shivering, wet, waiting. *Get up. Get up!*

A horrid stench betrayed the presence of more. Somewhere upwind they heard the call of the rifle, a Pavlovian bell, and ambled toward the feast.

She forced herself to stand.

If I reach the cabin, I'll warm up by the fire.

She took a step, fell up to her waist in a buried bush.

If I reach the cabin, I'll put on a pot of water, warm my hands around the cup, drink it down and have another.

She stumbled, resting on the rifle like a cane. She heard birds flutter out of a ditch at the edge of the woods. They were closer than she thought.

If I reach the cabin, I'll spend all night learning how to reload cartridges in the basement.

Over her shoulder, she watched the first one enter the woods. A man, middle aged, wearing a bright red lumberjack shirt, buttons missing, his chest ragged with tattered skin. His eyes, wide open, whites gleaming in the shadows, came to rest on her. He changed direction, a beeline toward her position. He stood between her and the cabin.

If I reach the cabin, I'll barricade the doors and shutters. I'll get in a few hours of sleep in the bed that... She fought down her emotions. In the bed she used to share with her husband and daughter. She could shoot the crowd in the morning, rested, reloaded, fed, warm, relatively sane.

Two more appeared behind him. Then another. The snow didn't slow them. It slowed her.

That odor worked to their advantage. She gagged, unable to control her body, losing sight of them as she doubled over.

I will never reach the cabin. The certainty of it struck her. It brought clarity, calm.

She was dead already. She had nothing to lose. All other consequences were insubstantial.

She had never run out of options before.

There was always another morning, another man, another fight. There was always a place to run or make a stand. No matter how bad it got, she always found her way through.

Now she was alone. Outside! This was new.

She needed new rules.

An old fantasy came back to her, something she swore she would never do. Fighting back, it only ever made things worse. But now.... all she had to do was reach out, take hold of the pipe, and swing. She hesitated. *What if I don't swing hard enough? What if I miss?*

What good is a fantasy if you never live it?

She unstrapped the pipe from her back, tore a piece of her shirt and wrapped it around the iron. "I'm not afraid of you." She held the pipe with both hands and...

...smiled.

"I'm done running!" she shouted.

Her breath clouded the air. Theirs did not.

"Can you hear me? All of you! And everyone like you!"

Her brave speech had no effect. They neither slowed nor sped up. Expressions did not change.

"Don't push me!"

The first one reached out with blackened hands and yellow nails. She swung as hard as she could. The pipe connected with the rib cage, knocking it sideways. Bones snapped. The vibration nearly shook the pipe from her hands, but she held on.

Elation flooded her. She felt the joy of action, newfound power, a world of possibilities.

The thing exhaled a putrid breath but didn't falter. Rib bones scraped together as it reached for her, fingers brushing her face. Bare teeth grinned.

In a near fatal instant, her confidence shattered. She took a stand, lashed out, to no effect! Now she would die for her mistake. *Stupid! Stupid!*

"No!"

She leaned back and swung again, crushing the skull into the brain pan. She pulled back just as the next one reached her. It toppled face first, head concave. Two more approached, only to meet the ground. Frantic, she raised the tube for another swing, but the woods were empty.

She should have felt some satisfaction. It worked! But the last of her emotion drained away into a numb ache. She was free, from fear, from hesitation, from aggressors, from her past, from herself, but there was nothing to take its place.

Only a cold wind and approaching darkness.

And more out there. More pain. More death.

She couldn't see them, but she knew. If she didn't move now, they would cut off her route to the cabin. She'd have to fight to get in.

She marveled at the thought.

She *would* fight them.

She laughed. A long, loud, hysterical laugh echoed from the same trees as that first gunshot. The sound of it only made her laugh harder.

"I *will* fight," she said out loud to the universe, like a prayer, like a promise. She wiped her hand across her mouth. "You hear me? I will fight you. I'll kill every last one of you."

Aggression replaced submission like a pendulum released from bondage. Some part of her wondered if she had become her oppressor, the only role model she ever knew.

She buried this doubt. Introspection would have to wait. She strapped the pipe to her back, picked up the rifle, and started walking, eyes forward.

Let them come.

SNOW

Snow.

The word "no" burrows in its heart.

No color. No heat. No life.

No music.

Instead, the earth belts out a cacophony of discord. Blown by the woodwinds, snow ekes out the voice of a trillion cymbals keening at the top of the audible scale. Trees hum like a whisky jar. And sometimes, sometimes, horns blow in the sky.

Stokes kept 4/4 time, each footstep thudding through the crusted snow. He was not the director. Not first chair. Not even percussionist. He was the metronome for a work that didn't need time.

At any moment he anticipated the falling baton, the symphony's end, the final bow. He knew the routine. Two knees in the snow, rest a measure, two hands, rest, count it out, collapse.

But he didn't know when. No conductor led this orchestra. No composer wrote the score. It played to an empty house. A warm up or a rehearsal or a farewell performance or nothing at all. Page after page of nonsense until the woodwinds died and all that remained was the measure of his step, adagio, step, adagietto, step, adagissimo.

Rest.

"I should be dead."

Even through tinted goggles, the snow pierced his hangover like a needle.

Cuba clapped him on the shoulder. "Cheer up, Stokes. No one dies anymore."

"Then I should have died when I had the chance."

Two days. Not a drop in two days. A lifetime of hangovers called in their IOUs.

Introspection stalked his brain like a wolf pack, waiting for a sign of weakness to tear him apart. He kept them at bay by focusing on the here and now, on the riddle of how snow managed to find its way into his boots despite being duct taped to his pants, on the distance between himself and Fifty's broad back marching into a world obliterated of color, on breathing the brittle air through his nose and not his mouth. Inside the opera house of his mind, a lo-fi record skipped, repeating the same cruel words, "What does a professor of Cognitive Psychology of Music do in a world of guns and teeth?" A question with only one answer, "Die."

He'd baited death his whole life, sneaking out of his parent's house to drink beers on the back of a truck at the butte, binge drinking his way through a bachelor's degree at the University of Nebraska, graduating to martinis and rusty nails and twenty one year old scotch sipped from eighteen year old navels. Alcohol took the edge off those tedious teaching assistant positions. It numbed the taste of ass at every faculty kiss-fest. Then came tenure, liberation from hangovers, a perpetual haze of escalating inebriation. He spiked cocktails from a flask after the bartender slid them over, smuggled hard liquor onto airplanes in little shampoo bottles even as the alcohol ate away at the plastic, kept a hidden reserve under floorboards, inside wheel wells, and above lampshades. He drank for others when he drank alone. He drank to feel like the person he could have been if he wasn't the person he was.

But death never took the bait.

A lifetime of training prepared him for the end of the world, ready to respond with a deep and killing tipple.

"We need to find a town," he shouted up the line.

Buck's voice drifted back. "They're around."

"I mean soon. I'm out. You said Ochre River would have something."

He heard Buck's laugh. "Ochre River did have something, until that something caught fire."

"One time!" Cuba huffed from behind. "One time, I take out an Eater with a torch instead of Mr. Crow, and now it's my fault."

For a moment, Stokes felt the flash of heat erupting from that golden liquid. "You didn't use a torch. You used a tavern."

"Worked, didn't it?"

"It didn't work for me."

"You see any of them following us?"

"The only thing following me is the specter of sobriety."

Buck laughed again. "Don't worry, Stokes. None of us want that. Wouldn't recognize you."

Cuba grumbled. "Next time don't send me in. Do your own damn fighting."

"With what? A swift *acciaccatura da capo*? A poke in the eye with my conductor's baton? Torture them with Philip Glass? I don't have your barrio skills, man. I'm dead weight in this crew."

Up ahead, Buck halted. Something in the distance occupied him for a heartbeat, then he backtracked past the hulk of Fifty, silent as a sentinel, straight toward Stokes. Stokes hesitated, not sure if he should get out of the way or stay put. Buck pulled up close, placed a hand on either shoulder and leaned in, speaking softly so only Stokes could hear. "We talked about this. You're important to us. Someday we'll live in a world that needs a music professor. Today we're walking through the Canadian wilderness, but we're walking toward the future."

Stokes blinked backed a feeling of nausea. "Does that future have a town?"

"I hope we get there soon." Cuba said. "I like him better drunk."

Buck smiled. "Not a town, but..." He pulled binoculars from his bag. "I think we've found our traveler. Have a look."

For the last hour, they'd been following footsteps in the snow. Not the stumbling drag of an Eater but small, deliberate indentations. A single pair. Someone on the run. Someone alive.

Cuba said the trail was fresh, but what does a guy from Miami know about snow?

Beyond them, the trees fell into a large field, pristine but for the trail of footsteps leading to a structure. Halfway out, clumsy furrows joined them.

Cuba took the binoculars. "Someone's alive in there."

Stokes wrenched off his goggles and raised his own binoculars.

A cabin.

Dung colored logs bubbled under low hanging eaves, gleaming with lacquer. This wasn't an old fashioned Abe Lincoln type log cabin. A flatbed hauled in trees grown in a different climate, assembling them by crane like a big toy set. It was the kind city people buy when they move to the country, a two story, air conditioned, interior decorated monster designed to inform the wilderness, "We have arrived." Smoke drifted from the chimney over a green metal roof. A smoking chimney meant warmth. Stokes hadn't felt heat since the saloon caught fire.

Sunlight sparkled on icy gutters. A three month old Christmas wreath hung from a gable in a scene worthy of Currier and Ives, except...

Eaters, at least ten, clawed at the windows and doors, trying to get at whatever hid inside. They pulled down the window flower pots. They dripped fluids on the welcome mat. They knocked railings over the deck. They beat against the walls. They ruined the pastoral scene the way teenagers ruin malls.

Above them, at least a hundred crows swarmed, diving to peck at the Eaters then retreating to perch on the roof.

Something in there smells alive, seasoning the air with the aromatic blend of hope and fear with a dash of remorse. Whoever hides inside that cabin, surrounded, has a few petals of patience to pluck.

Shuttered doors and windows keep the Eaters knocking, but they'll find a way to crash the party.

Father Time laughs behind them, arm in arm with Death in a good mood.

Bring out the shattered glass balls! Don the blood tinted lenses! Tell the bouncer to let everyone in! Listen to the crowd scream as the main act takes the stage. Time to shake that ass as fast as you can! This is the last disco! We're going out for breakfast when this is over!

"Shut up, Stokes." Buck hissed.

"Did I say that out loud?" Stokes let the binoculars drop and squinted in the morning sun. A crust of ice formed overnight to blind him. He peered through the binoculars again. Steam puffed from his happy-faced balaclava, fogging the lens. "What are we waiting for? There must be someone in there. Shouldn't we…"

"Wait." Buck favored caution over heroism.

Buck turned to his silent Hulk. "Fifty, what do you think our chances are?"

Fifty leaned his massive shoulders over an equally massive rifle. He surveyed the scene through a scope, finger on the trigger. "50/50."

"Are you correcting me or is that your answer?"

Fifty remained quiet, done talking for the hour.

"I like to ask. Cuba, what do you think?"

Cuba rippled with lethal energy even inside his bulky parka. He reminded Stokes of a leopard, or a snow leopard, under the circumstances. Cuba jerked a thumb over his shoulder. "Over there," he pointed at the churned up snow, "I found traces of a blood trail. The Eaters followed it like breadcrumbs. Either someone went out hurt and didn't come back, and then some stranger wandered in, or someone went for help with the wounded and came back home alone."

"Home alone," Stokes repeated. He laughed to himself.

Buck looked pensive. "Let's recap. We found one Eater with half a head missing, four more suffered blunt force trauma, something heavy, maybe a pipe."

Cuba chimed in. "I'm guessing our traveler ran out of bullets. From the footprints, our hero was tired. Tracks aren't in a straight line. They fell, several times. Didn't leave a big body impression, so they're small. Maybe a teenager, or a woman."

"So whoever's in there is one small, worn-out, unfortunate bastard." Buck's skinny face wrinkled in a smile. "Just my type."

Cuba corrected him. "Whoever's holed up in there is one hell of a fighter."

Buck shrugged. "We could use that, too."

Stokes felt again the pang of his position. What good is a professor in a world where books fuel the stove and most bipedals don't think? A leftover, cast to the landfill, buried without oxygen, unable to rot. He felt more akin to Eaters than the living.

Sobriety is a bitch.

"Ain't that the truth," Cuba said.

Fifty settled in the snow like a boulder, resting his rifle over his knee. Buck stopped him. "Don't waste your bullets. Cuba can take 'em. There's only ten."

Cuba rolled his eyes. "Why not? What's a few more strokes on the helmet."

In tandem, they moved into the valley, breath steaming from yellow happy faces. When they weren't far off, Fifty spoke. "Wait."

"You're chatty today." Stokes brought the binoculars to his eyes again. A woman leaned out of the attic gable window. The crows took flight like a cloud, kicking up such a ruckus he could hear it from where he stood. She pulled hard on a pail of liquid. It ran down the green roof and cascaded over the closest creatures like the medieval defense of a castle. What was she doing, pouring boiling water on them? Trying to freeze them solid? No. A tiny golden spark emerged from the dark. It hovered in the air over the liquid.

The concussion bent small trees, knocking Eaters into the snow, lighting them up like Roman candles. Unfazed, they stood up and resumed the attack, on fire, shoulders steaming. The roof belched smoke and fire.

"Yeah, we should go help her," Buck said and started jogging. "Anyone got any marshmallows?"

In snowshoes, even rushing to the rescue took them close to ten minutes. The woman never emerged from the structure, unless she walked away behind the house.

Six immolated creatures succumbed as brains sizzled in calcium crock-pots. Bodies hissed in the snow where they fell, twitching. Four remained standing. The cabin, on the other hand, burned. With so much beautiful new fuel, the fire would burn all night.

The crows dove through the black smoke, heckling the Eaters, tearing cooked scraps off the bodies in the snow.

Buck halted. "Stokes," he called out, panting. "Go in the back door and see if you can find the woman. Try to bring her out."

"Cuba didn't do his thing yet."

Cuba smiled. "Better you than me."

"Stunning logic." Internally, though, he wanted to rush in. *City folks always keep a pricey stash.*

Maybe even a wine room. No, don't go too far, you'll just be disappointed. He couldn't help himself. *And maybe, maybe, there'll be a piano.*

Careful not to attract attention from the remaining Eaters, Stokes circled around to the back door. He failed. Two caught his scent and trailed him. *Should have showered this morning.*

Half buried steps led up over a woodpile toward a steel and glass door. Broken glass wedged between the mullions and a piece of plywood secured from the inside. He wiggled the handle. Locked. Eaters rounded the corner. His crowbar splintered the jamb, and he ducked inside, pressing the door shut while he called "Miss? I'm here to rescue you!" He hoped for no answer.

Smoke slithered past him and out the door. The latch hadn't closed behind him. He banged against it with his shoulder but it bounced open again. The Eaters reached the steps. He had less than ten seconds to get this door closed or he'd opened the whole house to invasion. *Nice.*

An uncomfortable buzz filled his head. He turned to survey the room, frantic for an idea. To his left he found a couch, the real cushy type with built-in cupholders. He heaved it across the carpet and shoved it against the door. Then he stacked the cushions for good measure. The cushions fell down. The soft back of the couch gave a few inches for the Eaters to reach in, but the inner wooden frame wedged up against the door handle, blocking them.

Stokes congratulated himself. *Good idea.*

The frozen carpet crunched beneath his feet. He knelt down. Not frozen. Dried blood. *Someone died here.*

Backing up, he stumbled over a body. He scuttled back against the wall, but it didn't move. It was a man, once. A broomstick stood proud from one eye. Not bloated, it hadn't been dead long.

His guard rose. Maybe this wasn't the Traveler's house. Who sets fire to their own?

The temperature soared. He unzipped his parka. Every layer of wool and goose down sweated. Wood smoke parched his throat and dried his tongue. Booming sounds echoed from the second story as the tin roof buckled.

His priorities split. Look for her, a possible killer, or see what the kitchen had to offer and get out. His stomach clenched, needing a fix. If he had any hope of saving the woman up there, he needed a little liquid courage to do it.

Tearing open the cabinet doors, a welcome gleam issued forth. A poker game in progress! Daniels and Walker threw down spades for Courvoisier and Martin. Stoli and Smirnoff, the cool oppressors, cheated Don Julio and The Captain, starting a brawl.

Smoke blacked his lungs and brought tears to his already sympathetic eyes. He couldn't allow their party to end in flames.

He stole a blanket from the couch and rolled up each bottle to prevent them from clinking together. Some part of his frenzied mind realized the house still had electrical power. A safe fridge! He yanked it open and threw in whatever he found there – potatoes, sausage, onions. Fresh onions! Recently stocked! He took it all.

Now if I could find a piano, this would be a perfect day.

Something popped behind the stove. A low hiss, like a deflated balloon, stopped him cold. Any unnatural noise demanded immediate attention. He took his cue to depart.

Two Eaters clawed at the back door. Fire barricaded the front. A window above the sink glowed like a television screen, half covered in snow. *So it's through the rabbit hole, then.*

He smashed the window and fell out, careful to hold the treasure to his chest. The Eaters turned as he passed with his precious cargo slung over his back, like Santa Clause fleeing an AA meeting. Grinning beneath his mask, he strutted up to Buck and the group, triumphant!

"Where's the girl?"

"Girl?"

"Oh, c'mon, Stokes. Please don't tell me you liberated the liquor cabinet again." Buck threw off his pack and shuffled out of his snowshoes. "Fifty, cover me." He rushed across the front porch, leapt over smoking bodies, and dove into the flames.

Nonplussed, Stokes withdrew a random bottle. Reverence for labels disappeared as he unscrewed the top and tossed back a long draught. Out of courtesy more than desire, he held the bottle up to his companions with an unenthusiastic "Wansom? No?" Their eyes remained riveted on the house. He shrugged, answering himself. "Don't mind if I do."

The woman appeared again at the dormer, this time with a bucket of water. She tried to douse the flames, to no effect. Then she disappeared. Smoke billowed out the window she vacated. Enough time passed that Stokes assumed she'd died of smoke inhalation, but then she reappeared, dressed for the outdoors in a ruffed down parka, ski pants, heavy boots and a backpack with an old, lever action rifle, a shovel, and a pipe slung across her back. She tossed snowshoes into a snowbank then crawled up onto the dormer, avoiding the flames.

Kneeling on the roof-vent, she fired twice. Two Eaters fell to the cheers of the crows. *Nice shooting.* With the front now clear, she leapt off the roof into a snowbank beside the steaming husk of a barbecued creature. Waist deep in snow, she smashed its head with the rifle butt until there wasn't much left but a sooty black stain.

Cuba nodded. "This woman has issues. I like her."

Meanwhile, Buck tumbled out the back door, knocking the remaining two Eaters over a rail. The birds swooped down like a tornado, dozens of beaks stripping off exposed flesh.

Buck dodged the murder and ran back toward the group. "Did she come out?" The crack of a rifle knocked splinters off the corner of the house inches from his face. He fell backward, taking cover against the wall.

Stokes and his two companions hit the deck. They hadn't even seen her raise the rifle.

"Whoa, lady! We're alive! We're trying to help you." Buck pressed himself up against the wall like a chameleon trying very hard to change colors.

"You're looters! I saw you run out with a sack!"

"Stokes was supposed to save you. He's an idiot."

"Throw me under the bus," Stokes muttered.

The snow didn't offer much protection, but her attention, and her rifle, remained on Buck. Fifty inched up, his rifle raised, taking a bead on the woman.

Stokes whispered, "Not the living! Not even for Buck."

The two Eaters, hampered by the crows, lurched up behind Buck. "If you want," he pushed back with the butt of his rifle, smashing the head of an Eater, "I'll have Stokes put everything back."

Stokes whispered, "Shoot her!"

The woman swung the rifle back toward the trio, and Fifty ducked. "Sure, he can put it back. Oh, wait, *my house is on fire!*"

"That wasn't us." Buck picked up a chunk of firewood from the snow and smashed the last Eater in the face. Then he used it to beat back massive wings as the crows swooped over the body.

The woman took a few steps away, rifle at her waist pointing first toward Buck's corner, then toward the crew. "Nobody move."

As much as they wanted to, her instructions went unfulfilled. Something in the house, something flammable and unstable, blew up. The shockwave walloped them, a concentric circle of ice and fire. The back half of the house screamed across the field like a meteor. Whole logs impaled the frozen earth, skewering more than one black scavenger. The rest scattered in all directions, stirring the smoke with dark feathers.

Stokes recovered, head ringing, half buried in a snow bank. He wiped a gray film from his goggles so he could check the bag. The bottles were fine, *thank god.* Then he remembered to check himself. A splinter the size of a candle, spitting fire, pricked his left hand. He brushed it off, but the skin sizzled.

Shit. The cut didn't hurt, but the burn did. He thrust his gloved hand in the snow, with very little effect.

Buck lay face down beside an intact wall.

The woman sprawled across a cooked Eater. She scrambled to regain her footing.

Cuba blurred into motion. He sprinted across the yard to pounce on her. He plucked the rifle out of her stunned hands and then backed off, hands out in supplication. She leaned into a sitting position, mad as hell. Pieces of suburban bliss fluttered down from the sky as she shouted, "Give me that back you son of a bitch!"

Fifty appeared next to Stokes, calm as steam. One look at the damaged hand and he dug into the sack for a bottle of vodka. Sensing what came next, Stokes begged, "Not the Goose. Use the Stoli." He cringed as the liquid splashed across the cut, but the pain from the burn died down. Fifty produced a roll of white gauze from somewhere and rolled it around his hand.

Buck pulled himself out of the snow. He laughed, patting the logs. "I guess this is the good side," then scrambled backward as the wall fell inward in a plume of sparks.

The woman raised her head to see her house implode into a smoking ruin.

Buck approached her cautiously, shaking his head and tapping his ears. "Was there anyone else inside?" He showed genuine concern.

She hesitated for a moment before answering. "No. No one."

Stokes remembered the body on the floor but decided to keep his mouth shut.

Buck held out his hand. "I'm Buck." She ignored it.

Stokes and Fifty joined the little party. Up close, Stokes found her even smaller than he thought. Petite, but fierce, like a wolverine.

She bared her teeth. "My rifle, please."

"You'll get it back, I promise. But first, hear me out. Like I said, I'm Buck. Ugly here is Stokes. The big talker over there is Fifty."

Fifty waved.

"And the scrappy one who took you down is Cuba." Buck slapped him on the chest. "Say hello, Cuba."

Cuba grunted.

"I can't help but notice you are homeless, friendless, and in need of assistance. We've been there. Walk with us and we'll share what we have." It sounded canned. It was. He'd said the same thing to Stokes when they'd picked him up. "You're free to leave when something better comes along."

"How about now?" She thrust out her hand for the rifle. Buck nodded to Cuba to hand it over. He jacked out the rounds first, handing her the rifle and cartridges separately.

She took it, lowered it toward them, and started walking sideways.

Buck shook his head. "Um, I wouldn't go that way if I were you."

"Why not?"

"That's the way we're going. We're headed to Dauphin. There's a train with our name on it, and we're getting out of here. But you, you want to go that way," he pointed back the way they'd come, "past them bodies you dropped in the snow, back toward your personal tragedy. There's a good chance you'll get attacked, out there alone, but I'm sure you'll manage. Fifty, how many living people did we see in the last hundred kilometers?"

Fifty held his forefinger and thumb together.

"Yeah. Eaters outnumber humans, by our math, six hundred to one. Stokes, how much food you reckon she'll find that way."

"I think we brought it all with us."

"Oh, that's right. Well, I'll tell you what," he approached her. She raised the empty rifle to her shoulder. "Why don't you stay here by the campfire," he indicated the smoking ruin, "and keep warm while we get a head start. 'Course, the explosion got the attention of every Eater in Manitoba. They're headed this way now. But, like you said, you'll be fine."

"I don't need your help."

"No, ma'am, but nice to have sometimes. That pack looks pretty heavy. I'd be happy to carry it for you."

"I got it," she said, but softer. She took in her surroundings, as if seeing them for the first time.

What a sight they must have been. Each of them carried packs with at least fifty pounds of supplies. More than a few guns, axes, and blunt instruments hung in accessible places. Cuba wore a green WWII era steel army helmet. Fifty carried a rifle as tall as the woman. Mismatched parkas and snow pants puffed them up to three times their natural size. Even Buck, skinny as a pole inside that fluff, looked intimidating.

The manliness ended there. Duct tape ruined the effect, strapped loosely around the forearm up to the elbow and around the leg from the knee down, resembling homeless indigents stuffed with newspaper (which, technically, they were). To top it off, Buck made them wear black balaclavas with a massive, yellow smiley face printed across the front. Style gave up first chair to survival.

With a woman in the midst, Stokes felt more awkward than she did. He needed a drink.

Her rifle shivered a little, dropped an inch. "Where are you going?"

"North."

"What? North? There's nothing north."

"There's nothing south."

She struggled with the idea for a moment, incredulous, then put it off. She sighed, indicating for them to go ahead. "You stay in front of me."

"You have anything from the house you want to take along?"

They turned to survey the wreckage. If she needed a torch, this was the place.

They spent a moment collecting themselves, brushing off soot and feathers while she strapped on her snowshoes. She looked at them like they'd better get moving, so they trudged off single file across the valley. She didn't budge.

Stokes didn't like her behind them. Even empty, the bore of that rifle burned a hole in the center of his back. When he turned, she had it shouldered, but her eyes followed him. It was her gaze that hurt.

When they reached a respectable distance, she followed.

Clouds descended over the next hour. Snow fell, thick and wet.

Back to the familiar misery. Wet boots, tired legs, strained lungs, and now a pulsing hand. His glove rubbed against the wound with every step, but take the glove off and he'd lose his fingers to frostbite. He took a pull from a bottle every twenty steps, pacing himself, until he couldn't feel his hand anymore.

Buck halted them under a tree.

Cuba checked on the woman struggling through the snow. "Is it me, or are we taking more than the usual number of breaks?"

Buck smiled.

"I donmind," Stokes said, delighted by how slurred the words emerged. "Not like I got sommere to be."

"Hey! Look who's back. It's the old Stokes!" Cuba's dour expression didn't match his words. "Don't overdo it. I ain't carrying you, and we aren't yet in the tree line to camp."

When they moved again, the pace felt even slower than before, maybe because pieces of the journey were missing. The snow and sky blurred together. *Drinking in the daytime sucks. Well, outside.*

No one spoke, not even Stokes. He concentrated on forcing one foot to follow the next, avoiding falling into bushes. Three weeks trudging through snow hadn't made him any stronger.

The overcast sky muted the time of day. When his stomach complained, so did he. "Buck, I'm so hungry I could eat an Eater. Can we stop for lunch, please?"

"Another liquid lunch for you, Stokes?"

"Depends on what you got on the menu Maitre'd. If I spend one more meal eating..."

"Beans!" They shouted.

"It's unanimous," Buck said. "Beans it is."

"Dammit!"

The woman caught up after they got the stove burning. She sat some distance away, breathing hard.

On the camp stove, a frozen, brown mass bubbled and congealed.

Cuba dug in his pack for something. He handed a desiccated strip of meat to Buck and indicated the woman.

"Why me?" Buck asked.

"She shoots."

Buck crunched over, holding the meat out like a cross before a vampire.

She stood up, rifle ready. "What is that?"

"Dried rabbit."

"Ew. No thank you."

All four men paused. She had no idea what a delicacy that meat represented.

"I'll eat hers." Stokes made to walk over, but Cuba pulled him down.

"What did *you* bring?" Buck asked.

She didn't seem eager to share, but she pulled out a bag filled with olive green packets.

"MRE's? You got these from an Army Navy store? Big sale?" Buck picked up a package, reading. "Yeah, these puffy ones? Don't even open them." He tossed it over a bush. "This one? Expired ten years ago." Toss. "Which war did you get these from?" He whittled the pile down to a handful and shoved them back at her. "Dry ones like chocolate and crackers are fine with a can of beans." He indicated the way toward the camp stove like a bellhop.

She wore an expression of disappointment, not anger. Stokes guessed she didn't do the shopping. She hesitated, then moved to join them.

Stokes took a spoonful of hot beans with a cold swig of vodka to fend off any germs the beans might have. Can't be too sure.

The woman pointed at the stove. "Won't that attract... those things?"

"*Those* things?" Buck pointed behind her.

Three dark figures lurched toward them on the edge of the field, obscured by falling snow. Two crows circled overhead.

"Are those...?

"Eaters."

She chambered a round. "Let's take them out."

"Hold on, eager beaver. Don't waste your ammo. They're slow. Finish your lunch."

She didn't take her eyes off them as she ate. "They're getting closer."

"We'll be gone before they get here."

She picked up her rifle, spotted them in the scope. "I can take them down right now. I want to."

"Please don't. They're attracted by sound. I'd rather save the fighting for when we get to Dauphin."

Fifty pushed her rifle down with a soft hand.

"It's nice to find another human being alive on earth." Buck brightened. "This calls for a celebration." Out of his pack, like a diamond from a pirate chest, he pulled a can of pears.

"Now?" Cuba asked. "I thought that was for when..."

"Finding anyone alive in this wilderness is reason enough." He peeled it open with a can opener, slow, careful not to spill. He dipped a fork and pulled out a golden half-orb. Glistening syrup slid down over smooth flesh.

Stokes salivated. "That's the most beautiful thing I've seen in months." He stroked his beard in anticipation.

Buck proffered the first slice to the woman. When she reached for it, he held back. "What's your name?"

"Tara." She snatched the fork from his hand with a snarl.

"Welcome to the group." Buck's voice almost sounded flirty.

Everyone got a half. Stokes refused to swallow. He kept the slice on his tongue, suckling, savoring every drop of nectar.

Tara downed hers in one gulp.

How can she do that? Doesn't she realize this might be the last pear she ever eats?

Stokes didn't like her. She hadn't earned a pear. And she was grumpy.

He didn't envy her, though. First day out of the house is the worst. She didn't know how to scrimp or save, didn't know the value of a thing. Anyone who rejects rabbit has a steep learning curve or a shallow grave ahead.

She fidgeted as the creatures drew closer. Fifty didn't look too comfortable either.

Buck tried to reassure her. "Party crashers. We'll be gone before they get here. No good drawing more attention than..." He talked to footsteps. Her tiny form struggled through the snow toward the Eaters.

"Someone should help her." Stokes didn't mean *he* should help her, but somebody should.

Cuba gave a heavy sigh. He groaned as he rose, plucking a crowbar from his backpack, a rusty hook end crusted with human hair. Cuba slid his hand through a leather loop at the base. A black feather fluttered from the strap. Scribbled in white paint on the black iron shaft were the words *Mr. Crow*.

Buck jumped up, too. He looked like he had a purpose.

Not to look the coward, Stokes sucked on the pear a moment longer, swallowed it, and followed.

Tara started firing at ten yards, advancing like a Civil War soldier. Shots echoed across the plain. She missed twice but managed to take one down. Cuba caught up in no time. He dispatched the other two with Mr. Crow. The absence of vertical targets didn't slow her advance. She passed him, and proceeded to batter the bodies with her rifle. Cuba pulled her off, struggling.

Stokes nodded his head. "Better safe than sorry."

Tara retraced her steps, digging in the snow to pick up her spent shells. Then she came back, panting, and asked, "Why are they black?"

Stokes examined the bodies. "Except for what you did to the head, this is a perfect specimen. Frostbite blackens the skin. Purple blisters fill with blood. After about a week, the skin sags off the muscle like a cheap suit. When it catches on branches, it tears. My guess is, this one's been out here about three weeks. Takes that long for the eyelids to fall off."

Tara's breath came in panicked gulps. She was agitated. Excited might be the better word. "But there's nothing wrong with the eyes."

"The eyes," Buck spoke, pulling a piece of cloth over the ruined face, "don't decay. Neither does muscle. Don't know why." He arranged the other two corpses in some semblance of dignity. Two big birds hopped around them, waiting for Buck to leave. He shooed them away.

"Why is he doing that?" Tara looked offended.

"They were human, once." Buck said a prayer under his breath. "This is how we honor the dead."

"Honor them!?" Tara laughed over the protest of crows, surprised when no one else joined in. "I'll give you plenty of them to honor."

Cuba sat down next to the bodies. He slid off his hood and took off his helmet. He spit on it, rubbed away some writing with his thumb. A stick of chalk fell out of a hidden pocket. He wrote a few numbers, blew on it, and put the chalk away.

"What are you doing?" she asked.

"Someday, God will make me atone for my sins. I want to know how many to expect." He tossed on the helmet.

Tara read the words aloud, "513 down, 7 billion to go." She smiled. "That's how many you've killed?"

Cuba didn't say anything. He wiped down the crowbar with a soiled cloth.

"What's wrong with you people? You act like you're at a funeral."

"It is." Buck recited the words:

>*Triumph is not beautiful.*
>*He who thinks a triumph beautiful*
>*Is one with a will to kill.*
>*The death of a multitude is cause for*
>   *mourning*
>*Conduct your triumph as a funeral.*

"Who said that?"

"Some... Chinese guy."

"Some Chinese guy?"

Buck sighed. "The way I look at it, this is the first time these people died. However long they've been wandering in this state, well, we don't know what kind of torture it's been or if they felt anything at all. Did we kill them? You can debate that with your conscience. I like to think we're putting them to rest. So, yeah, it's sad. Even when they're trying to eat us, they're victims, too."

"That's bullshit." She spit out the words. "They're not victims." She turned to Cuba. "I want to keep track, too. To know how much catching up I have to do."

Without looking up, Cuba said, "Count on something you won't lose."

She ran her palm around the stock of the rifle. "I don't think I can fit three billion here."

Cuba laughed. "Thank you for splitting my sins!" He threw her a leather belt. "Notch this. You can use both sides." He watched her trying to count. He pointed to the first body a short distance away. The crows had landed on it and were busy pecking out the eyes. "That's one. We know you took down five last night. Another eight at the cabin this morning. Any more?"

She made fourteen strokes with a cheap, imitation K-Bar, bright scars on dark leather. "Two more before that." Another two notches. She hesitated. The knife hovered over the belt. Her hand shook. She didn't count; she weighed. Her eyes pinched in anger. She pushed the knife in deep for one more cut. She slid the belt through the loops of her jeans and hid her hands in her pockets. "How soon can I get some more?"

Buck frowned. He asked Stokes to pour a round of Jack. Buck toasted with his pear nectar. "To Tara, our newest member."

"To Tara."

Stokes liked her even less.

As the temperature dropped, the snowflakes condensed into pellets. A fierce wind blew them horizontally across the icy fields. They slashed his goggles and struck his parka with escalating sibilance. *We better hit a town soon.*

Stokes learned to welcome the distraction Tara presented. Schadenfreude. Life on the road didn't offer much intellectual stimulation. The only question, *Why?*, led to the only answer, *To stay alive*, which led again to *Why?*

Now he had questions, thoughts, even emotions. He wondered. Who was this woman? Why was she alone? Who was the man on the floor back at the cabin? Would it be a bad idea to bring it up? Was she a threat, maybe even psychotic? How could she shoot so well only to risk poisoning by expired rations?

He enjoyed the wondering so much, he made excuses not to ask her. The wind blew away his voice. The trek stole oxygen from speech. The answers would have to wait.

Snow granules rustled over his hood like sand in an hourglass. They built up on his goggles in pixels. Each time he wiped them, they came back like a fog. One moment he saw the trees, the next, not. As the storm increased, it became more and more difficult to orient himself. His companions shifted in a featureless landscape. He feared he might lose them. "I can't see a damn thing!" he shouted, panic rising in his chest.

Buck's voice filtered through the white noise. He pointed an arm at an old, blackened stump. "Aim for that broken tree!"

He latched onto the goal with single minded devotion. *Make it to the tree. Make it to the tree.* Buck had a way of finding goals when he most needed them. Even the smallest ones helped.

Several times he lost his way as it disappeared behind a drift. Heavy wind pushed him off course. Deep snow tugged at his knees. He made good time, though, approaching it faster than he thought he should. He watched a crow alight on one of the branches. Almost there, needing rest, he stopped.

The stump did not.

Its branches rose. Bony twigs scratched at his jacket.

A loud crack split his eardrums. Dark syrup plastered his face, blacking out his view. He wiped it off to see what happened. The stump fell over, headless now, blaspheming the virgin snow with an oily substance. The crow flew off into the storm. Stunned, Stokes peered through greasy lenses as Tara shouldered her rifle. He waved thanks, but she pushed past him.

Buck observed the fallen Eater. "Nice shot!" He shouted over the wind. "Where'd you learn to shoot like that?"

Tara shrugged. "Video games."

Cuba pushed them on. "Keep moving! If there's one, there will be more! We're getting close to town!"

"We should tie ourselves together!" Tara circled her arms around her waist in case Buck didn't hear her.

"I thought you'd never ask!" He pulled a rope from his pack and threaded it through his backpack. Tara and Fifty did the same.

Stokes fumbled with the ends, unable to make a knot. His hands shook. Either tired or drunk, his fingers disobeyed. He preferred 'tired'. Cuba helped him.

Tied to one another, the rope jerked first forward then back as the others struggled through the deep snow and punishing wind. He tried not to step on Tara, right in front of him, but she kept falling down. Whenever he tried to help her up, she shoved his hands away. After he did this three times she stopped and shouted, "Stop! Don't touch me. Ever." until the rope pulled taught and jerked her forward again.

A little too independent, he though. Rebuffed, he reached in his backpack for consolation. His gloved hand palmed the cap open. The rope pulled tight and sloshed the contents on his sleeve. As much as he wanted it, he wouldn't waste the precious contents in the snow. He put it back, shivering.

Then Buck disappeared.

Stokes suspected a hallucination. At the front of the line, the rope pulled forward, but Buck was gone. Then Fifty, then Tara, disappeared as well. An instant later, gravity buckled. He fell on his ass, driven into a dark hole. He started to scream but the fall ended gently. As his eyes adjusted to the darkness, he found himself under the vast branches of a snow-laden tree. The weight of the snow pushed the branches into the surrounding drifts, creating a hollow like a teepee. Small breaks let in enough light to see the others collapsed against snow banks, untying themselves.

Buck tore off his balaclava and glasses like a surfacing diver. "I know we're close to town, but we don't want to go up against Eaters in this weather. We'll be safer in here until the storm blows over."

Stokes pulled off his gloves. The air felt warmer. He tried to work the knot that kept his pack tied. His blunt fingers slipped off the curves. Couldn't Cuba *untie* the knots, too?

Buck chose that moment to ask, "Where's Cuba?"

Stokes tugged the rope. Cuba's backpack slid into the hollow. "Gone."

"What do you mean 'gone'?"

"Get a Webster's, man!"

"Shit!" Buck ducked outside for a minute and then came back. "I don't see him." He dug in his backpack for a longer, thicker rope. He tied one end around his waist and threw the other to Fifty. "Tie this around the trunk. I'll backtrack and find him."

Stokes waited. The wind blew through the cracks in the branches. It dusted his arms and legs. He shook. Even bundled up and in a shelter, the cold wouldn't leave him.

Minutes passed. Neither Buck nor Cuba returned. Stokes had the distinct sense that the others blamed him. Fifty wouldn't look at him, and Tara watched the hole Buck crawled out of, one hand on the rope. He defended himself. "Don't look at me. He was behind me. How was I supposed to know?" They *didn't* look at him. That made him feel worse.

Something big crashed through the canopy on top of Fifty. Stokes scrambled backwards. Tara flashed her rifle up as Fifty rolled out of the way.

She hesitated an instant, then lowered it, shouting at a prostrate form. "Where were you?!"

Cuba peeled off his goggles and mask, coughing. He couldn't answer until his chest stopped convulsing. He wiped his mouth, blood streaking his gloves. Clearing his throat, he said, "I had to take a leak. Why?"

Tara yanked on the rope. A few minutes later Buck reappeared. He saw Cuba, already asleep, cheek resting on the rough bark of the trunk. Too tired or cold to say anything, he settled in the snow next to Stokes, stripping off his gloves. His hands steamed in the hazy light. He closed his eyes.

It seemed like a good time for a drink. Stokes pulled a bottle out of the pack at random. Reading the label, he pointed at Tara, "Anybody want some of her Crown Royal?" To his disappointment, everyone did. Fifty knocked it back and handed it to Buck. Buck nursed it and kept it. Stokes pulled out another for himself.

Tara glared at them like lepers.

He hated that sanctimonious look. He got it so often. "What? I'm a spiritual man. I like my spirits."

"That's pathetic," she snarled. "The world gives you a beating and you turn to the bottle? Are all men this weak?"

"For your edification, I drank like this long before the world..."

"She's right," Buck interrupted. "Alcohol thins the blood. Drops the temperature of extremities, makes us susceptible to frostbite. None of us should be drinking." He handed the bottle back, well drained. "Except you, Stokes. God knows what you're like sober."

"You should have known me as a child." The snow surrounding them muted the storm to a low hum. Drowsy, he cuddled his bottle like a teddy bear. "And anyway, I'm not an alcoholic unless I drink before noon. So please don't wake me before noon."

Conversation died. The howl of the wind filled the hollow. After a time, Stokes asked, "We're not going to spend the night in here are we? I mean, together?"

"It's either sleep in here or die out there," Buck said.

"That's," Stokes took another sip, "a good argument."

Tara looked anxious. "Why do you ask?"

"The screaming. Hard to stay asleep."

"Who's screaming?" Tara gripped her rifle and backed away.

Buck reassured her. "We prefer to sleep alone. Every hour or so, nightmares wake a man, lungs first. We'll be tired tomorrow."

Tara pulled her knife out. "I appreciate all you've done." She stabbed at the snow until she'd built a small hole to crawl into. "But if any of you tries to touch me in the night, I'll be serving Rocky Mountain Oysters for breakfast. *Capiche?*"

No one answered. Fifty and Cuba already slept. Buck held up his hands in supplication. Stokes settled into a stupor, trying to ignore the porcupine in her den.

No one drank enough.

They had a new member in their little crew. New nightmares.

The first time she screamed, she kept it up until Buck lit a lantern.

As she became aware of her surroundings she broke down. "Oh, god. Oh my god. It's real. It really happened!"

That alienation hadn't crossed his mind in a long time. He didn't even dream it anymore. That former life, its complications and compensations, ceased to exist, may never have existed. All plans, ambitions, education, training, came to nothing. Survival's harsh light cast everything else in shadow.

Now he dreamt of what he saw during the day. And what waited for him in the night.

Caught in a state of sloppy insomnia, he watched Buck try to comfort her.

Buck sidled up close to the hole. "You don't have to go back to sleep. I'll stay up with you." She didn't respond. He tried another tack. "We came across the damage you did to the little hamlet of Ochre River. Had a lot of practice?"

She recovered a little. "First day on the job."

"You're a natural."

She laughed. "Thanks."

"Nice rifle, too. A .308 Savage 99? Lever action. Like the old westerns? An antique."

"Not so old. It was my husband's." Long silence. Stokes thought she might have gone back to sleep until she poked her head out of her hole. "What's with the, uh," she drew a semicircular motion with her finger and bared her teeth.

"Oh, the smiley faces? I thought they made us look friendlier."

She didn't smile. "It scared the shit out of me."

"Sorry. We tried going all black, but I thought we'd frighten survivors into shooting at us."

"I shot at you."

"Yes you did. Serves me right for trying to rescue you."

"Right." Tara turned her face. Her mood declined. She eased back into the hole.

"I know it's been a tough day."

"It's ok. I'll get through it."

"There are more ahead."

"That's comforting."

"You don't have to go through it alone. That's why we stick together."

She didn't respond.

"Let me ask you something. What do you want?"

"I want this to be over."

"It's been one day. Savor the adventure a little."

Tara responded with a sob.

"Bad joke. What I mean is, it's not enough to survive. That'll wear you down and kill you. You have to have something to live for. You have to tell yourself, this doesn't end until I get it. Get it? So what do you want?"

"For this to end."

"You can't wish for more wishes. I'll tell you what we want. Stokes is simple. He wants a piano. If he brings a little music back to the world, he'll find some peace. And Cuba? Despite his rough demeanor, he's looking for peace, too. It's a shame. He's so good at violence. I don't know what Fifty wants. Silence, I guess. The point is, we help each other find what we want in the world. That's the most we can ask."

"What do you want?"

"Pegasus."

She laughed through a sniffle. "Doesn't exist."

"It better. If you help me live long enough to ride it, how may I return the favor?"

Tara didn't answer. Maybe she fell asleep. Her first day on the road. Too early for her to know what she wants, to know what completes her. First, you take everything away. Then you narrow it down to what you miss most. No, not what you miss. What you need. The one thing you can't get in this world through scavenging and shooting. And the funny thing is, maybe you've been searching for it all along, even before, when you had everything.

"Quiet, Stokes. She's sleeping." Buck rolled away from the hole.

Tara's voice quivered with conviction. She knew. "The one who started this."

"We don't know what started this."

"Someone did. A man, I'll bet. I'll rest when he's dead. That's what I want. Can you do that?"

Buck shifted in the snow. "We don't kill the living."

"Why not?"

"Everybody's doing it. Gotta be different."

"So you won't help me? I'm on my own?" Despite her bravado, her voice broke on the last word.

"We'll help you till the end of the line. When you get there, maybe you'll want something else."

His reassurance calmed her, though. Her breathing steadied.

The night dragged on.

Fifty snored. Buck shouted. Cuba coughed. Tara mewled. And they accused Stokes of talking in his sleep.

He disagreed.

He didn't sleep.

He shivered.

The tree offered no security. Wind and driving snow had no effect on Eaters. If they caught a scent, they'd follow it straight through the blizzard. Any moment, one might crash through the branches the same way Cuba had.

Whenever he dozed off, that old, dark tree lunged for his eyes. He couldn't shake the fuzzy image. He never saw it clearly. That close to dying. If they hadn't found Tara, this might have been his day.

Every day brought a new nightmare. On the rare occasion it didn't, his brain offered up a library to borrow from.

More than once, Stokes sensed them waiting outside, surrounding the tree, trying to determine the source of that tasty human smell. Every hour or so he'd poke his inebriated head out the entrance, rifle first, for a quick peek. Drifting flakes obscured the landscape. Snow-covered saplings hunched in the darkness like something waiting. The wind blew trees against one another, creaking like arthritic knees. Hiding in the hole seemed a much better option, for the next hour or so anyway.

Stokes wasn't the only one. Cuba, Fifty, and Buck crawled past him at one time or another to waylay any doubts.

Morning couldn't come soon enough.

With the landscape so flat, they didn't see Dauphin until they passed the town limits. It began with a few industrial buildings and what used to be something flammable. Charred tubes the size of trailer homes littered the fields, some upended or stuck in the earth. Buck read the word Ammonia on one. A charred pile remained of the warehouse.

"Looks like your cabin!" Buck pointed out. Tara glared at him. "What? Too soon?"

Cuba growled. "You're in a good mood." Buck was the only one. None of them had slept well. No one sleeps comfortably outdoors in March.

"See this?" Buck pointed to a wide, flat area in the snow that bisected the town. On either side, low, weather beaten buildings stood against winter. Nothing moved. "That's what we've been looking for."

"More snow?"

"Railroad tracks! We can follow them straight to Churchill! Welcome to Dauphin, gentlemen and lady."

Tara frowned. "No welcoming committee?"

"Glad there isn't one." Buck had his binoculars. "No birds, either."

"That's good?"

"Could be. I can't see the train station from here. Must be on the wrong side of town."

A lump caught in Stokes' throat. Three weeks he'd followed Buck. Cuba and Fifty were with him even longer. They wanted a train, the train he promised them. Buck swore the town of Dauphin, with its little roundhouse, would have an engine, something to ride into the sunset, safe in the belly of a steel beast. "Are you saying there's no train station?"

"I'm saying I can't see it. I know it's there."

Cuba added his assessment. "Either the townsfolk slept in this morning or this is another dot we can scratch off the map."

Stokes chimed in. "Population zero."

Tara looked relieved. "No... Eaters either?" She said the word the way you taste foreign food.

"Hard to say. Up here folks tend to shut themselves in when things go wrong. Behind every one of those doors lies a variation of hell. Starvation, poisoning, suicides, bungled family murders. Every family history has the same ending."

"Surprise!" Stokes jumped out of an imaginary door. "Searching for canned food...It's Christmas every day. A whole new horror to unwrap. You better watch out. You better not cry." With that, he walked on.

Tara hesitated until Cuba waved her forward. She pulled the Savage off her shoulder.

Doom hung over the town. Silent. Dead.

As they approached, Buck gave Tara his usual pep talk. "Remember, try not to use your rifle unless you have to. If they're dormant, that'll bring them out at the same time."

"Dormant?"

"If they get you down, keep your arms up... Wait." Buck rummaged through his pack and pulled out a roll of duct tape. He stripped off a piece. "Eaters are ex-humans. They attack with their mouths, but they don't have sharp teeth. They can't bite through duct tape. That's why we wear it."

He took a step toward her. She backed up, suspicious, looking at the rest of them. They looked like poor kids dressed up as the Tin Man. "I thought it kept the cold out."

"Works well for that, too."

She held out one arm. He wrapped it like a mummy.

"It's not tight," she said.

"Doesn't need to be tight. Just needs to be there. When they get on top of you..."

"Don't you mean 'if'?"

Buck didn't smile. "When they get on top of you, keep your arms out in front of your face like this. Hurts like hell when they clamp down, but it should keep them away from your vitals long enough for help to arrive."

"And if it doesn't?"

"You won't have to worry about canned food. All right. We split up. I take the right side. Stokes and Cuba, you take Tara on the left. We rendezvous at the train station."

"You can't go alone," Cuba protested.

"Show Tara the ropes. Keep an eye on Stokes. Hey, that rhymes!"

"Why do I always get stuck with Stokes?" Cuba complained.

Stokes choked on his drink. "Cause you need me to protect you?"

Cuba scoffed. "What about Fifty?"

"He covers us from the tracks, right down the middle. You get into trouble, shout and move to his line of sight. We stick to the houses near the tracks. Don't go any deeper into town. Remember, we're good on medical supplies right now, so we're only looking for cartridges and food."

"And a piano," Stokes added. When the idea first came to him, it seemed a simple thing to find. After searching a hundred houses, the piano became a driving obsession, a life goal. He'd tackle a thousand rotting, infested towns to find one.

Stokes stood outside a one story, tin roof house, listening. A light wind blew. Snowflakes hissed across the ice. Loose roof panels tapped together. A wire creaked against a wooden pole. Somewhere a door banged open and shut, open and shut. No birds.

No dogs. Not a living sound. No music here, only the arrhythmic leftovers of civilization.

White paint flaked off wooden chip board walls. Windows sagged in rotting frames. Trash piled up against a cinderblock foundation. In other words, pretty normal.

"You know what I feel like? An extra."

"You're still on that topic?"

"I'm that guy on Star Trek you've never seen, the one they take on an away mission, and you think 'Who's that guy?' But then the apocalypse came, the writer died, and I outlived my scene."

Cuba shrugged. "I never watched Star Trek."

"You never... how could you...'"

"Focus, Stokes. Game time. This might be the last ten seconds of your life." Cuba sent a forlorn look towards Buck, hoping to change partners, but he was out of earshot. "C'mon man, let's do this."

Stokes tried the doorknob. "Locked. Bad sign."

"Why?" Tara's eyes widened. The unknown seemed to frighten her more than Eaters.

Stokes indulged her. "No one locks front doors in Canada. Means someone holed up inside. Ergo, they are now dead. Ergo, they are now undead. I don't think we should open it." He backed away.

Cuba gripped his collar and pulled him back. "First house of the day. We have to open it."

"Buck made that rule so we wouldn't chicken out. I'm not chicken. I'm saying this is a bad house. From experience."

Cuba pushed him out of the way and kicked the door. It broke off the hinges but only fell in a few inches. "Barricade," he said. Through the crack they could make out a tattered box spring mattress, buttressed against the frame.

"Not a good sign," Stokes repeated. "If we can't get in, no one got out. "Whoever's in there probably ate the food before they died."

"Maybe they went out the roof. Need to take a look." Cuba indicated Stokes look through the door.

"Not me. You're the one who said, 'First house...'"

"All right!" Cuba bent over, peered into the dark space beyond the broken jamb. An arm thrust through the bedsprings at his face, skin hanging off in dry strips. "Shiiii..." he said as he fell backward into the snow.

"Feels good to be right." Stokes said, laughing. He helped him up.

"Yeah, Mr. Expert? You get the next house."

"What about him?"

Tara broke the reaching arm with a swing of her cast iron pipe, trapping the Eater behind it in the bedsprings. "It isn't going anywhere."

The next house, a two story with similar décor, stood with its front door half open. Snowdrifts blew in, curling up against the couch and television.

Mr. Expert smiled. "Now that's a good sign." He turned toward Tara, falling back into his old Professor mode. "Open doors mean one of two things. Either someone already looted the place or the previous owner fled in a hurry, leaving behind his supplies. No signs of forced entry, so I bet on the latter.

"What happened to the owner?"

Stokes flashed on the tree in the snowstorm. "No way to tell."

Cuba pressed a finger to his lips as he beckoned Stokes in. The living might be out, but the dead...

"Show me what's behind door number two!" Stokes whispered.

Light filtered in between drawn shades. Cuba passed through each room, silent as a ghost on the brown shag carpet. Old furniture, faded photos of outdated hairstyles, floral wallpaper, the hallmarks of an elderly home.

Stokes went straight for the kitchen.

Day of the week pillboxes littered the kitchen table, pills inside. Stokes sorted through them but didn't find anything interesting or recognizable. He had one drug of choice anyway.

He rummaged through the cupboards, finding a few sardine cans, a box of crackers, and a can of prunes. "This will keep me regular," he said. None of the flour, pasta, or other baking goods survived the mice. Black droppings contaminated everything. He opened the crackers. Still good.

Tara reached for the handle of the refrigerator.

"Don't open that." Stokes ate another cracker.

She opened it. A hoary frost covered meats and vegetables. "They're frozen. They look fine."

"Buck calls that a puke machine. When these towns lost power, everything inside spoiled. Then the cold got in and froze it. If you need one, that's a good way to die."

Cuba clumped down the stairs, no longer quiet. Nobody home. "No piano," he said to Stokes' expectant face. "Headless old lady in bed. Looks like a botched suicide pact. Grandpa must have done her in, freaked out, and bolted. You find anything?"

"Cwkas."

"You know you're not supposed to eat until we split it up later. What if we find some peanut butter?"

"Ft chns."

At the third house, a trailer home half buried in a snow bank, the door was closed. Cuba tried the knob. "Unlocked," he whispered.

Tara proffered, "A treasure trove of untapped supplies?"

"Or an extended family of Eaters waiting on the other side."

Cuba raised Mr. Crow as he reached out with his left hand. "Only one way to find out."

The door opened without a sound onto a typical floor plan. One hallway led down the side between the living room and the back bedroom. Standing in that hallway, silhouetted by the broken bedroom window, stood a tall, black creature.

Cuba mouthed the dreaded word. *Waiter.*

Stokes stopped. His loins shrank.

It lingered in the hall, in front of the bathroom door, head down, arms limp, immobile as a charred log. Whatever it chased in there never came out.

"That is why I drink." He whispered. "That! Right there!"

"Shut up, Stokes!"

Tara looked ready to run it down, but a fear of the unknown stopped her. "What is it doing?"

"When they don't have anything to chase, they... shut down. They wait."

Stokes hated Waiters more than any other Eater. In his worst dreams, he hid, hurt and alone, trapped in a place he couldn't escape, Waiters outside, patient as time.

Cuba stole through the living room into the kitchen to get closer, silent as a snake.

Stokes stepped across the threshold. His foot found a frozen puddle on the carpet. The ice cracked.

Lidless eyes turned on him. A toothless mouth gaped a gummy grin. The old creature raises its arms for a final embrace, ready to take us down to hell, to join him in this eternal game, to steal the warmth of our blood for...

"Shut up, Stokes!" Cuba leapt out of the kitchen and backhanded the creature. Its head snapped back and up, smacking against the bathroom door. Cuba brought the next blow down square on its forehead. It went limp.

"Christ, Stokes, why you gotta talk to yourself all the damn time!" He kicked the body once for good measure. "And why am I always the one who does the slaying? I'm tired, man!"

Stokes spoke around the shaking bottle at his lips. "Because I miss."

A thudding, scratching sound came from inside the bathroom.

"Shit." Cuba put his ear against the door. The door rattled, but no one spoke. "Someone's in there."

Tara stepped forward, "Let her out."

"Wait!" Cuba held up a hand. "I don't think it's alive."

The rattling continued. The thing inside never tried the doorknob.

Stokes laid it out for her. "This guy chases his wife into the bathroom. With no other distractions, he waits for her to come out. If she comes out, she dies. If she stays, she starves to death. When that happens, you get two Waiters, one on each side of the door. Undisturbed, they might stand like this for eternity, one on either side of the door, waiting to eat each other, oblivious of time."

Tara held up her pipe. "So let her out. Let's take care of her."

Cuba waved her back. "You'll get plenty of chances. No sense letting this one out. Even the easy ones can kill you."

Cuba left the hall and started tearing apart the kitchen, bashing up the cabinets and smashing the counter tiles.

Stokes stood out of the way. "You won't find anything intact that way."

"Nothing! They ate it! Greedy bastards!" Cuba broke down, coughing, leaning on the crowbar, one knee on the linoleum floor.

"Temper, temper." Stokes held out the bottle. "You want a drink?"

"No!" Cuba spit blood on the floor.

"Are you okay?" Tara asked.

"Peachy." He pushed his way outside.

Two hours later, they circled back to Fifty and walked along the tracks toward the station, a beautiful building in comparison to the rest of the town. Red brick stretched along the track punctuated by carved limestone cornices. Deep, wooden brackets held up a wide roof that hooded the platform from the snow. A second story protruded like a miniature pyramid through dark roof shingles.

Buck sat on the deserted platform, elbows on his knees, head in his hands. He didn't register their arrival.

A caboose stood out bright red next to the station. Stokes' hopes soared. "I'll be damned. Buck was right!"

Buck's muffled voice said, "It's a museum piece. It isn't even on the tracks."

Stokes wasn't listening. Something even more exciting emerged from behind a stretch of shrubs.

A liquor store.

Somewhere, Stokes heard angels. Maybe it was his imagination. The angels, not the store. The store was real. He took a step toward it.

Buck stood up, kicked the steps, and screamed into the forest. "Dammit!"

Stokes, not willing to take his eyes off the prize, asked, "What's the matter with him?"

"Guess we're not worried about attracting attention."

"There's no train?" Tara asked.

Buck was livid. "It's not even a train station anymore! It's a damn government office. I don't even know if the trains stop here."

Stokes, distracted by the vision across the street, attempted to console him. "You... there must be something. What about the roundhouse?"

"Nothing. I looked. I... I didn't go to any houses. I couldn't wait. There are several cars. No engines."

"What about the caboose?" Stokes was grasping at straws. "Can we get it going somehow?"

"How? It's a caboose. It doesn't have an engine."

"I don't know, push it with something?"

"Yeah, you push it."

Buck stood aloof, his body language warning them away. Cuba and Fifty moved into private spheres of silence.

For 300 kilometers, Dauphin waited for them, the first important milestone on a long, dark journey, a wellspring of hope and anticipation. Now dry, desolate, empty. Just like everything else.

"'We walked here," Tara offered. "Why do we need a train?"

Buck spoke through clenched teeth. "Because there are 1400 kilometers of track between here and Churchill, and that's not a distance we're walking."

As broken-hearted as Stokes felt, he felt worse for Buck. "Look, you came at least that far from Oklahoma, right? And Cuba came all the way from Miami. And Fifty, he... well, we came a long way to get here. Distance doesn't frighten us."

"In case you didn't notice, it's -25 today. Here's a hint: it isn't going to get warmer *up there!*"

Tara stood dumbstruck. Stokes credited her for being smart enough not to say anything.

"I've never..." Stokes wasn't sure how to say it. "I've never seen you mad."

"I've never seen you mad either," Cuba added.

Fifty nodded.

"I'm not m... I'm... I'm mad at myself. All right? This was my plan. I should apologize to you for making you come up here with me. This was my plan, it was a dumb plan, and now I... I don't know. I don't have another plan."

Cuba stopped him. "Hey. We followed you, not the train. We'll find another way."

No one else knew what to say. It had been no easy task to make it this far, but Buck's plan got them here. They even dragged Tara into it. What were they supposed to do now? Separate?

In the silence, Stokes heard something the others didn't. He cocked his ear toward the station. A sonorous hum vibrated the window and wafted over the new snow like a pleasant odor. "Am I drunk, or do I hear music?"

Buck perked up. "Both. Let's check it out."

Cuba popped a door open with Mr. Crow.

Music bounced off vinyl tile floors, redirected by paper tacked to white walls, laminate desks the color of mud, and uncomfortable metal chairs. The music cast a warm hue over the cold furnishings, like the glow of a fireplace.

First the strings, then the horns, then a chorus. The voice of Frank Sinatra haunted the space, crooning *Forget Domani.*

Let's forget about tomorrow.
Let's forget about tomorrow.
Let's forget about tomorrow for tomorrow never comes.

Stokes wanted to cry. He memorized every note like a dead lover's face. His fingers twitched out the notes on an imaginary instrument. *How long has it been since I heard music? A lifetime?* He followed that wisp of paradise into a sunlit office behind the ticket booth. A black, government issued player blinked with a red light. "How?" he mouthed, enraptured.

Buck pointed at the window. "Solar powered. Playing on a loop."

"I'm taking this with me." Stokes hesitated. To disturb it would stop the music.

"You'll have to ask this guy's permission." Buck pointed to an undefined shape in the shadows. The outline of a man disfigured a chair. A dark spot stained the acoustic tile ceiling above him with a matching one on the floor. A pair of empty boots caught the sunlight, one on top of the other. Buck smirked. "I don't think he'll object."

Tara held back, "What is it? Is he dead?"

"Oh, he's dead alright. Looks like he used a box cutter to slash both arms from wrist to elbow." Bloody icicles hung from the chair. "He bled out for a long time."

"So he killed himself?"

"Not that way." Buck held up his hand when Tara started to move closer. "While he bled out, he put a shotgun under his chin and pulled the trigger with his toes."

Tara made an involuntary glance at the stain on the ceiling and covered her mouth.

"Pretty thorough."

Tara asked, "Why would he do that?"

"Bad marriage?" Stokes offered.

Cuba fingered a piece of paper on the desk. "He left a note."

"What does it say?"

"You tell me."

The rest of them crowded around. A fountain pen scrawled out three short words in a hurry on City of Dauphin stationary.

They're inside us.

Tara asked, "What's that supposed to mean?"

Cuba got tight lipped. Buck looked away, too. Even Fifty seemed to know.

Stokes didn't. "What? What is it, some kind of code? What does it mean?"

"It means there's no train," Buck said. "Let's leave this man alone." Buck stepped outside.

They filed out into the sunshine on the platform. Stokes, as much to his surprise as anyone, didn't feel like raiding the liquor store. He didn't feel like doing anything. A great apathy gripped him. Emptiness has weight, and the vast expanse surrounding them bore down on his chest. He felt lost, and scared.

But not alone.

He clapped Buck on the shoulder. "I have you to thank for that, Buck."

This time, he hadn't been speaking out loud, but Buck seemed to follow the thread of his thoughts.

"Me, too," Cuba added.

They were all thinking it. Their world centered on Buck, the source of what they could do, of what they had done. They were here. They were alive. That would have to be enough.

"Well," Buck said at last. "If you're not going to hit the liquor store, I will. Friends of mine held up liquor stores in their youth. Time I did the same. Anyone have an objection?"

"I do."

Stokes often mistook that deep baritone for an avalanche or an earthquake or some other force of nature. Fifty was pointing to a lump in the snow beside the railroad track. The earth rumbled again, "I think we should dig out that truck."

How Fifty knew it was a truck, or even a truck they needed, Stokes couldn't figure. "We can't drive in this snow. What good does that do us?"

Buck dug down until he exposed the wheels. "See that?" The truck had some kind of attachment on the front, miniature railroad wheels on a pneumatic arm. "Those fit the tracks. We can drive on the tracks! This is even better. Our own personal train."

It took them half an hour to dig it out, another two hours to attach a snow plow to the front, and another half to finagle it onto the railroad tracks.

They even managed to get old Blue Eyes relocated into the stereo. All the while, Buck gleamed like a kid who got what he wanted for Christmas. "Next stop on this line is Hudson Bay."

At this point, dusk approached, but Cuba cleaned out the bed and started loading the packs. He lifted Tara's with a groan. "What did you bring? A rock collection? You've been carrying this yourself?"

Tara dithered. "Wait." She turned to Buck. "The trains come out of Winnipeg. Maybe they'll send one out. Why don't we just wait here?"

"No reason for the train to stop," Buck explained, though he was smiling. "Even if there is one, it might blow right past."

"But there are houses, we could look for food. Couldn't we..."

"This looks like a sleepy town, but we wait and we risk being surrounded. Stay here long enough and every Eater in the county will smell us eventually. Got to keep moving."

"And we'll be on the rails in a truck with a train possible any minute."

"Not likely, but it's a risk I'm willing to take. Besides," he opened the door, "I'd rather sleep in a warm truck than Suicide Station."

Stokes chimed in, "If you don't mind, I'd like to throw a few things in the back before we get going."

"I'll go too," Tara volunteered.

"After that speech last night?"

She shrugged. "They might have a good Chardonnay."

Walking back to the truck, arms laden with a box of flavors he never thought he'd taste again,

Stokes reflected, "This is the best I've ever felt, drunk or sober. Well, I can't remember a time I felt good sober, but..."

"I know what you mean." Tara said it with a smile, but it faded as her own memories crowded in.

Stokes volunteered to drive, but that got vetoed fast. "Not even on rails, in a straight line?"

Fifty drove. He would have filled the backseat, otherwise. Tara took the front seat out of deference to her gender. That left Buck, Cuba, and Stokes squeezed together in the back seat. It took ages for the heater to warm up the cab, but once it did they started to sweat. They fit better with the coats off.

When Buck took off his coat, Tara noticed his T-shirt. Block letters on the front read STILL ALIVE.

"I don't get it," she said.

Buck looked down as if he'd forgotten what he was wearing. "Oh, this? Double entendre. If I die, survivors will appreciate the irony."

"Before you eat their brains?"

"Competitive advantage. Eaters don't laugh. Check out the back."

She read it out loud. "Good guy."

"Removes any ambiguity. How did your first Hunting and Gathering go?"

"I touched one."

"Kinky."

"It was warm!"

"They all are."

"Why?"

"I try not to think about it."

With coats off, the cab filled with the pungent odor of human sweat. Showers were a distant memory, but Tara smelled maddeningly good, floral. Stokes felt sorry they couldn't return the favor.

Between the body odor and the beans, this would not be a pleasant drive. At least one of the five senses suffered at any given time. Every now and then someone cracked a window until it got too cold to bear.

Windshield wipers beat out a rhythm as the plow threw powder across it. Low trees and open fields slid by on either side. Snow, snow, and more snow. The heater blasted. The warmth had the immediate effect of putting them to sleep.

Stokes woke last.

Tara sat sideways in a heated discussion with Buck. "That doesn't make any sense. There's nothing up north but more of this. Civilization is down south."

"That's where we came from, lady. There's nothing left of civilization down there."

"There must be something better than this."

Stokes took an interest in the conversation. "Tell her your theory."

Buck turned shy. "It's... she'll think that's crazy, too."

"It's why we're going north."

"Not the only reason. We're going north because we can't go south."

"Yeah, but," Stokes wouldn't let him off easy, "Tell her your theory."

"I'm up for it," Tara crossed her arms, already resisting Buck's theory. "What is this theory?"

"Global warming," Cuba pitched in.

"Let's not get ahead of ourselves."

"You're going the wrong way for warming," Tara laughed.

"Ok, ok, here it is. See, the day before this... happened, I was reading an article on global warming..."

"You worked in the oil fields..." Stokes corrected.

"Yeah, why is that important?"

"It lends perspective."

"Ok. So I used to work the oil fields in Oklahoma, where I grew up. I'm an oil man. I heard about this global warming and how I'd lose my job if some idiot in Washington passed a law..."

"A carbon tax."

"Right, so I'm curious. Wanted to know what this talk of an apocalypse was all about."

"There, see?" Stokes smiled. "Shows you have an inquisitive mind and can consider both sides of an argument. Shows a strong character."

"Anyway, so this article said the Northwest Passage is now ice free all year long." Buck paused for dramatic effect, as if waiting for applause.

Tara wasn't impressed. "So what?"

"Well, it didn't mean anything to me at the time, but after this whole business with the Eaters started, I found myself driven north. I got as far as Minnesota when I realized I was about as far from any ocean as a man could be in North America."

"So?"

"South wasn't an option anymore, so I needed alternatives."

Cuba entered a coughing fit that killed the conversation. He rolled down the window, cold air and snow swirling inside. He spit into the wind. A red and black gelatinous mass smeared across the back window.

"Nice."

"Sorry."

"I'll let Cuba tell you why we can't go south after I finish my story, but I was thinking, 'North America is an island of death, and I want off.' How do you get off an island? By boat. That's when I remembered that article."

Tara rolled her eyes and faced forward. "Why couldn't I have been rescued by normal people?" She turned again, a little angry. "What're we going to do? Swim the Northwest Passage?"

"No. A boat. I just said..."

Stokes couldn't stand the tension. "See, there's a town called Churchill, the only port on the Northwest Passage, and they have a ship that winters there. These tracks lead straight to it. We get there, take the boat, sail it to someplace warm, maybe a private island somewhere, and sip margaritas for the rest of our lives." He embellished that last part, but he liked the sound of it.

"What makes you think the people of Churchill didn't already do that?"

They didn't say anything. Stokes had never considered it.

"You mean, we're going to travel thousands of miles into the Canadian wastelands to look for a boat that you read about in a magazine once? That's your escape plan? You've really thought this through, haven't you?"

"I have. I think it's the best option."

"It's suicide!"

"No," Cuba intervened. The gravity of his voice gave her pause.

He seemed to gather himself, holding his throat.

Tara grew impatient. "This is the part where you tell me why we're not going south?"

"There is no South."

Stokes felt the need to fill in the back story again. "Cuba's from Miami. He knows everything in between. If he says there's no South, it's because he's been there."

"That makes no sense."

"The nuclear reactors failed. Meltdown. Everything south of Canada is a dead zone." Cuba coughed, lightly, to emphasize his point.

"Which one?"

"What?"

"Which reactor?"

"All of them."

"That's not possible."

"I'm not arguing what's possible. I'm saying what is."

"Nuclear reactors have backup systems. They have backup systems for their backup systems."

Stokes tried to stop her, but she was on a roll.

"Even if the power grid fails, they generate their own power."

"Don't –"

"And even if, in the highly unlikely event that one failed, it would have no impact on any other station."

"He's – "

"They couldn't, ever, ever, fail at once."

Stokes got her attention and mouthed the words to her.

Cuba brought it up before she comprehended it. "Ok. I'm sure you're right. Now turn off the lights and watch me glow."

Tara put two and two together, his knowledge of the power plants, the black sludge frozen to the back window. "Oh! I'm sorry... I..."

"America is a nuclear wasteland from the Mississippi river east. I know this for a fact. I passed through those areas. I saw the same story everywhere I went. Plant after plant. Whole states wiped out. My passage north zigzagged around nuclear hot zones. I'm no engineer. I don't know how it happened, but I damn well know it did."

That last part came out as a whisper with the force of a roar. There was no arguing. His dead serious tone and coughing fits proved it, but he added one more statement.

"I used to carry a Geiger counter, but I got tired of listening to it. When I walked away from it... it stopped."

Tara turned to look out the windshield, quiet for a moment. "So. The Northwest Passage."

Buck shrugged. "I'm afraid so."

"Having only one option makes life simple." It also made life scary. Stokes needed another drink.

Tara digested the information without asking more questions for almost an hour. No one else felt like talking. They slept on and off. Fifty drove on like a machine. Frank crooned on.

At some point, Buck asked, "Can we give Frank a break? I'm more of a country western guy myself. What's on the radio?"

Tara fiddled with the dial. Static. Static. Static...

"Keep trying."

"I have it on 'search'. What did you expect? Top 40?"

A weak voice broke out, then fell away again.

"Wait! Find that! Find it!"

Tara lunged for the dial, pressing keys until she found a voice again, soft, hidden behind a hiss, but human.

"...now that you've heard the Chinese broadcast, you know there's hope. But the government, your government, doesn't want that. They won't give you the truth! You'll only hear it from me. Stay warm, stay alive, stay free, and stay tuned. I'll be back tomorrow, same time, unless the black helicopters come for me. This is the Captain signing off from Churchill, last port in the free world."

Static resumed.

Buck lifted his chin. "Is it a recording?"

"Doesn't sound like it. Not if he's coming back tomorrow." Stokes couldn't believe someone would broadcast over the radio, only to offer *talk* radio? They couldn't play music the rest of the day?

"Sounds like you were right about Churchill," Tara nodded to Buck.

"Sounds insane," Cuba scoffed. "The government? Where have we seen any government? Some conspiracy nut broadcasting from his shelter."

"What's the truth coming from China?" Tara asked.

Buck leaned forward. "See if you can find more." The radio crackled and hissed. Nothing. After fifteen minutes, he gave up. 'So we wait. At least we know there's a crackpot at the end of the rainbow."

The message validated Buck's direction, but little else. They would have to wait.

Tara turned with another question. "Why do you call them 'Eaters'? Why don't you call them 'zombies'?"

All four men stiffened, as if insulted. Stokes snorted, a practiced sound. "What? Like, in the movies? Arms out, eating brains and such? That's too weird."

"But that's what they are, right. I mean, some version."

Buck butted in. "We use 'Eaters' for short. The whole name is Dust Eaters, 'cause they're slow."

She made no sign of recognition.

"You know, 'Eat my dust!'"

Tara rolled her eyes. "I get it. I can't believe you spent three months fighting zombies but you won't call them that."

Cuba chimed in. "Technically, we're not even sure they're zombies."

"Really? Plagued humans who reanimate after death, become aggressive, and try to eat you? What's not zombie about that?"

Buck's voice went flat. "Zombies aren't real. Eaters are."

That worked for Stokes. He couldn't spend his days fearing and fighting an imaginary creature. "Naming it makes it real."

They went quiet, lost in horrible thoughts.

He took a swig out of the bottle and reiterated, "Dust Eaters. That's what we call them," as if that ended the discussion.

Cuba, however, grew philosophical. "It's a good point. I've never seen the dead and buried reanimate. Only the recently dead. I used to sleep in graveyards. They offer great cover and the fewest unexpected visitors. No hands reaching out. No empty graves to fall in."

Stokes gave him a look. "You sleep in ... that's a little creepy."

Tara didn't buy it. "Maybe because they're stuck under six feet of dirt. I'll bet if you dig down, they'll try to get you."

Stokes chimed in. "Mummies either."

Fifty piped up. "No brains."

When Fifty didn't elaborate, Cuba went on, "Egyptians use a crochet hook to pull the brains out the nose during the mummification process. And brains rot out fast in a graveyard."

"Cuba's right, though." Buck joined in. "The only dead who ever turn are the recently dead. I was hitchhiking once," he interrupted himself, "I didn't tell you guys this one. Funny story. This was before we met you, Stokes. When you guys lost me during the run-in at the factory, before we circled up again in, what was that town?" He got his story turned around, trying to decide whether to fill in the back story for Tara and Stokes or just tell the story to the guys. He chose the former. "Anyway, so I'm running like a bat out of hell from this pack of Eaters that found us in a factory we'd camped out in. Before I knew it I'd lost the rest of the guys. You know how it is when that happens."

Tara shook her head, no.

"When the shit hits the fan, it's every man for himself. You focus on the Eaters attacking you and that's it. Anyway, I get to this road and I keep thinking, 'Head north. Head north.' Five minutes later I hear a car coming. I figure Cuba found us some wheels. Eaters don't drive, so I'm safe, right?

"I stick out my thumb to hitch a ride. The window rolls down. It isn't Cuba. I don't know who it is, but this jerk slows down and passes right by me, a fifty megawatt grin on his face. He drives right past."

"He didn't pick you up?"

"No! I mean, probably he was high or tripping on something, but I didn't think of it at the time. I was mad. As he pulls out of sight around the corner I thought, 'That son-of-a-bitch! I hope he crashes.' Right then, BAM! I hear the soda can sound of metal hitting something solid. I jog up the road. Sure enough, he hit a patch of black ice and drifted off the road, smack into a tree."

"Karma."

"Right? So I catch up to the car. The car is totaled, no use to me. The guy's still in there, pinned to his seat by a huge branch sticking through the windshield. I know he's dead. I know this because the tree is now growing out of his throat."

"Ew," Tara says.

"Then he starts to moan."

"He turned?"

"Yup, he turned right there. Not one minute after that branch took him out."

Tara looked hard. "What did you do?"

"I, uh, finished him off. I didn't want him getting loose and following me. That's not the point. The point is, he turned right away. Those are the people who turn."

Tara looked confused. "Wait, so he turned? Was he bit or something?"

The men looked at each other again. Stokes' heart skipped a beat. She didn't know. He looked at Buck. So did Cuba.

Buck shrugged. "So that's another thing to add to the non-zombie list. Zombie bites don't make you turn."

"Oh, come on. How do you get the disease, then?"

"Uh, we think it's airborne."

It took a moment for that to sink in. Tara gave them an incredulous look, a kind of half-smile of disbelief. She leaned forward like she wanted to speak then sat back again. The smile faded, replaced by a look of genuine concern. "Wait, so you're saying.... no."

"Yes."

"That can't be."

"It is. We're already infected. When we die, we turn."

"Bullshit."

"Sorry."

She mulled that over for a while. "So how do you know you're infected? I mean, is there a blood test or something?"

Buck looked like he'd swallowed a bug. "No. You don't need a blood test. You have it."

"Except me," Stokes added. He hated how serious the conversation turned. It ruined his hard-earned buzz. He held up the bottle. "I'm self-medicated. Let those little Eater germs shrivel up and die."

Tara fought some form of revulsion then held out her hand. "Do you mind, Stokes, if I have a swig of my own alcohol?"

"Be my guest," he said, but had the courtesy to dig out a fresh, unopened bottle. He hesitated between the cognac and the vodka. He gave her the cognac. That was a girls' drink anyway.

"Don't drink so much," Stokes panicked when she started chugging. He pushed the bottle down. "Uh, 'Alcohol lowers your blood pressure, makes you cold'," he said, winking at Buck.

Tara handed the bottle back to Stokes. "I'd rather kick some zombie ass."

Stokes accepted it. "'Eater ass. Thatta girl."

"Eater ass. Right. Sorry."

For at least ten minutes, no one spoke. The tracks rumbled beneath them. The rails stretched on in front and behind to infinity. The trees marched alongside, meeting on the horizon. It looked less like a path, more like a tunnel, a bright white tunnel of conifers. Snowflake banshees shrieked across their path, whistling through the uninsulated cracks around the windows.

"You know what else is weird?" Cuba kept his vision out the windshield, but that tone in his voice sounded like he was about to tell them something they didn't want to hear. Stokes shivered when Cuba spoke this way. It always meant an impending glimpse of hell.

Cuba spent three months fighting through some of the most infested regions of the country. He saw horrors no one else could ever dream. When Cuba speaks, he has the unnerving ability to peel back a piece of the earth, to let a little fire escape with the sound of a million tortured screams. He invites you to look inside, beckoning with those powerful hands, his face calm as a mask. Come on, look, or are you man enough? Look at this Earthfire. Look at the unspeakable terror my eyes have seen. See for yourself that menagerie of tortured flesh, that veil of gloom, that Love Killer. See the sparks fly off the anvil of hate as the devil beats your heart into a flat sheet of pure iron. Let me show you the masks of death so you may choose one to fit your skull. Let me guide you through the Valley of Death for I have a summer house here and know the neighbors by name. See how...

"I just wanted to tell you about a dog." Cuba said.

"Was I talking out loud?"

"Yes!" they chimed in.

"You're from Miami?" Tara asked.

"Born and raised."

"What the hell are you doing up here? Why didn't you hop on a boat and head south to somewhere warm?"

"South is a big thing for you," Buck mumbled.

Cuba shrugged. "My family came on a boat. They made a lot of sacrifices so I could live in America. It would dishonor them to go back that way. North. That's the only direction for my family."

"That's so noble."

"It was stupid. I don't know what the hell I was thinking. Should have hijacked a sailboat and kicked it in the Caribbean for the last three months."

"You mentioned a dog?" Stokes couldn't stand the tension. He'd been holding his breath this whole time. He had to know what was so damn scary about this dog.

"Right, the dog. I was casing a house outside Kansas City. It looked untouched, so I figured there was food inside. I called out, made my presence known, told them I'd walk away if they were home, you know, so they wouldn't shoot me."

"You would have walked away? That's nice."

"Of course not. I wanted to know how many people I was up against."

"Oh."

"Anyway, no one answered. I waited a few minutes, but no one showed. So I went for it. As soon as I opened the door, something big hits me in the chest. I fell back onto the lawn, this big thing on top of me. It was a dog. Well, if there's one thing I'm protected against, it's a bite. That dog only clamped on to an arm guard and duct tape. I used my other hand to grab my .44 and blasted it in the chest. An instant later it knocked me down again and went for my throat. I managed to crawl into a car in the driveway. It beat itself against the window, slobber and blood plastering the glass. It had a gaping hole in the side where I shot it, but it wasn't bleeding. That's when I noticed it. Patchy fur, skin falling off its face. I rolled down the window a crack and stuck out my gun. When the damn thing bit it, I pulled the trigger.

"After I got out of the car, I inspected the carcass. Not much left to inspect, but by then I knew. It was infected."

Another bombshell. Stokes' hands shook. "Thanks Cuba. Now we know the world is even more fu..."

"How could a dog get infected?" Tara interrupted.

"That's what I wondered."

Buck joined in. "Viruses spread through multiple species, but they don't affect them in the same way."

"Just saying what I saw."

Stokes clung to hope. "Maybe he had rabies. I had a dog once that..."

"It wasn't rabies. I've seen enough Eaters in my time to recognize the signs. Even in a dog. I'm telling you. It was infected."

Buck laughed, one short burst.

"What's so funny."

"I shot a squirrel once for target practice."

"Ha ha. How funny."

"No, I mean, I remembered it when you mentioned the dog. The shot took out his entire midsection. I'm looking through the scope and damned if that squirrel wasn't crawling away. It had little more than two front legs and a head, but it crawled away. I dismissed it at the time. Nerves, I thought. But, now that you mention it, yeah, I've seen a few animals that I thought were infected."

Tara spoke, quiet. "I saw a deer."

"Where?"

"On our front lawn, gnawing at the birch tree I planted there last summer. A bare skull for a head. Ugliest thing I ever saw. My husband shot it. Thought we'd use it for food, but he told me it wasn't edible. I thought…. I thought it was just sick."

"It's never the birds, though," Cuba added. "I've never seen a bird affected, even though…" He didn't finish his sentence.

Stokes flashed on the stationmaster in the chair. *They're inside us.* "When… wass… the lass time you blinked?"

Buck laughed. "Dude, you are so drunk."

He was drunk. Drunk enough to voice his crazy theory out loud. Drunk enough to slur, "I'm sris. Serus. Se…"

Tara looked confused. "I don't know. I didn't think about it. There, I blinked. So what?"

Stokes wanted to know he wasn't crazy. He noticed it a few weeks ago, staring at the snow until he almost went blind. Did anyone else experience this problem? Maybe this wasn't the best time to explain it. "There's nothing stopping you from blinking. You just don't do it automatically. You find yourself staring, wide-eyed, waiting to blink. If you don't... I think you're infected." That's not what he said, word for word, but he got the point across.

"Why would a disease have anything to do with blinking?"

"I don't know. I don't know. I just think, no one blinks anymore." Then, because he felt emotional about it, he added, "I miss blinking."

He regretted saying it, the word 'miss', like an emotional minefield. Survivors never talk about it. He hoped Tara wouldn't pick up the thread, being new to the life and not knowing any better.

The others let it slide. The cab lapsed into silence again, but there seemed to be an unnatural bit of forced blinking for the next half hour.

They fell asleep. Fifty kept the truck moving. Maybe he slept a little too. Not like he'd go off the tracks.

The rumble of the engine stopped, drifted to a halt. Only the heater fan kept blowing.

The lack of movement woke them.

Buck wiped a speck of drool off his lip. "What happened? Are we there?"

Fifty tapped the dashboard. "Out of gas."

Cuba swore in Spanish. "How far to the next town?"

Tara checked a map she'd found in the glove compartment. "Another 40 kilometers."

Dusk slashed the horizon into bloody ribbons, but only the headlights illuminated the track ahead.

"Fine. At a steady pace we can make it by tomorrow. Grab the gear out of the back and let's get moving." Buck stepped out of the truck and closed the door. No one followed. They heard his muffled voice say, "Holy Saints it's cold!"

"It's warm in here," Stokes pleaded. The heater fan continued to blow, but the air already cooled.

The others stepped out, letting more cold air in. Stokes shrugged his coat back on, complaining the whole time. He dreaded emerging into that frigid winter after so many cozy, warm hours. It was like birth. He wanted to scream. He stayed inside.

Cuba spoke up. "We can't leave the truck on the tracks. What if a train comes?"

"Doubtful, but good point." Buck thought a moment. "Fifty, tie off the winch. We'll pull it off. Then we walk."

Stokes watched Fifty lug the heavy hook out into the darkness, loop the cable around a pine tree, and secure the hook to the line. He had no intention of going out there. He shouted through the window, "I'm not moving. I'm fine right here."

"Good, you volunteered." Buck indicated he roll down the window and then stuck his head inside. "The battery has juice, so the winch should work. Pull this lever here. That should pull the truck off the track toward that tree. When you're done, catch up."

"You want me to drive?"

"Hell, Stokes, you're drunk. If anyone is qualified to drive into a tree, you are."

Backpacks on, Tara and Fifty plodded down the tracks, blending into darkness beyond the reach of the headlights.

Dammit Buck. He knew what Stokes hated more than cold. Solitude. This wasn't the first time he got him moving this way.

He shouted out the window. "All right! I'll do it! I'm coming!"

Buck waved over his shoulder as he and Cuba started off.

Stokes cursed under his breath. "Damn it. I don't know how to do this." He pushed on the lever. The motor whined, but nothing happened. "Aw c'mon!" He pushed again. The cable stretched out at a forty-five degree angle to the left of the truck. Stokes felt the vehicle twisting, straining to stay on the tracks..

The winch groaned. *Maybe I'm not drunk enough*, he thought. He took another swig of fortitude.

The base of the tree, where Fifty looped the cable, sat below the rails. The tightening cable pulled the front end down, leaning on the plow. The rear axle, lighter without the packs, rose up off the rails. With a lurch, the whole truck pivoted perpendicular to the track.

Stokes watched four black specks walk around a bend in the rails, out of sight.

Alone.

"Cmoncmoncmon." He jammed the lever forward. The rear end lifted higher. Stokes slid on the vinyl seat as the front end dug in.

Stokes clenched his teeth. His cheeks felt heavy and numb. This is what it must feel like to be an astronaut, he thought, drifting away from the space station after the tether snaps. No hope of return. A long cold trip to the end of the universe, to the end of time. The thought terrified him. Humanity, what was left of it, seemed infinitely remote.

A branch cracked as the cable twisted on the pine. With the back suspended, all the weight transferred to the front left tire. It blew, dipping the hood further until the third wheel left the track. At this point the whole truck rolled over sideways. The window shattered, spraying chunks of safety glass. Cold air rushed in, like filling a vacuum. The winch whined and smoked. The tree split. It fell forward, crushing the hood. One branch swished through the vacant window, narrowly missing his head. Suddenly free, the winch wheeled in the slack so fast that it bound itself with a biting groan.

Stokes shut it off. He crawled sideways out the rear window and stood up. Now the truck lay *across* the tracks... with a tree on top of it. Alone, there was no way of moving this mess.

"If you can't take the truck to the tree, take the tree to the truck. Say that ten times fast." He took another shot from his friend Mr. Daniels. "I succeeded in wrecking it. That will have to do."

To his great disappointment, no one unloaded his liquor box from the back. It now lay open, half of the bottles smashed on the side of the pickup, a multi-hued liquid dripping out, melting the snow. He salvaged the few remaining bottles, played taps in his head, fished his pack out of the snow, and ran down the track into the darkness.

There are no weekends in survival. No vacations to request. No hard deadlines to look forward to.

You forget the past in its irrelevancy. You disregard the unpredictable future. To survive you live in the everlasting now.

No matter how adverse the present, take comfort in the undeniable and infinitely consoling truth: right now, you are alive. Through most of universal history, you did not exist, nor will you see the eons that remain. But right now, *Cogni ergo sum*. To think is to live. The body is but the servant of the mind. Even to feel pain and hunger and loss is a luxury, a gift. If each coin has two sides, then each side is...

"How can you talk and walk at the same time? I have barely enough breath as it is!" Tara complained. "And Fifty, isn't that gun heavy?"

He nodded.

"Is that practical, carrying that weight? You have zero chance of finding spare ammunition for a .50 caliber. Why do it?"

"Eaters scare me."

Buck stopped and turned. "That's the most I've ever heard you say."

Sometime in the night, Buck held them up. "How far do you think we walked?"

"Ten kilometers," Cuba guessed.

"It's getting cold. We better hunker down for the night. Let's make camp here. Stay close to the rails. We sure as hell don't want to lose them if it snows."

Fear froze Stokes' heart. The rails were their only path through the wilderness. Losing them meant wandering into starvation and death.

They set up camp beside a thicket. Bushes provided cover from the wind.

Tara didn't bring a tent. No tent in her ridiculously heavy pack. *Stupid.* Buck solved the problem. "Stokes, you and Cuba sleep in one tent. Tara can have yours."

"How chivalrous of me," Stokes whispered. He didn't like the idea of sleeping in the same tent as Cuba, coughing up blood on him in the middle of the night.

Cuba set up Stokes', now Tara's, tent. He pulled branches out of the woods and stacked them against each other, forming a lean-to. Then he started throwing snow on top of that.

"I thought the point was to keep the snow off?" Tara asked.

Cuba's labored breathing kept him from answering, so Stokes did. "Snow is an insulator. Traps air inside it. Keep a layer of it over your tent and you'll be nice and toasty." This woman wouldn't have lasted a night without them. He hoped she realized that. She might be a crack shot but that wouldn't keep her warm.

Cuba set up their tent the same way and crawled in. "Damn I miss Miami." He passed out almost immediately.

Although exhausted after the trek, Stokes couldn't sleep. Tara's presence woke something in him. Maybe the scent of a woman. Maybe her fresh ties to the old world, the world he tried to forget. He stayed up late, drinking, thinking, trying not to think. He thought about the life he left behind, of faculty parties and nights at the piano, about warm houses and warmer grad students, weekends of repose with a book and a fireplace, days on the beach during sabbatical, and those lovely nights. A glimmering utopia so remote as to be difficult to believe.

He drank to the memory of every memory.

He listened to the night sounds. The wind flapped the tent like a sail in luff. Over that, a miserable symphony played out in the night, a dirge, a mass, all in a minor key. Fifty roared like a wounded lion. Tara whimpered like a teakettle. Buck howled in an open mouthed moan. Cuba stopped breathing altogether, seconds ticking by before apnea gave ground to a racking cough that somehow never woke him.

It's impossible to concentrate on my own misery.

Stokes' skin burned like a furnace. He shed his coat and hat, but it didn't help. He needed some air.

Outside the tent, the wind buffeted him. It felt good. Starlight froze to the ground, enough to make out shapes and obstacles but little more. Stokes took a few steps, but the ground whirled around him. Bushes blurred. A nausea rose in his throat. He realized he might have had too much this time, but the numbness offered a welcome relaxation.

Still warm, he stripped off his shirt and gloves, let the frigid air cool him. He peeled off his boots and tossed them back toward the tent. Then his pants went too. It felt so natural. Human. Alive. The ice broke under his feet, cut into the soft places between his toes.

He shivered. Even warm, his body vibrated uncontrollably. He had trouble gripping the bottle. *It might be a good idea to put my clothes back on*, he thought.

He lost his sense of direction. He found himself on the tracks. The wind scoured the snow away, exposing the rails and even the gravel in between.

The shivering increased. He dropped the bottle, reached to pick it up, but couldn't convince his fingers to close around the glass.

His heart beat his ribcage like a tympani. That chest, hot as a jet engine, couldn't stop shivering. Panting in short, quick, breaths, he looked up at the sky.

The sky calmed him. Tiny points of light. Like him, they travelled so far through the darkness and cold. That light would continue to travel, forever, until it hit something solid - ice and snow, iron rails, Stokes. *I am stardust*, he thought. He touched the starlight on his chest. *It found me. It will bring me home.*

The lulling piano of Arvo Part's *Alina* came to mind. He never understood the piece before, never had the patience. Now the stars twinkled, one for each note. He counted them, measure for measure.

He lay on the tracks. He couldn't remember how he got there, in the middle of the wilderness, at night. Who brought him? In dreams, you can't remember how you arrived.

He tried to roll, to sit up, but couldn't feel his limbs. They didn't want to move. They liked it here. So peaceful. So warm. His heart slowed. His breathing slowed. His mind relaxed.

He closed his eyes. He felt starlight on his eyelids.

Starlight is warm, he thought. *So space is warm. Darkness is warm.*

It took time for his brain to die. He explored the cosmos. He held a long conversation with his mother. He argued with the department head and won. He went back to that beach in San Juan. He tried to cry but laughed. This went on.

That singing again. Like angels. A single note impugned his fantasies, soft at first, but rising. *B flat*. Behind it, a bass rumbled. He didn't hear it so much as felt it in his back, transmitted through the gravel directly into his spine. *The earth is singing to me.*

His skin crawled, like something kicked into action beneath it, even as his heart stopped. His breathing, already slow, ceased. His body went limp, ice taking advantage of this immobility to freeze his skin to the rails. Numb and fading, he hardly noticed.

He stared up at the sky, eyes wide open, unblinking, even as darkness settled on his mind like a thick blanket. His thoughts faded. He stopped wondering at the itchiness, like subdermal teeth trying to get out. He no longer registered the ringing in his ears, the singing steel rails, even as the sound grew louder, louder, insistent, like a warning scream from a long lost love.

Something important begged for his attention, insisted that he wake, recover, run. He did not, could not respond, but it fired off in his mind a single synapse, a connection, an understanding, one final thought to take with him into the afterlife, two words for what was coming, for all the hope he left behind.

A train.

THE TRAIN

Today I die.

Before he opened his eyes, Cuba whispered his mantra. Certainty removed the fear, the doubt, the paralysis of indecision. It helped him rise, prepare, and meet another day. If night found him alive, he felt not relief but anticipation. If not today, then tomorrow. Each morning reduced the odds. Each hour increased the certainty. This must be the day. *Today I die.*

A strong pain bit into his chest. He coughed a piece of lung into his palm. He flicked on a head lamp. Blood oozed across his lifeline. He wondered if he should keep it, if a doctor could put it back in. He unzipped the tent, reached out, and rubbed his hands in the snow until they chapped.

It was inevitable, he reasoned. Fuck Death long enough and she'll impregnate you. He felt it growing larger, night after night, a malignant black lump under the ribcage. Its birth would be the death of him.

Darkness hid their tents from dawn. He listened to the familiar sounds of Fifty snoring, Buck breathing. He didn't hear Stokes' drunken murmering. His arm dragged across the sleeping bag beside him. Empty. The head lamp confirmed it. "Stokes?" Maybe he went to take a piss. He waited an appropriate amount of time, but when Stokes didn't come back Cuba shrugged on a coat and stepped out.

His breath clouded like a beard. Toothpicks formed in his nostrils. The chill invigorated him.

The wind swept clean any trace of their tracks from the night before. No new footsteps marred the snow in front of the tent. With mounting concern, he realized Stokes left a long time ago.

His mind raced through a dozen scenarios. Did Stokes wander off in his sleep? He didn't have a history of sleepwalking. He had been drunk, but that wasn't unusual. Was he pulled away by wolves? No, that would have woken him. Did he run away, ashamed at his uselessness? Cuba felt a pang of guilt for not making Stokes feel more useful. Did he exit the tent to relieve himself, only to be attacked? Again, no, the Eaters would have smelled everyone, would be upon them. So he wandered off?

Cuba walked the perimeter, checked the other tents, then stood on a hillock to scan the area.

An orange glow illuminated airborne flakes on the horizon. Too small to be the rising sun, something approached through the woods. Something big. It groaned, a long, ringing moan that shook the ground. Three glowing eyes pierced the forest.

His breath caught. Was this a dream? He must be hallucinating. A red haired giant stalked the gloaming. Huge, unblinking eyes cast their orange light his way. Spotting him, it bore down, steady, growing larger.

Those eyes terrified Cuba more than anything he'd seen in the last three months. It took him several moments to realize it wasn't a hallucination, not a giant.

A train!

Hope and fear and desperation fought for control of his emotions. Crib notes of frustration ran through his mind. He never believed Buck's plan would work. He didn't care. He stayed with the group because he wanted to spend his last days with the living. Now that he realized Buck might be right, there might be somewhere to go, he felt an instant of remorse and longing. His death might be today, just when he found something to live for.

For a moment, he forgot Stokes. That could wait.

"Buck! Buck! A train!" He shook their tents, knocking the lean-tos apart. "Fifty, wake up! A train!"

He needed to stop it, to get on somehow. How could he flag it down?

Forgetting the cold, he stumbled toward the tracks. The light approached, billowing in a plume of snow. He waved the head lamp in his arms as high as he could reach, tried to make himself big and bright.

If it didn't stop, they would never make it to Hudson Bay in time to catch it. What if this was the last train? What if they were stuck out here in the cold, waiting for a train that would never come?

Missing this train would be worse than never expecting one.

The engine crawled through the wilderness, slowed by drifts, a huge plow tossing snow off the tracks. Desperate, Cuba began kicking snow onto the tracks, hopelessly hopeful. His boot snapped something stiff.

A narrow cone of light erupted from the forest long enough to reveal a naked form lying on the rail bed as if in deep slumber. Two hands rested on the rails, one finger now askew.

"Stokes!" Cuba knelt to throw his coat over the prostrate form. His gloved hands dug into the snow beneath the body. Warm. What was he doing out here? Why wasn't he in the tent, talking in his sleep? *Why the hell is he naked?*

Exploding snow thundered across the valley as the train blasted through a snowdrift. Cuba couldn't leave Stokes on the tracks.

Frantic now, torn between stopping the train and digging out Stokes' body, he glanced back at the tents for help. No one came. He had to do this alone.

His ears picked up a low keening, the sound of steel torturing steel. Did it see him?

He glanced up to gauge the distance.

Hope melted.

Something was wrong. The back of the train flickered in a haze of emberglow.

The train is on fire.

As it neared, the details twisted into focus. Windows belched fire over the roof. Stainless steel skin smoked and blackened. Thunderclouds whirled above, alive with cinders. Sparks shot from the wheels like roman candles.

Over it all, he heard the screams.

Long shadows stretched across the snow. Horrible shadows. Like Thai paper puppet shows, human forms wavered across that stage, running, chasing, dying. The shadows fell. The stage consumed the players. Even as he watched, a body crashed through the fourth wall, plunging upside down, stopped in an instant by an callous tree.

With all his attention riveted on the train, he nearly missed the movement beside him. The body stirred. Matted hair clung to black iron. Skin separated as hands broke from the rails. It rose up on one elbow, reaching for him. The jaw cracked open.

An irrational sense of elation filled Cuba. *He's alive! It's not too late to save him!*

Then instinct drove him backward, away from the mouth that breathed without steam, out of the way of the thundering train.

Stokes shook as the tracks rumbled. His head turned, eyelids wide open as if sewn.   Fingers stretched out, and Cuba, paralyzed by fear and awe, did nothing but stare as they closed around his boot.

Two massive hands seized Cuba from behind and wrenched him away from the tracks.

Stokes let out a purr.

600 tons of flaming steel obliterated him.

A maelstrom of sparks and fire and frost and snow erupted as the train engine blew past. Wheels shrieked in tandem with hundreds of dying voices. Cuba covered his head and ears against it all. A heat wave scorched his face. Smoke left him choking and blind but not before he glimpsed the inferno inside, a cauldron boiling plastic and flesh into a stew. Through it all, dark forms moved, on the hunt, unfazed by their own charred oblivion.

In seconds, the train passed, leaving in its wake a black stain on the snow, some of it soot, some of it oil, some of it Stokes.

Cuba caught his breath. Fifty let go of his shoulders.

He stood up. Three kilometers down the tracks, the train slowed, drifted, and came to a stop. The fire erupted in earnest, engulfing the last carriage in a fireball.

Buck came up behind them, tousle haired, rubbing sleep out of his eyes, late to the party. "That's my train."

Sprinting toward the flames, Cuba described to Buck how he found Stokes.

"Dammit, I told him not to drink so much," was all he said, too excited about the train to mourn Stokes now.

Cuba couldn't help but feel slighted. Stokes may not have been with them as long as Fifty, but he mattered. As he ran down the tracks, Cuba's thoughts were torn between that last image of Stokes and the approaching horror. He never had time to mourn anyone. They'd come back to haunt him someday, the forgotten. He prayed he'd be dead before then.

"Hey Fifty!" Buck called out, giddy with excitement. He must have slept well. "What are the odds anyone's alive in there?"

"50/50".

"That good?"

With a popping noise, the rear door flew outward. A chunk of metal fell from the ceiling behind it. Something charred, creaky, and bipedal stumbled out of the opening, flaming. Steam rose from its footsteps. "Is it alive?" Buck shouted.

Tara took aim through her scope, pulled the trigger. The creature's head exploded in a ball of fire and sparks. "Nope."

"That reminds me," Buck went on, apropos of nothing, "Why do they call it Texas Barbecue? We had some damn good barbecue in Oklahoma. The secret is maple syrup. So good. And dry mustard." He took a shot at another corpse falling out of the train. "Dry, not that stuff in the jar."

They approached the back of the train, ready for anything. The last two cars were a total loss. Fire tore through the sleepers. Gutted husks groaned and buckled under intense heat. Paint bubbled and smoked like a forgotten omelet.

The third car suffered at its coupling. A trio of human torches tumbled out into the snow. Before they could stand, Cuba batted their heads with a crowbar. Burning hair and black bile arced across the carriage to hiss and smoke where it stuck.

"Get inside and see if you can salvage anything!" Buck pointed to the fourth car. It smoked, but not every window belched flames.

Cuba leapt up the steps and through the door. Fifty brought up the rear. They checked the door between cars. The fire had fused it shut. Nothing would come through behind them.

Smoke obscured everything but the walls two feet away. Cuba raised his .45 to eye level. The heat penetrated his boots, sticky like tarpaper. The acrid flavor of melted plastic crept into his lungs and forced a cough. He couldn't stop coughing. He bent over, spitting blood. *I'm disintegrating.*

A dark shape erupted out of the smoke, hands reaching. Fighting for breath, he pulled the trigger on instinct. The shape blew back into the gloom. He shook his head to clear it as the report echoed down the narrow hall, bouncing off smoking panels of fake wood. His ears rang.

Fifty bent to inspect the body. Blood pooled out of a middle aged woman's head, saturating the thin carpet. "Dammit," he whispered.

Cuba wiped his mouth. "Don't tell Buck," he said when he could speak. He was more concerned about what Buck would say than that he'd shot the living. Wasn't the first time.

Fifty nodded.

Cuba shouted out the window, "Some of the passengers are alive! Hold your fire until you're sure!"

Moving on, he jerked the pistol toward each compartment. Most lay empty.

A window imploded. A pipe raked the frame, knocking out shards of glass like broken teeth. Tara's voice followed. "Buck says to throw the suitcases out!"

Fifty rummaged through the overheads, dropping cases and bags for Cuba to toss out. They flew through the air and stuck haphazard in the snow.

The dining car offered little loot. He yanked open drawers and refrigerators, tossing microwave packets out the window. Condiments followed – tea, creamer, salt, pepper. The instant coffee he stuffed in his pockets. The packets of mustard he left. "Dry my ass."

He placed the back of his hand against the door separating the dining car from the last carriage. *Stupid. Of course it's hot.* He yanked hard, drawing back the curtain on the puppet theater of Hell.

The stench hit them first, the smell of vaporized plastic, meat, and burning hair. A gust of wind surged behind them and pushed the smoke aside. He wished it hadn't. Now they could see.

Bodies piled up against the far end, a volcano of limbs and blood. The living crawled and slid up its slope, trying to break down the far door. Eaters chewed up the rear, overwhelming the living, clawing back the writhing bodies like fresh meat. The living and undead broiled in a ball of death. Blood ran thick until every pale arm, every screaming face, every piece of clothing went monochrome.

The fire started at the rear of the train, pushing survivors toward the engine. With that door locked and the crowd crushing from behind, the lead car transformed into a death trap.

Cuba cut loose on anything standing. He emptied a magazine, reloaded, then started pumping out the next. Heads exploded, bodies fell. Smoke stung his eyes as his sight narrowed to a cone directly in front of him, a field of view clotted with bloody faces, eyes of wild desperation, and gnashing teeth.

He waded into the dead, pushing forward, a hunter of hunters. Arms clutched at his pant legs. Bodies writhed under his feet. A pair of jaws closed on his calf, unable to penetrate the tape. He kicked it off. Adrenaline kept the pain at bay.

When he went empty, he flipped the pistol and started smashing heads.

In the narrow confines of the corridor, Fifty could do nothing but watch.

Cuba fought through knee deep corpses to reach the last few biters. Three of them had a woman by the throat. Before he could reach her, their teeth rent an artery. Her blank eyes stared as she mouthed the words '*help me*'. His arm rose and fell four times, the last for the woman.

There was no one left.

The cacophony of torment quieted. The fire crackled. Cuba's breathing slowed. His temples pounded.

He stood in a puddle of gore, wary of any movement, flinching when a body twitched. The floor wriggled and dripped with blood. At least eighty people piled up in the corridor. A few moments earlier and he might have saved someone. Now, aside from the hiss and pop of the heated cab, nothing made a sound. He looked up at Fifty, blank, unfeeling.

Fifty did the honors of saying "Clear!"

Another window imploded. Cuba nearly pitched over as he swiveled toward the sound.

Buck's voice filtered in with a blast of cold air. "Any survivors?"

Cuba didn't know what to say.

Fifty gave him a look, somewhere between shame and pity. "Us."

"I thought you said there were... Shit, Cuba."

Cuba whispered. "Past tense."

Buck grumbled inaudibly before saying, "Any more baggage?"

Cuba shrugged. "Nothing clean."

"Then get out of there before you burn up."

On the way down the steps, Tara tried to push her way in. "There must be lots of stuff in there we can use." She hesitated when she saw Cuba. His bloody boot slipped on a step.

Fifty held her arm and shook his head.

A thumping startled him from behind. The lavatory door shuddered. Cuba caught Tara's rifle, swung toward the door for a quick shot, but Fifty laid a beefy hand on him to wait. He brought a finger to his lips.

Buck shouted, "Someone in there?"

A young voice answered, "Occupied!"

Cuba rolled his eyes. "When you're done shitting yourself, you can come out. They're all dead."

"It's the dead ones I'm afraid of!"

Fifty laughed.

The latch clicked. The door slid open a crack. One clean eye peeped out, attached to a young, male face. "What are you smiling about?" he said.

Cuba pulled the balaclava off his face. "Go play outside, Kid. The weather's lovely."

A thin young man stepped out of the lavatory dressed in a black t-shirt and jeans. He rubbed his arms in the cold wind. "Where are we?" he asked, as if disappointed by the unscheduled stop.

"Middle of nowhere. Where were you headed?"

"Hudson Bay's the first stop." He waved his hand up the rails, then looked back at the burnt cars. "Weren't supposed to make any local stops."

"Good thing we didn't stay in Dauphin," Tara muttered.

Buck puffed himself up for his speech. "I can't help but notice you are homeless, friendless, and in need of assistance. You're in good company. Walk with us and you'll have the support you need. Leave at any time."

"Ok," the Kid shrugged.

"What's your name?" Tara asked.

He said something unpronounceable in Russian.

Buck didn't catch it. "Ok, uh, Kid, let's get you something warm to wear."

The Kid turned to the train. "I left my suitcase back in the..." The sight of the last two cars melting stopped him.

Buck turned him toward the suitcases on the ground. "Let's see what we have out here, shall we?"

Then he turned to Cuba. Cuba knew what Buck wanted to say, but Buck didn't bring it up. "Cuba, why don't you get... cleaned up."

Cuba excused himself. He melted into the tree line. Alone, he stripped down to nothing but his trunks and gloves. His chest steamed. A blanket of adrenaline kept the cold at bay.

Bruises, scratches, and healing wounds covered his body like a map of pain. The damage to his body didn't bother him.

He inspected his hands. They shook.

"Sorry little brother," he whispered.

That old problem. He smelled the creosote and tar of the streets of Miami, the sea breeze mixed with sweat and blood, the cordite of gun smoke and singed hair, the faux leather seats and brass gun casings after a drive-by. Everything he fought for, everyone he fought against, the long battle to control himself, to move on, to become a Big Brother and keep other young soldiers off the streets, in school, at home, at work, focused on the future. *Look at me*, he told them. *It can be done.*

Those little 'bangers. He told them they'd be safe, they'd live a better life, get away from gangs and drugs. Become productive citizens.

They became something.

Dead.

All this death, and his self-esteem forced him to mourn one more, a dozen more, a hundred. Not the marks on his helmet, not the ones he couldn't save. The ones he could.

He wondered where the balance lay. Did he save more kids, back in the day, than the living who got in his way now?

A Berserker I have been. A Berserker I have become.

I'm better than that. He rose above it once, why couldn't he do it now? The old days, those were brutal times, but with a system in place, police, judges, neighborhoods, gang loyalty, family. Out here, he was the system. *Do the right thing.* Life and death was his decision. *Not the living.* But once that tunnel vision kicked in...

How many times had he broken his promise? Rationalizing didn't work anymore. He had fewer and fewer excuses. One remained. When his little brother turned, his promise died, too.

Ice granules made for decent soap. He scrubbed everything - jacket, trousers, boots, gloves. When the snow around him resembled a killing zone, he moved to another snowbank. Now he worked on his hair and face. It felt good.

He carried a length of electrical wire in his pack and used it as a clothesline. He used it often. Sweaty and wet, his clothes would freeze in no time. Clap them against a tree, shake out the ice, and they'd be dry. Not a trick he'd learned in Miami.

Waiting for the ice to form, he stood there in a blanket, feeling the cold attack his skin. The silence comforted him. It also scared him. He imagined being alone in the world, everyone he knew either dead or killed by his wayward hand. It centered him, made him glad for the company he kept. He gathered himself, stopped shaking, stopped crying.

He asked his little brother, long dead, for forgiveness.

Again.

He shook the ice out of his clothes and rejoined the crew.

"Oh, look, you're all clean," Buck said. "Just in time to get dirty. We need to get those bodies away from the door so we can get into the engine. That's our ride north."

Cuba shuddered.

He felt those jaws clamped to his leg. The idea of going back in there...

"The door to the engine is up front. I can get in from the outside," The Kid volunteered. Before Buck could say otherwise, he moved toward the engine. Moments later, he had the cab door open.

Cuba owed the Kid one. Even worse than killing was going back in. In the heat of the moment, he could forgive himself. Later, seeing what he'd done...

"How did you know how to do that?" Impressed, Buck looked for other uses for the Kid.

"I love trains. I got into engineering so I could build them some day."

"You know how to drive one?"

"You mean this 4400 horsepower F-type engine? Only on a PC simulator."

"Good enough for me."

Cuba took point, climbed up on the cab to look through the windshield. The engineer lay slumped over the controls, bleeding from a massive head wound. His body applied the brakes. He never even turned.

Lucky for us.

He peeled the body off the console, threw it out in the snow like luggage, and wiped away the blood with a rag. The Kid took the controls and, after a few wrong guesses, released the coupling. The cab rolled forward.

A screech got his guard up. "What is that?"

"There's something lodged underneath!" Tara called from outside.

Cuba didn't want to get down and look. What if he found... Stokes?

Tara disappeared then stepped back again. "Looks like part of a truck!"

"Which part?"

She shrugged. "The part that goes 'screech'?"

The Kid checked the brakes and then jumped out, leaving Cuba alone. The engines rumbled in the floor. This cab was the safest place he'd been in weeks. He savored it as long as he could. All that steel to protect him. That powerful engine to take him away. He fought for a world like this. Sane. Rational.

Safe.

Buck called him. He had a hard time leaving. The cold clutched him as soon as he stepped outside.

"Nice work!" Buck admired the separated trains. Firelight flickered on his face. Even though the sky was bright, the sun hadn't risen. "You and Fifty try to get that thing out from under there. The rest of us will play baggage gorilla." He tucked up his arms and made an ape face as we walked back to the others.

Tara stalked around the train, looking for something to shoot.

Cuba lay down under the chassis. A fender spiraled around an axle with one bare hub attached. It took them a good half hour to pry it loose. "I got a feeling," he said to Fifty, straining on Mr. Crow, "I know where this came from." Fifty nodded.

When they finished, they joined Tara, Buck, and the Kid as they piled luggage into a big heap. "The Kid told us a campfire story about his little train adventure. Why don't you fill in the Big Boy?"

"I'm legally an adult. I'd prefer you don't call me The Kid."

"Sure, Kid." Buck patted him on the head and turned to Cuba. "This is the last train out of Winnipeg! I was right!"

"Winnipeg is dead." The Kid tossed a bag to Cuba. It crunched like broken bones when it hit the snow. "I went home for winter break when all this started." The next one thudded like bodies in a pile. Some broke open, resembling a flea market. "My parents convinced us we could wait it out. They kept me from going back to school. We had some food, supplies. That lasted longer than we thought it would, but eventually we ran out of water and medicine. We had to wander out." He disassembled the baggage pile as he talked.

"We heard about one last train, headed north. The police, a small force at this point, cordoned off the train station. They tried to maintain control... My parents knew they couldn't get us all through, so they sent me and my sister. Hundreds of people tried the same thing. It was chaos. My sister held my hand, but... I lost her in the crowd..." He stopped, focused on breathing.

Buck put a hand on the boy's shoulder. "It's all right. We all know this part of the story."

The Kid looked at each of them. Did he see a team, or four lonely individuals? They were both. The Kid shook it off and took a deep breath. He kept his eyes on his work as he continued. "Refugees crowded the station, packed twenty deep up and down Main Street. The staff, even with a few police, didn't stand a chance. A conductor," he made a sound, a half-laugh, half sob, "a conductor called out for tickets! Can you believe it? The ticket booth was empty! He tried to kick off a family because they didn't have tickets. They had two little girls!"

"Lucky for them, it turns out." Buck dumped out a red suitcase and sorted through the debris.

"No." He seemed interested in a man's necktie. "The mother threw the girls on the back of the train." The Kid glanced at the burning cars. "The crowd tore that conductor apart. They stampeded to get on. Everyone inside tried to shut the doors, but they swarmed on the cabs, climbed on top, grabbed every handhold underneath. I managed to crawl through a window as the train moved forward. It dragged that crowd right out of the station. Bodies rolled under the tracks for miles. People on the roof dropped off as they froze. People were jammed so tight in the passages, some even suffocated. They turned. When I think about being crushed up against one of them, unable to move or get away, those teeth clicking at my ear... Somehow we managed to get most of them tossed out before they did much damage.

"A few miles out, the heating system failed. Even with all that body heat, most people weren't prepared for the cold. We had no water on the train. By last night, we'd lost a lot of people. It wasn't long before the dead started to outnumber us. They started to tear into the living."

"How did you survive?"

"I hid in the bathroom and locked the door." He tossed a hair dryer aside and dumped out a board game. "I heard the screaming all night, footsteps up and down the hall. No one knocked anymore."

"How did the fire start?"

"I don't know, but a few kilometers back we hit something big. The train jolted, and I slammed forward against the wall. A fireball blew past the window. Must have started the fire at the back of the train."

"Everything happened so fast. Next thing I knew I heard renewed screaming and the heat started again."

"Goddamn Stokes." Buck whispered to Cuba. "Too drunk to crash a truck properly. Worked out well, though. That train would have sailed past us if not for him."

The Kid kept talking. "The train stopped, I heard shooting, and then you opened the door." He pulled a handful of feminine products from a cloth bag. He grimaced and made as if to throw them away.

Tara appeared and tore them from his grasp. "I'll take those, young man. You see any more, you let me know."

Buck urged him on. "You hid out in the bathroom the whole time?"

"Not my first choice." He selected another bag, a leather one. "But it had a strong lock."

"And your sister?" Cuba regretted the question as soon as he said it.

The Kid only shook his head.

"How old are you?" Tara asked.

"Nineteen. I know, I look younger. Everyone says that."

"You're lying! You look fourteen!"

"No! I'm in college. I'm studying engineering... *was* studying."

Buck clapped him on the shoulder. "Don't worry about it, Kid. No orphans among wolves. Time to study the art of ass kicking. No better teacher than Cuba over there."

Cuba gave him a don't-saddle-him-with-me look. He wasn't a Big Brother anymore. People around him ended up dead. He didn't want the responsibility. *I can't do it, little brother.*

"Yup," Buck continued, "Don't ever leave that man's side. He'll teach you a thing or two."

Buck sorted out several hard-shell cases and separated the supplies by case. Food in one, sweaters in another, medicine in the third, and so on. "We have a whole train now, so don't be picky. We can carry anything you think might be useful."

The last three cars were nothing but billowing black smoke. A steel skeleton leaned outward, held in place by the weight of the undercarriage. Snow melted down to the gravel on either side. Even at the front of the train, Cuba felt the heat. For once, he preferred not to.

There wasn't much room in the cab. A few seats, but not enough room to lay down. Everything had to be strapped on outside, but surface area wasn't a problem. This thing was huge.

Once everything was loaded, The Kid volunteered to take the controls. "Aw, man, this is great! You don't know how many train sets I had as a kid. I never thought I'd get to drive one. My five year old self is real jealous right now."

He fiddled with the controls, moved a lever or two, tapped a gauge. His smile faded. "This doesn't look like the simulator."

Buck frowned. "Can you get it to work?"

"Yeah, yeah. Give me a minute."

"Today?"

The Kid pulled a lever. A horn blasted, so loud and unexpected that everyone jumped.

Cuba shouted, "Jesus Christ, Kid!"

He looked even more nervous. "That's the horn."

Buck remained calm. "Never touch that again."

The Kid talked out loud, "Engine brake, train brake, dynamic brake."

Cuba pointed. "Did you try the one with blood on it?"

The Kid hesitated to push it, but when he did, the engine moved. "Here we go."

The train eased up to speed. Trees blurred. Snow whirled.

Buck tapped him on the shoulder. "We're going too fast."

"No way. At this rate, we'll be there in no time. Uh, where are we going?"

The train leaned into a turn. It shifted to the outside, wheels squealing, carriage moaning. Centripetal force threw the occupants to the walls. Cuba reached for the controls, eased the speed down.

Buck grinned. "We could probably go a little slower. We have until spring to get there."

"What happens in spring?"

"Another layer of permafrost melts and the tracks drop into the tundra. No maintenance crews to fix it."

"Great."

Fifty hunched over a disassembled rifle, cleaning it with a toothbrush and a tiny rag. An oily smell sweetened the cab.

Tara surprised them by pulling her own cleaning kit out of her pack and set to work on the Savage.

Cuba laid out his own weapons, an impressive amount. The Kid looked over his shoulder. "What have you got there?"

"These are my friends. This is Mr. Crow," he indicated the crowbar. "This is Babe," he pointed at an aluminum baseball bat. "This is Shiny," to brass knuckles. "Mr. Chuckles," a semi-automatic rifle. He continued on for some time.

The Kid looked impressed. He stepped over to Fifty. "What's yours called."

Fifty didn't look up. "Barrett."

Buck called back, "That's a Barrett fifty caliber sniper rifle, son. Those two are like big, silent, deadly twins. Hence, his full name. First name, Fifty. Last name, Fifty."

The Kid moved to Tara, "And yours is?"

"The Savage."

"Can I get one?"

"Get your own." Cuba hadn't meant to sound so brusque. The others even stopped to look at him. "I mean, I'll give you something when we get somewhere. I don't need you accidentally shooting up the cab."

The Kid retreated, cowed, but returned a few minutes later, after all the weapons were put away. Cuba had his helmet off, waving his finger in the air, stabbing imaginary creatures. "What are you doing?"

"He's counting." Buck said. "Can't count corpses in the hot zone."

"I have to picture them in my mind," Cuba said. "Replay events. Slow it down. I have a good memory."

"That's a blessing."

"No. It isn't." He wiped a hand across his bald head, then used the sweat to smudge a chalked number. He blew it dry and wrote 529.

"Not even making a dent," Tara frowned, as she added notches to her own belt.

Cuba looked at those numbers, so insignificant on their own, but remembered every one. Especially the first.

Buck sat down next to Tara. He reached over to her face, "You have something on your..."

She jerked her head away before he could touch her.

Buck paused, then resorted to pointing. "Some blood or something. Wipe that off."

Cuba knew that look. The girls in his barrio had it, the ones with drunkard fathers and boyfriends with anger management issues. Tara was fighting more battles than the one on the ground, and hers started long before this mess.

Until then, Cuba thought of her as a burden, a civilian they rescued, a shield for him to sacrifice at some later date. She was none of those things.

She was a survivor.

She might be clumsy in the outdoors. She might be an Eater tyro. But Cuba knew those weren't the things that get you killed out here. Not really.

He'd seen it enough times to know. People die when they're ready to. When they've had enough fear. When they pass the threshold for deprivation. When they give up.

The body is capable of extreme longevity, eating away at itself, repairing itself to survive.

But the mind is not so elastic. When the mind is done, it's done.

That's when he'd seen people sit down during a fight, walk out of a safe place, lie down to sleep and not wake up

That would never be Tara. She'd lived with predators a long time, recovering and recovering, growing stronger, like a Damascus steel blade rolled over on itself again and again.

She would survive them all.

She would certainly survive him.

Cuba coughed until he tasted blood.

They all would.

A reluctant sun lit up the town of Hudson Bay in contrasts of bright white and darkness. Cuba had the Kid stop short of the platform. "Wait. At least fifteen minutes. See if we attract any unwanted attention."

When no one appeared, living or otherwise, Buck took offense. "Where are the brass bands and ticker-tape parades?" He was still high on finding the train.

"I don't think the train was scheduled," The Kid said.

"Good thing, on account 'a we got only one original passenger." Buck allowed the Kid to ease up to the platform. He waved to Fifty. "Get up on the roof of the station. We're going to town!"

Cuba looked at the Kid. *Time to give him the bad news.* "Gear up, Kid."

"What? Why?"

"You're coming with us." Cuba hated to prep newbies. They didn't have a high rate of survival. It felt like a waste of time to train one. Hiding in the bathroom didn't give this one marks for creativity. Buck wanted all hands on deck. For Cuba, it was one more warm body in the way.

"I don't know..."

"You're in the country now, city boy. You have to hunt to survive. Let's get you ready."

Cuba dug into his rucksack and fished out a roll of duct tape. "Armor," he said. He stripped a length of duct tape from the roll.

"That's it? Don't I get something harder?"

"Don't need it." He wrapped the tape around the Kid's arm several times. "They typically get you in three places, the arms, legs, and throat." He said, stropping tape around each. "If they get an artery, you're done. They like the jugular. Keep your hood up." Cuba wrapped a length around the Kid's neck like a high collar.

"There. Ready to shoot you to the moon, Spaceboy."

"Do I get a weapon?"

Cuba handed him Mr. Crow. He held it out with both hands, bowing his head.

"That's it?"

"Mr. Crow is your best friend. Heavy enough to cave in a skull. Light enough to swing all day. And Mr. Crow is popular. He'll get you into *all* the best places." Cuba pried open a phantom door.

"Can't I have a gun?"

Cuba hesitated, then found him one. "You can have this one." He held a black .45 in his palm. Looked like it survived an explosion. Shiny scars gleamed through baked paint like a starry night.

The Kid did not look impressed. "A word of advice. Guns are a last resort. The head is damn hard to hit, even at close range. The skull is round and hard. Even if you hit it, the bullet might glance off or not penetrate. Better to swing than shoot. "

"I notice you name your weapons. Tara has the Savage. You have Mr. Crow. What did you call this gun?"

"Doesn't matter. It's yours now."

The Kid smiled. "I'll call her 'Betty'."

Cuba raised an eyebrow.

"I'm old fashioned." He started to tuck it inside his waistband.

"Betty's a lady. You put her in your pants, she'll blow your balls off." Cuba held out a tangle of leather. "Use this holster. One more thing. Nothing brings more Eaters like shooting. Mr. Crow keeps his secrets and won't tell anyone where you are. I want him back when we get on the train, so keep an eye out for one of your own. Nothing is more valuable than a crowbar."

Buck caught the Kid on the way out. "Hey, do yourself a favor. Stay out of Cuba's way when the fighting starts."

"Oh, I don't want to get in the way."

"No, you don't." He gave Cuba a significant look and let them go.

The Kid looked at Cuba. "What does he mean?"

"He wants to keep you alive. Nothing personal, Kid, but I'm not too discriminate when the killing starts. You can ask Fifty if you need a second opinion."

Fifty nodded, wide eyed.

Of course, when the action started, that's where Cuba wanted the Kid to be. In front, between him and the bad guys.

No one waited for them inside the station, no Waiters in the waiting room. Cuba was glad for that. There must not have been a train for some time.

Buck rammed the butt of his rifle against a vending machine. The glass shattered, skittering across the wood floor. He harvested single serving packages and tossed them into a sack, complaining. "Fat free chips? What the hell?"

Once outside, Cuba took point, as usual. He thought he'd have to fight Tara for the lead, but she seemed content beside Buck. The Kid trotted up the rear.

Fifty climbed up to the roof of the station with Barrett to set up a clear line of fire. As he reached the peak, he disturbed a flock of crows. Their noisy caws rippled through the town.

Cuba held his breath. It didn't seem to attract any attention, but that was a bad sign. The crows took roost on another rooftop nearby, watching him.

The rooftops. Now that he noticed, there were a lot of birds. Ravens, eagles, hawks, owls. They perched on peaks and gables, telephone poles and trees. They fidgeted, squawked, fought, and preened like an audience before a show. Wings outstretched, they watched, necks turned to impossible angles.

"Lot of birds here." Buck had noticed the same thing.

Tara shifted the grip on her rifle. "Is that bad?"

"It's not good. Birds mean meat. Unless there's a convention of mice, our friends without skin better keep their eyes covered."

The Kid took notice. "Birds *eat* those things?"

"Not much else to eat up here in the winter."

"Do they..." he hestitated, apparently afraid to look stupid, "...turn?"

"No," Cuba answered. Now wasn't the time for a conversation. "Let's get through this."

He hated towns. He had fought through too many. The whole Eastern seaboard is one big town, an endless mass of houses with no discernible borders.

Houses were a necessary evil. Most shops and factories were looted in the early days. Whatever they managed to take, people hoarded at home. If he wanted supplies, he had to hit the houses.

The structures themselves never bothered Cuba. From the outside, they looked normal. The doors bothered him, that terrible sense of anticipation. What horrors waited behind them? A warm home full of survivors and life? A live human with a shotgun? An Eater? A Waiter? A dog? Best case scenario, nothing waited behind the door, but that wasn't any better. With each empty house, the world felt a little more...

....empty.

All those pretty little houses, decorated by loving hands, yearned for by eager families, paid for with years of labor, now left vacant and rotting. Shops, businesses, factories – these he preferred. They had a certain urban decay charm. But houses... an empty one was nothing but the husk of someone's dreams, the joy and love inside eaten away leaving only an exoskeleton. A house is the hide of hope.

"We'll split up," Buck said. Buck and Tara teamed up. Cuba got the Kid. "Go down this street. We meet back at the station in an hour."

An alarm bell went off in Cuba. "Wait. You want to come back the way we came?"

"It's a small town. Not a lot of options."

As they walked away, the Kid looked concerned. "Is that bad?"

Cuba didn't want to tell him. Eaters follow you, follow your scent. Backtracking is a sure way to encounter one. "Don't worry about it. Stay close to me. I'm going in each house. Your job is to stand outside and make sure nothing comes in after me."

"What if there's something already inside?"

"I'll take care of that. Keep your eyes open. You see something coming, knock on the door. *Don't* call out. *Don't* shoot your gun. Knock. I'll hear it."

He made sure they kept a clear line of sight back to the station. On the roof, with a full view of the street, Fifty would clear a path for them. If anything showed up, all he had to do was run.

Half an hour later, Cuba stood in the second floor bedroom of a withered white clapboard home, immobilized in front of the dresser. Reflected in the mirror in front of him was a man he didn't recognize. An older man, grizzled, a yellow grin floating over a dirty beige parka splattered with blood. His blood, some of it.

Looking for a distraction, his eyes drifted to another reflection. Rotating, letting his eyes adjust to the shadows in one corner, he stretched out one hand to touch the object.

A piano. Not a grand piano but grand enough for the times. An upright clad in lacquered walnut with minimal details.

"Dammit, Stokes." He hadn't time to think about it until now. "You only had to live one more day."

The world seemed quieter without him.

Cuba wondered if it worked. A part of him hoped not, not when Stokes was so close. He pressed an ivory key.

The note didn't sound right. Not out of tune, but concussive, harsh, like the report of a .45 being fired by a young moron in a town full of sleeping dead. Before he could depress the ivory to test his acoustical hypothesis, he heard it again. Leaning toward the window, he saw the Kid's profile, legs splayed over Mr. Crow, both arms extended stiff and horizontal, Betty spitting fire from his fingers. An Eater approached, slow, but unharmed. He fired again, wild. Step by step it advanced. The Kid froze, rooted to the spot like an icicle. The Eater closed the gap to a few steps.

Cuba sprinted downstairs, erupting out the door.

The Kid's composure melted. He jerked the trigger, emptying the magazine in a blinding haze. A lone chip of flesh flew off the Eater's shoulder. The hammer clicked again and again, the chamber empty, the trigger yanked in desperation. Then the creature's head vaporized in a black mist.

The Kid smiled, triumphant. "I got him!"

Cuba twisted the gun from him. "You're lucky if you hit the Earth. Wave to Fifty."

Halfway across town a small dot waved over a smoking barrel.

"You can thank him later." Cuba picked up Mr. Crow, abandoned in the snow, and dusted it off. "Next time, use this."

"I'm sorry. I didn't... I didn't listen."

"Don't be sorry. When I say 'next time' I mean two minutes from now. You woke up the whole town."

The telltale scent of rotting meat drifted into the street. The birds went crazy, swooping down out of sight behind the houses, rising back into sight with strips of flesh dangling from talons and beaks.

Tara and Buck came running. "What happened?"

"The Kid invited everyone to a block party. Guess what's for lunch."

Eaters lumbered out of side yards and broken front doors, closing in on the road to the station like the Red Sea behind Moses.

Buck smiled. *"Gray skies are gonna clear up..."*

Cuba rolled his eyes. "He's singing again."

"He does that?" Tara looked puzzled.

"All the time."

"Put on a happy face." Buck slid on his balaclava, tilted his cap, and pulled out a baseball bat.

This fired Cuba up. He pulled up his balaclava, unhooked the Babe, and regretted giving up Mr. Crow. He felt the bloodlust coming.

"Brush off the clouds and cheer up," Buck smacked the first comer along the temple. *"Put on a happy face."* Home run.

Cuba pushed the kid forward "Go! Run for the middle. Don't stop for anything."

Cuba jogged behind the boy. He tried to avoid using the Kid as a human shield, but if the Kid didn't listen to instructions, Cuba wouldn't die for it.

Eaters poured in from everywhere, every alley and home and open shed. Their mass grew dense, like walking the wrong way in a parade. Hands reached out, teeth chattered, blackened skin shone blood red in the morning light, a grotesque menagerie of pustules, blisters, punctures, and wounds.

Buck waded in. *"Pick out a pleasant outlook, Stick out that noble chin."* He took a swing, smacked an Eater up under the throat. *"Wipe off that 'full of doubt' look,"* Connected. *"Slap on a happy grin!"*

Buck's theatrics did nothing for the Kid's nerve. He stopped in his tracks, posing for a last stand. Cuba pushed him on. "Your only advantage is momentum!" Then Cuba lost sight of the Kid as a wave of rotted meat crashed between them.

Cuba pushed with the bat. They were within arm's length now, and there wasn't room to swing it. To get through as fast as possible, he chose to weave and duck. He held out one arm like a quarterback to connect whenever they got too close, crushing sternums and clavicles, deflecting energy to send them flying. He aimed for muscle mass - shoulders and pectorals. Even when they didn't go down, they spun out of his way.

The crowd closed in. The chill air filled with the purr of Eaters, the heavy breathing of the living, the sickening crunch of brittle bones whenever the two met, and the insane racket of the birds.

Every now and then a head popped as Fifty did his thing, but there were too many for it to make a difference. Cuba slipped on a patch of ice and went down. The first Eaters to lean over him got a bat in the face. He leaned on it to stand, regained his footing. His focus narrowed to the path in front of him. He forgot where Tara and Buck were, forgot the Kid existed. He tunneled in on the station two blocks away and tenderized anything in between. He felt, rather than saw, when Babe connected with a skull. His arms fought on auto-pilot, on meat radar. Anything that entered his peripheral vision went down.

That included birds. They didn't wait for the carnage to end. They attacked the Eaters from above, dive bombing the heads, tearing off anything loose and fleshy – ears, scalp, strips of frozen jerky. They liked the eyes. Cuba kept one arm up against the onslaught of giant wings, feathers slashing the air, talons pulling at his hair, glad more than once to be wearing goggles.

He broke free of the horde at the station, scrambled up the steps, and slammed the doors behind him. To his surprise, Tara stood there in the broken glass of the vending machines, reloading. She shrugged at his expression, "I went around."

"How'd you do it so fast?"

"Same way I catch my bus at Penn Station." She pushed past him out the door, letting the Savage address the crowd. From the porch's high vantage, the Savage spoke to every head that paid attention. Cuba could hear her laughing.

The heavy thump of Barrett on the roof reverberated through the space, shaking snow off the eaves, dusting her hair as she launched back into the fray. If Fifty still fired, his friends were still out there.

"Where's Buck?" he shouted to Tara.

"He went back for the Kid."

Cuba looked out a safe window over a sea of bobbing heads. "I don't see them." Did he hit the Kid? He couldn't remember. The Kid ran in front of him, a bad place to be, a bad place to put him...

The rear door crashed open. Cuba raised the bat against a black creature silhouetted by the blinding snow.

"Get on the damn train!" Buck shouted, stepping into the room. "Where's Tara? Get her out of here!"

Cuba tugged on Tara's arm once. She shrugged him off. She kept shooting and then stooping to pick up her shells. He pulled harder. "The train's leaving!" When that didn't work he lifted her, still firing, and dropped her inside.

She slung the rifle across her shoulder and skipped to the door, as if leaving was her idea "Aren't you coming?"

They stepped outside to see the Kid and Fifty pulling themselves into the cab.

The creatures clustered around the front of the station, leaving the back empty.

Cuba helped Tara up into the cab as the Kid jammed the controls forward. The train inched away. The steel cab offered plenty of protection, but at a maddening pace.

They hadn't gone thirty yards when Buck said, "Hold on, hold on. Stop it here." The swarm followed the train like iron ore toward a magnet. Buck didn't even wait for the train to slow to a stop before he jumped to the ground. He twirled his long coat once, flashed a showman's smile, and bowed for the cab.

Fifty shook his head.

Cuba smiled and shouted out the window, "C'mon, man! Have some respect for the dead!"

Buck threw a bird over his shoulder.

"Is this some kind of inside joke?" Tara looked annoyed.

Cuba grimaced. "Watch."

Buck stepped up onto the platform in full view of the crowd. When he raised his arms, the Eaters raised their arms, trying to reach him. He turned around, winked at the cab, and unbuckled his pants.

"I can't," Cuba said.

"I can," Tara laughed. "What happened to, 'Treat your victory as a funeral?'

Buck dropped his trousers, his manhood swinging in the breeze. He bent over, swaying side to side so all the night creatures caught a glimpse of the moon. "The Chinese guy also said, treat your escapes as a buffoon!"

"He did not!" Tara pretended to cover her eyes.

Dressed again, he strode back at an Eater's pace, sashaying and blowing on his fingernails. He swung up to the cab ahead of the crowd. "My adoring fans," he said, blowing a kiss to the moaning, rotting mass of ex-humanity. "Sometimes, to get to the top, you have to crush the little people." He reached for the lever.

A bullet smacked the window. The windshield wiper automatically squeaked across a spider web of glass.

"What the..."

A middle-aged woman, very much alive, stood at the fringes of the melee, hunting rifle aimed at the train. Beside her, an elderly policeman in uniform waved his arms in the air. He mouthed the word "Stop." He looked concerned. Behind him were two teenagers with shotguns blasting, but they weren't shooting Eaters. They aimed above the exposed skulls, pelting birds as if they were the real enemy. Black bodies fell from the sky like rain, and the boys didn't hesitate on their mission to clear the sky even as the Eaters closed on the ground.

All of that was unusual enough, but what held Cuba's attention was the last member of the group, a uniformed deputy with a stick.

Over the past few months, Cuba had witnessed every reaction to Eaters, from surprise and alarm, to terror, to retaliation and even resignation. He'd seen people sit down at the first sight of one, too weak to resist. He'd seen fanatics run toward a front of Eaters, swallowed whole. Hell, he'd experienced many of the same emotions himself. But this guy....

An unlit cigarette dangled from the man's lower lip. He leaned against a tree, unaffected by the horde that approached him. In one hand, he held a coffee cup with a donut on top. He tried to sip the coffee without dropping the donut or his cigarette. In the other hand, he held a metal rod, but it didn't look substantial enough to bludgeon a skull.

The Eaters shifted toward him, surrounding him. He let them get close, utterly unconcerned. Finally, he tucked the cigarette behind his ear and bit the icing off the donut. When the first one got within biting distance, he raised the stick to waist level.

A blue spark jolted the Eater into twisted paroxysms. When the next one approached, the man jabbed it with the stick, too. Soon he'd managed to herd the whole crowd back into the street. *Herd* them! Like sheep! Moments later the whole crowd dispersed and disappeared back into the town.

"You can come out now." The old policeman beckoned.

Cuba cocked his pistol, but Buck shook his head. "Not the living."

"What do we do?" The Kid asked.

Buck sized up the situation. "They know how armed we are. They wouldn't be stupid enough to... "

Smack! Another round bounced off the window frame.

"All right! Stop shooting my train!" Buck shouted out the window. "What do you want?"

The policeman swung up to the cab. "You're late." He frowned. "Where's the rest of the train?"

"They were all smoking cars. I don't smoke."

"Son, we expected this train at 5:20 this morning. We had family and friends coming in from Winnipeg. Now you hot shots show up with no cars, no passengers, to start a looting spree and a riot. You'll have to be more specific, or we're going to detain you." He said it like it would ruin *his* day, not theirs.

Buck took a breath, his cocky smile fading. "Fine. But answer this question first. How did you get rid of those Eaters?"

"Cattle prods. They don't like electricity. Convinces them to move in the other direction."

"You *herd* them?" Buck echoed Cuba's thoughts.

"Not so hard when you get used to it."

"Why don't you just..."

"Kill them?"

"I was going to say shoot them, since they're already dead, but, yeah."

"This is where our opinion differs. I say they're undead. If I shoot one, that makes me a killer," he spat on the ground, "like you. Now I got one simple question, and I'm looking for a simple answer. If I let you into my town, can I trust you?" The man held his gaze.

"Yes." The nodding heads behind him backed up Buck's words. If Buck said something, it was so.

"'Kay, then leave your guns here. Come over to the Tim Horton's for a double double and let's talk."

"I'm not comfortable leaving my guns." Buck's eyes followed a few Eaters who lingered near the station.

The policeman followed his gaze but dismissed him with a wave of his hand. "Awww, they won't hurt ya."

Cuba worried more about people with guns, like the two kids and the woman, but this man seemed so oblivious, or crazy, that it was hard not to trust him.

As the man stepped down from the train, he waved, not to one of his men, but to *an Eater nearby*.

He *waved*. "What the hell?" After fighting two thousand miles north, Cuba thought he'd seen everything. Consider his mind blown.

"This is the weirdest town I've been to," Buck said. "But I could use a coffee. It's been a while."

They stepped out of the cab, without weapons, hands raised.

The man laughed. "Can't shake your hand with them up like that." Buck lowered his and the man took it. "Sheriff Otley, Hudson Bay PD."

"Buck," he said. "How are you?"

"The very best! This here's my daughter Anna." Otley indicated the woman with the rifle. "She's a crack shot, wouldn't you say?" He pointed at the windshield of the train with pride.

He's making a joke, with Eaters still wandering around. *This is like some kind of weird dream.*

Anna smiled at them, at Buck in particular.

"And these are her two hellions, Rory and James."

The teenagers yawned.

Bored! With Eaters on all sides! Cuba still shook with adrenaline from running a gauntlet of molars, from thinking he'd killed the Kid, and these two little twerps were bored.

Otley introduced the Juggler last. "And this is my Deputy, Payton."

The man raised the prod to his hat, his attention on Tara, but Tara was watching the Eaters. They hovered on the perimeter like scarecrows, shifting from foot to foot, watching, waiting, but no longer approaching.

Buck made introductions all around, then stood waiting for what may come.

"Well, come on." Otley turned and waved them on. "Sally doesn't serve coffee outside."

Twenty minutes later, they found themselves seated in a nook at the local Tim Horton's as if the last three months never happened. Anne Murray sang Snowbird on the sound system. Patrons dressed in pajamas and fuzzy dug into flapjacks with plastic knives and forks. A man with a mug of coffee chatted up the waitress. Warmth emanated from the kitchen where a chef toiled away on their order. The air filled with the smells of dark roasted beans, sugar, and even a woman's perfume. He heard laughter.

At that moment, Cuba might have believed in time travel. Might have believed he stepped through a portal into an alternate universe where Eaters only existed in books and the world worked. Might have thought his body lay in the snow somewhere and this was an undeserved glimpse of heaven. Might have, if he didn't turn toward the plate glass windows.

Outside, Eaters wandered around, drawn to the smell of grease. A pimply teenager in a white apron stood near the door with a prod, shooing them away when they got too close.

Otley watched him and, as if he could read minds, said, "We've kept the place up. Kind of a local landmark. Makes life normal if we can get a coffee at Tim Horton's."

"How do you keep it going without resupply?"

"Well, we ran out of branded serviettes long ago, but we re-use our cups. Everyone pitches in with flour, greenhouse vegetables, and meat from the few animals we keep. We strongarmed the coffee from every household, so we've got enough tins to last us another year or so." The idea of running out must have saddened him. He frowned, took a sip of his cup, and paused in consternation. He brightened again when the food showed. "When was the last time you ate a decent meal?"

The waitress brought plates of food, steaming hot from the griddle.

"Thank you, Sal," Otley said. "Much obliged."

The shock of a normal meal made it hard for Cuba to focus. Until now, food was something you killed or canned. Seeing wasn't believing. He needed to eat.

Buck and Fifty had the same look, but the Kid dug in with no hesitation. Tara was too busy struggling with her murderous urges to eat. She looked ready to forego the meal if the Sheriff let her resume the carnage.

Maybe the Eater outside distracted her. It stood against the window, eyes wide, head bumping rhythmically, black sludge from an open pustule oozing down the glass. The skin, where it had skin, clung tight and hard to the muscle beneath, the tissue frozen black and destroyed. Ears and nose had long ago fallen off. Hair clung to patches of scalp stretched thin over a dome of bone. Chilblains and frostbite ravaged anything that wasn't muscle. Not an appetizing view.

"Is Earl bothering you? I'll pull the shades. Poor bastard loves flapjacks."

"You know that one?"

"I know all of them. Been Sheriff here almost thirty years. Earl used to work here."

"Did the Department of Sanitation know about this?"

"He looked better then." He waved Earl off as he closed the shades. "Not much better."

"You're saying," Tara overcame her shock long enough to speak, "you *co-exist* with them?" She looked like a child whose parents told her they weren't going to Disneyland after all.

"It's a small town. Everybody knows everybody. We're family."

"What the hell does that mean?"

"See that one over by the tree?"

Buck turned his attention to a blackened corpse chewing the bark off a nearby pine. The shredded remnants of a dress exposed a tough bronze and black colored muscle mass.

Buck said, "I see the family resemblance."

"That's my niece, Alice. I raised her like a daughter when my sister died. Helped her through college, got her a job when she got out. She lived with us until she could afford a house of her own, then bought the one next door. She and Anna were best friends. Probably still are. Just be damn glad you didn't run her over, or we might not be having this conversation. I wear a badge, but I've been known to take it off now and again. Your turn. What brings you here?"

Buck told the chief the annotated version, downplaying the violence and accentuating victimhood. Headed to Churchill. Train on fire. All dead save the Kid. Stopped here to forage. "We're not used to seeing these towns populated by the living."

Otley took a moment to recover from the news that there were no other survivors from the train. The weathered wrinkles around his eyes and mouth deepened. He ran a hand over his sparse hair, down over his eyes, and took a breath. "Starting to get used to loss here, too."

Cuba watched his plate. In his mind, an image of another middle-aged woman emerged from smoke and fire, covered in blood, screaming. His memory twisted her into a resemblance of Otley's daughter. Another relative? Did the sheriff know her? Could he guess what Cuba did to her?

"That saddens me," Otley said at last. "More than a few people have a bad day ahead when they hear the news. You don't get used to hearing," he wiped his mouth "bad news."

"I'm sorry," Tara held up a hand and shook her head. "I'm having a hard time with this. Your whole town is infested with Eaters, and you do nothing about it?"

"'Eejas. Huh. I like that. Hey Sal!" He called over to the waitress. "These folks call them Eejas."

"Oh, they do that," Sally consented. A few patrons laughed.

Tara again, "And all you need is a few cattle prods?"

Buck tried a more tactful approach. "You understand, there isn't much left of your relatives in those bodies walking around out there. What gives you the strength to not... fear them." This welled up from a deep, personal place.

"Ey, what if they find a cure?"

"Little late for Earl."

"Don't laugh! We got a radio up here. We listen to the Captain. He says China found a cure."

"We heard part of his broadcast." Buck leaned forward. "What else can you tell us?"

Ortney smiled. "About the Captain? He's a bit of a lunatic, but who isn't these days?"

Cuba grunted assent.

"He broadcasts out of Churchill. It's the only news we get from the outside world. I have no idea where he gets it."

Otley turned toward Tara. "Listen, I'm not stupid, I realize this tissue damage can't be reversed, even with a cure, but would you give up on your husband or kid just because they turned?"

Tara and Buck and Cuba all found somewhere else to look, somewhere far away.

"Hell no," Otley went on. "If they're walking, there's hope. Hope keeps us alive. Hope keeps *them* alive." He pointed out the window. "It's a win-win."

Cuba noticed this struck a chord with Tara. She looked away, out the window, lips pursed, wiping her eyes. *All of us have those dark strings, plucked and vibrated at the wrong moments,* he thought. The analogy made him think of Stokes, and for the second time this morning he felt a heavy pang of loss.

Tara shook it off and asked, "Do you know what causes it?"

"That's the skill-testing question, isn't it? As remote as we are, we didn't even notice it at first. Heard stories from down south. Started seeing refugees come in by train. They didn't stop here long, moved on looking for something else.

"One day, a few oddballs get off the train. Wandered around like normal tourist types. No one thought they was, heh, Eejas. We thought, 'Hm. Awful lot of Newfies up this time of year.' Folks tried to help them with directions. They were the first to go. After that we had a bit of a kerfuffle, contained it, and now you get what we have here." He rapped the glass toward Earl.

"We've reached equilibrium. Haven't had a new case in almost three weeks. They stay within the town limits, we keep them at bay with the prods, and nobody gets hurt."

"Come on," Buck laughed. "Eaters don't feel pain. I've seen them shot. I've seen them cut in half. I've even seen them set on fire. And that's just this morning."

Otley frowned at the reference. "No, but they have muscles. The brain sends out electrical pulses, tells those muscles what to do. Zapping them confuses those signals. It isn't fear or pain that drives them away. They're disoriented. All we do is... orient them away from us."

"You make it sound so simple."

"It is simple. And we're careful. They're dangerous when they bunch up, like any living mob.

We try not to let that happen. Like it did this morning." He threw the words back at Buck.

"How do you keep them from congregating?"

"Radio tags. The local Conservation officer used to tag wolves in the area. We borrowed the equipment so we could track the population." He smirked, covered his mouth. "Now the officer has one. How's that for cosmic justice?

"What good do the tags do?"

"A radio receiver tells us where they are. Too many in one area and we go see what's going on. Sometimes it's a relative that got too familiar. We show up and herd them away. Usually it's a rabbit they got cornered. You ever watch one of them try to catch a rabbit? Funniest damn thing."

The Kid excused himself to go to the bathroom.

Buck stood up to let him out. "Mind if we take a few of them cattle prods with us?"

"I wish we could spare a few. I don't like your methods, but we don't have enough as it is. Where're you headed again?"

"Churchill, after we stop in The Pas."

"Oh, yeah. Those poor kids. Well, there's not much up in Churchill, besides the Captain. Heard they don't have one case!"

"Sounds good to me." Cuba savored the last bite of syrupy pancake. He accidentally smiled.

Otley saw it. "You're welcome to stay here." He must have surprised himself with the offer. He looked ready to backtrack. The conversation paused, filled only by the thud, thud, thud of Earl's head on the window.

Buck looked over the tables to where Anna and her teenagers sat. She'd been watching him the whole time. To Otley, he said, "You mind giving us a minute to talk?"

"Take your time. Get warm. In addition to them, we keep hospitality alive."

When the sheriff had moved out of earshot, Buck ducked his head low and spoke quietly. "We're not a democracy, don't need a vote. Any one of you wants to stay, you go ahead."

"What about you?" Tara asked.

"I've been chasing a dream a thousand miles. I won't stop until I get to Churchill. But you, you've been homeless for all of two days. You should stay here. Now, wait, don't object yet. These are good people. In all my travels this is the most intact town I've ever seen. They have a chance, and they'll be stronger with you around."

Tara sat back in her seat, frowning. Cuba recognized the angry silent treatment. He'd been on the receiving end of too many such feminine punishments. Cuba attempted to save Buck with, "Don't take offense, Tara. He's right. I've never seen a town I didn't have to fight my way out of."

Buck continued, "No one's ever offered to let us stay. No one. If you're looking for a secure place to settle down, this is as good as any."

The Kid slid into the booth. "What're we talking about?"

"You can stay here, Kid. They'll take you. Hell, you're probably related to one of them, anyway."

The Kid looked anxious. "Well, what about Cuba? Is he staying?"

What difference does that make? Was this kid bonding to him? Cuba prepared a snappy retort, but a whooping cough shook loose another bit of lung. He lost his wit trying to breathe. When he recovered, he saw Buck, Tara, and Fifty waiting for an answer. He sighed. "I been with you, Buck, for a long time now. I'm not letting you go back out there without me."

Buck shook his head. "There's probably a doctor here..."

"I said no." Cuba didn't mean it to come out so terse, but there it was.

"I'm going then," said the Kid.

Great.

"I can't make you stay. Tara?"

"Pass."

Fifty nodded in consent with Tara.

Cuba sipped his coffee. As much as he wanted to live in peace, to never kill again, to make his brother proud, the thought of staying in this place made his skin crawl. He couldn't sit here, waiting to die, while Buck fought on. If he learned Buck or Fifty or any of them died while he still drew breath... No way. He wasn't in it for the journey like Buck, or the fear like Fifty, or the revenge like Tara. He was in this for them. That's all he had left.

Buck waved Otley back over. "Appreciate your offer, but we've got a train to catch."

Otley, Cuba noticed, brightened up a little.

It felt good to climb back on the train, like arriving home after a vacation. He owned this world. The discomfort was comfortable.

The good townsfolk of Hudson Bay supplied them with greenhouse vegetables and fresh water for the journey. Buck turned down a can of coffee. "We don't have any trouble staying awake. It's sleeping that's hard."

Otley handed up a burlap sack. "Letters for the Captain." He smiled a sheepish smile. "Fan mail.

Say hello to him for us. He's the only celebrity we've got." He shook hands with Buck and hopped down.

Warm, fed, and somehow devoid of fear, they pulled out of the station better than they arrived. They also made a better exit, careful not to run over any 'Eejas' as the train moved out.

Otley stood there a minute, waving, then jogged along aside and swung up again. He rapped on the window. "Hey!" He wore a look both dubious and hopeful. "If you find the cure, come back."

Cuba's heart sank. That warm fuzzy feeling disappeared. It was a hoax, a hat trick. These people prayed for a cure, sent letters to the Captain, clung desperately to hope. They weren't living a new reality, one built on harmony with Eaters. They clung to the past. They insulated themselves from the horror, put off the inevitable. It was only a matter of time before Hudson Bay collapsed as well. In a few months, a year tops, the coffee would run out, resupply from down south would never come, the crops would fail, a winter of starvation to follow, and Hudson Bay would look no different than Dauphin.

The town wasn't any more alive than the Eaters in it, shambling along, trying to act normal, while it rots on the inside. By this time next winter, there would be no one left. Mother Nature stacked the odds in the Eaters' favor. Everybody dies sometime.

Cuba made the right decision. Not because he would have lived to see the fall. He wouldn't. But if he'd stayed, he'd be living a lie.

Back to the real world. No cure. No hope. Just today and what it might bring.

Abandon all hope, ye who enter here.

Born in the fires of hell, only hell was home..

No one spoke for the first thirty kilometers.

The Kid... he seemed lost. This was his first day in the wild. What a day. Maybe he thought every day would be this good. Maybe he didn't know what he passed up. No. He'd suffered in Winnipeg, lost his family, maybe even watched his sister die. It might be his first day on the road, but he'd been through a lot. Cuba thought of cutting him some slack.

Before long, boredom set in. The monotonous trees and snow seemed to go on forever.

Buck convinced the Kid to teach him how to drive the train, then he took over.

The Kid looked for something else to do. He opened an old copy of Frankenstein he found in one of the suitcases, read it for a while, tossed it aside, then started fishing letters out of the mail sack. "Who is this Captain guy? Look at all these letters!" He tore one open and read it out loud. "Dear Captain. Love the show. Keep it up." He ruffled another. "Dear Captain. Is there really a cure in China? Tell us more." He plucked out a red envelope. It smelled of perfume. "Darling Captain. If you're ever in Hudson Bay, look me up. I'd love to..." he blushed as he scanned the page and then set it aside. "A very literal woman."

"I'll take that one," Buck said, snatching it out of his hand. Tara laughed.

The Kid took out another one. "Dear Captain. Have you heard anything out of Europe? My wife was visiting when..." He put that one down in favor of another. "Hey Captain. What happened in Winnipeg?"

He let the letters slide to the floor as his hand went limp.

Tara put them back in the bag. "These aren't for us." Conversation over.

The Kid went back to Frankenstein, lost in fiction.

Tara gravitated toward Buck. They seemed to have some chemistry going. Under the circumstances, it wasn't romantic. Buck had that effect on people. He drew them in; they followed.

Cuba sat with Fifty. He appreciated the quiet. The Kid, however, kept lurking, watching everything Cuba did, mimicking him even. He labored under the delusion that Cuba gave a damn.

Cuba polished Mr. Crow, chipping at the hard chunks that accumulated on its jagged edge. If he concentrated on a task, he didn't have to think. He hated downtime like this. Thinking led to dark places.

The lethal instrument distracted the Kid. "How many zombies have you killed?"

"'Eaters'," Tara corrected him. "Look at his helmet."

The Kid fidgeted like a puppy. "What do you feel when you pull the trigger?"

This was not something Cuba wanted to talk about. "Recoil," he grunted. An old joke.

Without a chance to debrief after the fight, the Kid bubbled over with a bagful of questions bigger than the one for the Captain, ready to pop. "Wow. All I can say is, wow! I mean, Buck talked about you like you were some bad-ass, but I had no idea. Back there in that town, you were a hurricane. You're like a ninja or something!" He air jockeyed a joystick. "Up down left right - KO. You're a hero!"

"Kid!" Buck shouted. "Come over here." His voice softened when the youth approached. "I don't know what it was like for you in Winnipeg, but out here, the things we do to survive... it isn't pretty. We rarely talk about the shit we see unless it's something to help us next time. Ease off a little."

That put off the inquisition for no more than five minutes. Cuba watched the steam build in the Kid's head until he blurted out, "C'mon. Tell me how you got so good. Teach me everything you know. I want to be like you. I want to be a hero!"

Swift, Cuba collared him, shoved him up against the wall, got in real close. He looked at the boy with calm, indifferent, narrowed eyes. "You want to be a hero?" He dumped the Kid and walked as far away as he could. It wasn't very far.

This boy had it all wrong. Cuba didn't need his past thrown in his face. He felt caged. He wanted to get away. He wanted to get away from himself.

The Kid looked like he couldn't decide between crying and pissing his pants. "What's his problem?"

Buck didn't even turn around. "Only one kind of hero – a dead one."

"What?"

"You think this is like something you saw in the movies? Sure, experience counts for something. It's an edge. But like they say, experience comes from stupid mistakes. Mistakes that maybe got other people killed.

"We're not alive because we're good at this. I've seen men stronger than me, faster, smarter, better trained, go down. You know what that does to your self-confidence? So you lived. So what? That doesn't make you special. It makes you alone.

"The real horror is, when you've been fighting this long, what you're too terrified to admit you already know: it's random. Luck.

"Live. Die. Every day is a new day, like being born. What you had to do yesterday to stay alive...."

Cuba listened to this and had to jump in. "You know what a hero is? Suicide. A hero's someone who lets emotion override common sense. He doesn't try to preserve himself. Self-preservation is our god-given right. No one can excise that." He pointed at the boy. "When you find yourself in that situation, when you think you need to be a hero, you do what's right for *you*. You run or you die. You die, and your story is over."

"He's right," Tara chimed in, back to polishing her weapons. "You're only a survivor until you die."

"Right." This morning, Cuba would have thought she hadn't been on the road long enough to contribute, but he knew what she was. She'd been on the road her whole life.

"Kid," Buck said. "Why don't you come and drive."

That shut him up for a while, and with the silence, the tension eased.

Buck unfolded a map on the floor, studying it. He pointed at The Pas.

That must have prompted Tara's memory. "Hey, back in Hudson Bay, what did that cop say? 'Those poor kids,' he said when you mentioned The Pas. What do think he meant?"

A dark terror descended over the Kid's face. "We're not stopping in The Pas, right?"

Cuba realized the Kid had excused himself to the bathroom while they discussed the route.

"We have to. We need supplies. Thompson's too far, and that's the last outpost of civilization before Churchill."

The Kid shook his head. "Nothing there. I visited a few years ago on a lark. Had a few beers at the Algonquin. Even less there now, after The Pas Eleven."

"The who?"

"The wh... you're kidding, right?" No one answered. "You've never heard of The Pas Eleven?"

Buck snorted. "I'm not Canadian."

"Everyone... it was an international..." He stared at the blank faces. "Alright, I'll tell you." His body went rigid. He kept his eyes on the rails. His voice went soft and monotone. "This is a college town. Kids come from all over. Mostly degrees in agriculture.

"My parents held me over after winter break, thinking things would get worse, but most of my classmates went back. The students of The Pas did. I guess they thought the whole thing would blow over, or maybe it hadn't gotten up here yet. Anyway, things started to get bad and school morale flagged soon after the semester started in January."

Kids were in school in January, Cuba thought. *While I cut my way through Florida.* He couldn't reconcile the two images, the atrocities he witnessed while these kids worried about grades and getting laid. How could the two worlds exist at the same time?

The Kid continued. "So these eleven students, The Pas Eleven, they decided they'd had enough suspense. Some of their parents and families back home disappeared. One of them lost a boyfriend in that whole mess in Toronto. You heard about that, right? No? Geez! Do Americans even know where Canada is? Anyway, in remote areas, whole villages stopped communicating, dead or defensive, it didn't matter. The kids at the school, they couldn't go home. They heard about what happened in New York, Paris, and, my god, Sao Paolo. The bloodbaths, the retribution. It was too much for them.

"They formed a suicide club. Talked about offing themselves before the plague came. They published a manifesto in the school's paper extolling the virtues of sacrifice, the ascension to God before the demons of Hell could take their souls, the unfairness of admission policies, the lack of soda in the cafeteria, esoteric stuff. The paper ran it and no one paid attention.

"The school board voted for a pep rally, unite the community, a light in the darkness, something like that. Dumb idea, but, like, everyone was on edge, right? They weren't thinking straight. So when the Eleven said they wanted to read something at the rally, nobody questioned it. They needed speakers, they got speakers.

"There's a video of this next part. I can't believe you didn't see this on social media, but, whatever. It was, like, so viral, even with everything else going on in the world. Six hundred students and at least twenty staff attended the assembly. Several recorded it.

"The Eleven stood up on the edge of the stage, each reading one paragraph of the manifesto. The last one, a skinny Venezuelan exchange student, read the final words '...now we rise!' All eleven held something in their hands, and together they brought their hands to their mouths. They popped a pill. Cyanide, stolen from the chemistry lab, or made out of cherry pits, no one was sure where they got it. A second later their bodies hit the floor, tumbled off the stage like wet sacks. That was pretty horrifying, but that was just the beginning. As the professors and staff ran toward them..."

"They got back up." Tara smirked.

"... You saw it!?"

"No, it seems so... student filmy."

"You can tell them in person. See, not only did they stand up, they tore into the teachers with the kind of rage only the oppressed know. Students fled, but where could they go? Before the speech, the Eleven chained the doors shut. They *knew*. They wanted to turn, wanted to take everyone with them.

"Someone reported later they'd set pipe bombs under the stage as a *coup de grace*. The electronics malfunctioned. The result was... much more comprehensive.

"There are two hours of video on record. None of the cameras had a clear shot. The first hour you see feet and hear the screaming. By the second hour the screaming dies down, replaced by wet sounds of chewing and rending.

"Not until that night, hours later, did anyone react. Spouses, parents, babysitters, friends who ditched. Calls came into the police department. Missing persons. First a few, then dozens, then over a hundred. The police department sent a deputy over, found an empty school with an auditorium locked from the inside. Called for backup.

"The town's lone reporter covered it, filming from his car. He did puff pieces, local news, weddings. Followed the police scanners in vain. He didn't expect much.

"The police made a lot of noise banging on the doors with nightsticks, shouting, trying to kick them in. The audio captures the howl of those inside waiting to be let out. The police knocked the hinges off the door. They rushed in as a stream of people, drenched in blood, rushed out. Hundreds of them, torn to shreds, limbs missing, faces eaten off, a bloody mess! The cameraman bailed. The police went down.

"Later, as the horde wreaked havoc on the town, this cameraman went back *in* to the assembly hall. He collected the dropped cell phones and cameras and security footage. He spliced it together and released it.

"The Pas Eleven? You never heard of them?! The horror of that scene caused the Montreal Riots! People panicked. It was all over the news, back when we had news. I never heard what happened to this town, but I'm willing to bet it's nothing but... Eejas."

Tara smiled her malicious grin. "Yeah," she said out loud to some internal dialogue.

Cuba laughed. "Sounds like your kind of party."

The weather turned bad. The sky darkened with clouds. Ice rain skittered off the wind screen. The wiper blades cut across, but the shards accumulated.

The Pas huddled beneath a hard mist, buildings appearing, disappearing, reappearing behind a wall of ice.

"We're stopping in this?"

"No choice. We won't make it to the next town unless we refuel."

The Kid corrected him. "Trains refuel in Thompson. They take on water in The Pas."

"Well we better find something or we're going to be pretty damn cold in a few hours."

"Can't we wait it out?"

"Look." Buck pointed outside. Dark forms approached from the tree line. "The engine is loud. We must be pulling them in for miles. The longer we wait, the more of them we attract."

The Kid fiddled with Mr. Crow. "Can't we pull forward, until the storm ends, then come back?"

"Sorry Kid. The only thing that'll improve is the weather. Those things out there will congregate on this spot and wait."

"Wait?"

Cuba didn't want to explain everything to this Kid, so he said, "If this town fell as fast as you say it did, it's a treasure trove. Way out here, with no visitors, there'll be food, ammunition, medical supplies, everything we need to make it to Churchill."

Buck added with no compassion, "Way out here, with no one to shoot them, there'll be a lot of Eaters." Then he added, "Look alive."

He and Tara snickered.

"The rails curve around the town." Buck pointed at a map. "If you three move down this street, you can turn and meet me on the other side of town, before this bridge. The engine will serve as a distraction, so if you're quiet they might ignore you and head my way. It looks like there might be fuel near the bridge. That's a bottleneck, a defensible position. We can wait there, but not for long. You three search the town for supplies. I'll move the train around to the north side, where the refueling station is. Fifty will cover your approach. If I can, I'll get her fueled up while I wait for you. Don't be late or I'll have a swarm around me by the time you get there."

The Kid put his hand up. "*I* can drive the train around."

"Sorry, Kid. You're the tour guide. You've been here before, remember?"

"That was... a long time ago," he whispered, but it was drowned out as Tara and Cuba stood up with their gear.

The Kid looked ready to choke.

Cuba felt bad for him. Second battle in one day. Not the best day for a newbie. "Hey," he said to the Kid's back. "I'm sorry about roughing you up earlier. Things get tense, you know."

The Kid didn't respond, so he decided to give him a few pointers. "Listen, they're slow. That's your only advantage. Stay ahead of them. Don't fight unless you have to. When you have to, use the crowbar this time. Don't get fancy."

The Kid looked like he was ready to throw up.

Buck whispered to Cuba, "He didn't look this way in Hudson Bay."

"Guess Hudson Bay wasn't famous enough."

"I don't want him to freeze up on you." Buck raised his voice for the Kid. "Keep it simple. I knew this guy, real badass, Southeast Jujitsu Champion. Favored swords. Got carried away one day and kicked an Eater in the chest. His foot caught behind the ribcage. Before he could free it the zombie got real friendly in the groin area. You do not want to die that way.

"The best option, always, is to run. Even if you're armed to the teeth wearing a sharksuit and body armor - run."

Cuba jumped in. "If you have no weapons and absolutely must get close and personal, push it on the ball of the shoulder. That's what made me the Hudson Bay Hurricane." That self-referencing joke made the Kid smile. "There it is! That's what I'm talking about. Let's do this!"

Buck chimed in. "What about that time when you..."

Cuba smiled. "Well, I wouldn't recommend..."

"He tore off the Eater's leg and brained it with the hip bone. And the two behind it."

"Only after you cut the muscle with an axe."

"It worked!"

Cuba turned back toward the Kid. "Don't try this at home."

Cuba surveyed the town. This felt good. This felt right. He was back in his element. He could apologize to his brother later.

Snow blew across a gravel road. The sky, overcast as a caul, muted the shadows. Eaters already wandered toward them. Even without the sleet, this would be one hell of a fight.

"I'm dropping you off right after that mural!" Buck pointed to a long row of painted plywood. Wolves and polar bears cavorted across an arctic scene. The engine slowed to a crawl. "Now!"

Tara was ready to go, but Cuba forced the Kid off the train first. "It's a tradition," he lied. The truth was he wanted the cover. That pep talk wasn't to keep the Kid alive, it was to keep the Kid's arms working so there would be fewer Eaters for Cuba to fight. His earlier advice was the one he followed. *Do what's right for you.* He wished he had ten more

Kids. This Kid was too skinny to make a decent shield.

As soon as they stepped free of the cab, the Eaters caught their scent. Cuba kept the mural between them to gain a few yards.

"Whatever you do, Kid, don't stop. Make your way to thin spots. Stay away from groups."

"You have any more obvious advice?"

"Sure. Don't die, or I'll have to kill ya."

"Noted."

At the end of the mural, they turned onto a wide street making a straight line into the fog. Two Eaters waited for them there. They were far gone, clothes tattered beyond recognition, skin flaked like dried mud, yawning skulls. A bunny ear flopped out of one abdomen, half digested.

The Kid froze. Cuba bumped into him. "What did I tell you?"

"I don't know what to do."

The Eaters were almost on him.

"Swing for the skull!" Cuba slapped the Kid's head to get the adrenaline going. A light switched on. Mr. Crow swung up and bit into the Eater's chin. Cuba took the second.

The Kid shivered, shoulders hunched, breathing hard.

"See?" Cuba patted him on the shoulder. "Easy as pie. Keep that up all day. Oh, look, here come three more."

Tara called out from the sidewalk. "I know you don't expect to hear this from me, but go around them! Let's get moving! I want to be back on that nice, warm train."

Sleet fell from the sky. The ice made it hard to keep a footing. The cold bit his lungs with every ragged breath. He wanted to cough but fought it down, fearing he wouldn't stop.

Despite the weather, the next hour was routine.

How many times had he done this? How many towns had he scavenged? They encountered a few Eaters, downed them. They had some trouble with a bear trap someone left out. They found a cache of weapons, food, medicine. The usual.

Cuba almost resented his perfection. The trouble with a spotless resume is you get that job over and over again. Killing was a prison he couldn't escape.

Tara tore into the head of an Eater with an iron pipe she picked up on the road. As the body fell, she paused to see Cuba laughing.

"What's so funny?"

"Who would have thought," Cuba said, "that hunting Eaters could get boring?"

She didn't look like she agreed.

Cuba felt old, older than time. Three months and every day a year. He'd been fighting ninety years. How the hell did he get here?

Cuba lost his patience as Tara bent over the fifth car tire. "What are you looking for? Let's go!"

She popped something off the tire with her knife and dropped it in a bucket. "Tire weight. Pure lead. I can melt it down for bullets."

What the hell is she talking about? "Sure, if you had the reloading equipment."

"What do you think I've been carrying in that big pack on the train?"

Cuba thought about it, then smiled. "Holy shit! The load of bricks! You came prepared."

She didn't look as pleased. "Hard to find ammo for the Savage."

She was right, and it was the only rifle she had, until...

"Hallelujah!"

Cuba brought his gaze about. Tara picked up the pace, headed for a store called *The Gun Shack*. "How much do you think they'll have left?"

"Whatever this guy couldn't carry." Cuba kicked a mound of snow in the street. A frozen corpse lay on a stack of rifles. "It looks like he looted the store, walked out with an armload of guns, slipped on the ice, and hit his head. How's that for bad luck?" He started to go through the stack. "None of them even loaded."

Tara started to pick them up.

"Don't bother," he said. "They're shotguns. Unless you're real close, they're worse than useless. Stick to the Savage. And leave the damn tire weights. We'll have bullets now."

Wrong. The store shelves sagged under the weight of small bore shotgun shells, but not many casings for what they carried. They found a few single shot rifles.

"Doesn't matter," Tara said. "Look what I found." She handed Cuba jugs of gunpowder and a carton of primers. "There's boxes of this stuff. Looks like my reloading equipment will come in handy after all."

Cuba grumbled. "Kid, carry her lead."

By the time they exited the store, a sizeable crowd gathered.

Tara smirked when she saw one Eater in a short red dress. "I'll be damned. A cheerleader. I thought those were a cliché."

Cuba grinned. "One last pep rally."

The Kid didn't look happy to see his admirers. He looked to Cuba. "My arms are so tired."

"Here, Kid. You take Babe. He's lighter, more your speed. I want Mr. Crow back." He pushed the Kid forward. "Go get get 'em."

Cuba did the duck and weave like a prize fighter. Outside of arm's reach, he had little to fear. He fought less and danced more, but they grew thicker by the moment. "Keep running!" He shouted at Tara. A gaunt giant in a basketball jersey blocked his path. He felled it like a tree only to find another right behind it. He brought it down on the back swing. It began to feel like T-ball as a kid. Swing. Connect. Back. Repeat.

Routine.

Then Mr. Crow connected with something stronger than bone. The impact shook through his gloves. He backed up.

A big woman blocked his path. Black jacket, black ski pants, black boots. Out of instinct, Cuba swung again, but again Mr. Crow refused to bite.

This one wore a helmet.

It reached out and grabbed his sleeve.

Something ricocheted off its head. Gun smoke drifted past Cuba as Tara said, "What the hell?! It bounced off!"

"Don't fight it! Run!" Cuba ducked around.

"Like hell!" Tara lunged, but it caught her hood, jerked her back. The Savage dropped to the snow.

Tara whirled, caught the arm under hers and broke it at the elbow. She shoved the helmet with both hands. The creature lost its balance, arms flailing, and toppled over. Tara picked up her rifle and spat.

"Can't die, but can't bite me either, bitch!" She thrust the Savage under the chin strap and pulled the trigger.

Cuba admired her reflexes. "Nice moves. Where did you pick that up?"

"Rape prevention class at the 93rd street Y."

New York? She used to live in New York? "You get threatened by a lot of overweight lesbian snowmobilers in New York?" he wanted to say, but there was no time to talk. The Kid joined them as they pounded their way through to the end of the street, all the way back to the train.

Buck reached out a hand to pull them aboard. "I've got bad news, and I've got bad news. The bad news is, I didn't find the fuel pumps. You need to go back out there and fuel us up."

"What's the bad news?"

"I don't know what they look like. Better find 'em quick, though. You guys brought a lot of friends."

"I'm guessing it's a hose next to a tank."

"A tank would be nice."

"There!" The Kid pointed to some pumps under a small shed, close enough to the tracks for one person between the train and the shed.

Buck doled out responsibilities. "I don't know how long it takes to fuel. Might be ten minutes. Might be four hours. Need all the fuel we can get. We have to stay till we're done. Tara, you like the south. You and Cuba take the south end of the engine. I'll take the north. Fifty on the roof. Kid, you refuel."

No one looked happy about their assignments, except Fifty.

The train eased down the track to the shed. Eaters followed, drawn in like leaves in their wake. On the plus side, the sleet died down.

Buck counted them, a grim line for a smile. "Fifty, what do you think our chances are?"

"50/50."

The Kid cried out with surprise. "What kind of math is that!? There must be three hundred Eaters out there and only five of us. How many do you think you can kill?"

"Doesn't matter, Kid." Buck lifted his bag on his shoulder. "They're coming."

"Even if we kill ten a piece, the odds are…"

"Only one of two things happen out here," Buck interrupted. "We live or we die."

Fifty shrugged. "50/50."

"Too bad you didn't find a shotgun," Buck said. "Those are good for up close battles like this."

Tara flashed Cuba a dirty look.

They slid up to the shed. Buck shouted "Positions!" as he opened the door. He jumped out first.

Cuba hustled past the pumps and leaned up against the metal siding. Tara came up beside him. The Eaters followed the tracks in a beeline toward the train. More filtered out of the streets and adjacent buildings. The Kid's estimate of three hundred was already obsolete. Cuba shouted out, "They're coming!"

The Kid stood transfixed.

Buck prodded him. "Game time, Kid."

"There's so many of them."

"More for me," Tara said.

Buck waved him toward the panels. "Kid, I don't want to be Grand Marshal of their parade, so if you don't mind..."

Tara's first shot startled the Kid into action.

Nothing fell.

Cuba patted her on the shoulder. "Lie down. You won't miss." He pointed at Fifty, lying on the train at eye level with Barrett on two little legs.

She fell into a prone position. With her next shot, a body twisted backward.

"Nice shot."

"I'm catching up."

"So this is a competition?" Cuba scoped in on an old bastard's head, pulled the trigger. It exploded. "Better shoot faster."

She did. Between the four of them, bodies fell.

Not fast enough. It took time to aim for the head, even with so many heads to aim for.

Tara kept her cool, even as she reloaded. He recognized it as an element of a novice. She never witnessed a feeding. She never had any close calls. For her, right now, though she might deny it, this was a therapeutic sport.

Not for long.

Cuba shouted, "I haven't stood against this many Eaters since Cleveland! And back then I had forty armed men at my back, a small army!"

He squeezed the trigger.

"What happened?" Tara asked.

"You don't see them here, do you?"

"Not helping morale!" Buck scolded.

The boom of the .50 ruined a shot. Getting hit by the ice chips that blew off the train from the brutal concussion didn't help his concentration. His scope bounced whenever Barrett spoke. *Damn that thing is loud.* Fifty never positioned himself so close.

With the Eaters packed tight, one word from Barrett ended four other conversations, ripping through multiple Eater heads like tissue paper.

While Tara fought with bravado, Cuba could not. He felt one emotion, the same one he felt every day, the one that never faded.

Fear.

"How much fuel we got?" Buck shouted.

"Quarter of a tank." The Kid's hands shook.

"Good. Keep pumping."

Buck kept their spirits up, but Cuba knew better. This took too long. As he fired into the crowd his mind made a few quick calculations - distance, quantity, ammo supply.

No chance. He came all this way to have eleven mopey college dickheads end him. Looks like Cuban on the menu. To make matters worse, he tasted blood in his mouth.

Today I die.

The little band kept up a steady *pok pok pok* with an occasional thump from Fifty. The Eaters kept coming, stumbling over the bodies of their dead comrades, unstoppable.

Buck turned to fire at Eaters approaching the rear of the shed. "How much fuel?!"

"Quarter of a tank!"

Tara's cool crumbled. She spilled a box of cartridges, digging in the snow to find them.

"Get a new box."

"This is the last one."

Shit. How long had they been here? Minutes? Years? Eaters paced meters away, numbers undiminished.

She looked at him with frightened eyes. "I never had a chance to reload."

Cuba felt her pain. "Buck, let's get out of here!"

"Not enough fuel! We'll starve to death on the tundra!"

The slow tide threatened to wash over the train like a tsunami.

"I'm not the one worried about eating!" Cuba's legs wanted to turn and run, as fast and as far as possible, until he couldn't run anymore. It took a conscious effort to fight the urge.

Maybe he didn't have to.

"Stop firing," he shouted. "Everyone hold still. I have an idea."

They stopped, stopped moving, stopped breathing. Grunts and the shuffle of snow broke the silence.

"You better have this idea soon…"

Cuba dashed straight toward the horde. He ran close, real close. Wretched fingers scraped against his jacket when he veered left at the last moment. "Don't be a hero. Don't be a hero. Don't be a hero."

At first, the ruse worked. The front line turned to watch him. A few followed. Then they turned back. They couldn't resist the roar of that diesel.

Cuba's vantage point gave him a new concern.

Fighting between the building and the train, they focused on the horde on the track. An equal number converged from behind the train.

Surrounded.

"Get on the train! Get out of here!"

Barrett drowned him out.

"Dammit, Buck! They're all around us! We have to go! Now!" He pumped his legs to rejoin them, but a contingent from the north converged to cut him off. He collided, bowled through them. His foot tripped over buried equipment. He fell, sprawled across the gravel and snow. Pain drove up his shin like spikes. They were almost on top of him. He rolled aside.

The shed lay between him and the train. Buck couldn't see him.

Buck couldn't help him.

He tried to stand, but the bone ground against his skin. He used Mr. Crow as a crutch and hobbled, faster than the creatures behind him. The chase would be comical if it weren't for the inevitable ending.

The Kid appeared, rounding the corner with his pistol blasting. He missed, but it looked good.

Cuba shouted at him. "Are you trying to be a hero?"

"Yeah, how am I doin'?"

"I'll tell you when you're dead."

The Kid made an abortive attempt to get to Cuba, but the crowd thickened around them. "Stay there!" Cuba didn't need some punk to come to his rescue.

He had a plan.

He had Tara's gunpowder in his pack.

The Kid couldn't find an opening, so Cuba shouted, "Did you get enough fuel?"

"Buck says 'no'."

"Why not?"

"No electricity to pump it. Only residual pressure in the tank."

There are other things fuel is good for. "Tell
Buck to pull across the bridge. I'll take care of this
crowd and meet you there."

The Kid had doubt written on his face in block
letters. "How will you..."

"You want to make yourself useful," he shouted
to the Kid, still taking potshots at the air, "throw me
your flashlight."

"It's broad daylight!"

"Goddamn it, do as you're told."

The Kid threw him a Maglite. It soared over
reaching hands and nearly hit Cuba in the head. He
grumbled as he dug it out of a snowbank. "Now get
back on the train!"

"Not without you!"

"Shut up and do it!" Cuba hopped on one foot to
swing at an encroaching corpse.

The Kid disappeared. A moment later, the train
rumbled forward. It parked in the middle of the
bridge. As Cuba predicted, the horde funneled onto
the tracks.

There were two bridges, parallel to one another,
a rail bridge and a road. With their attention on the
engine, there were no Eaters on the road. A plan
formulated in his mind, but he needed to get under
the bridge.

Growing up back in Miami, Cuba made pipe
bombs at home, throwing them under cars for fun.
Back then, he never had three gallons of gunpowder
to play with. Now he needed a metal container.

He circled back to the pile of debris that tripped
him up. A small contingent of Eaters, twenty or so,
stalked him. He arced wide, ending up almost where
he started, but they were too dumb to stay there.
They followed him like magnets.

He had to do this twice before he found what he needed. Two propane tanks with the heads attached. Now he had to get to the bridge.

That might be tricky. When the Barrett took down Eaters in the middle of the track, they fell, knocking others over and down the bank. There were more and more down there, scrambling to get back up or wandering off into the river. They were right where he wanted to be.

Buck shouted to him from the bridge. "What the hell are you doing over there? You're going in circles!"

He didn't want Buck to know about the broken leg. He didn't want him to know about the cough he suppressed. If he started coughing, he wouldn't stop. He didn't have much lung left. "Ram them! I need a clear path!"

No Otley here. There would be blood.

Buck put the engine in reverse. The squishing, popping noise of an engine backing up over three dozen Eaters was indescribably horrific. Even Cuba felt squeamish, but he had his opening.

The train moved forward, and for one instant a gap in the crowd opened near the bridge, on the track. He knew Buck expected him to run along the tracks and catch the train. Maybe that's what Cuba thought, too, but he could feel his chest and his leg and knew things weren't working right inside.

He dragged the tanks up the tracks. They pinged and scraped on the gravel like a dinner bell. He slipped and lost his footing on the gore on the tracks, then fell back down the other side.

Buck leaned out of the cab. "Where are you going? Let's go!"

"Get clear! Get clear!"

He fell under the bridge supports.

He had less than a minute to pull this off. He unscrewed the pressure valve in the tanks and poured as much black powder as they would hold. He fished his clothesline out of his pack and stripped the ends down to the wires. He pulled the bulb and spare bulb out of the Maglite, broke off the tips of the bulbs, wrapped the wire around the poles, and buried them in the powder. He stripped off the duct tape around his wrists to hold the valves in place. Not the best option, but time was short. He used a bit more and strapped it to the leg of the bridge.

He glanced up. Most of the crowd followed the train but a few of his old disciples came sniffing his way. Time ran out.

His chest convulsed. He couldn't breathe. Racking coughs pushed against his diaphragm. *Not now!* He fell to his knees. The Eaters edged closer. He felt his insides ripping out. That familiar taste of blood.

A pocket of air dodged the cough and caught in his lungs. He fought to keep it, hold it, like a diver under ice. He forced himself to keep moving.

Through tears, holding his breath, he watched his hands move as if separate from himself. He taped the other tank to the second support. So far, no one behind him. With the Maglite in one hand and the clothesline in the other, he backed up, spooling it out as he went. He doubted he had enough gunpowder to pull this off, but he shrugged off the doubt. *This is going to work. You got this. Buy enough time to hobble across the second bridge, and meet them on the other side.*

He backed up as far as the slope to the roadway before the wire ran out. *Not far enough, but it'll have to do.*

The silent mob swarmed around the fuel shed.

Time to warm up.

Cuba pressed the wires to the flashlight battery.

A flash split the air, flaring across the bridge supports, white smoke obscuring an inferno behind it.

The explosion knocked him to the snow, on top of Mr. Crow. The crowbar bit deep into his side. He pulled it free, holding back the blood with one dirty hand.

The plume cleared to reveal thirty or more eaters lit up like immolated priests. The bridge held. One tank remained. But it had the effect Cuba wanted.

The Eaters scattered, disoriented by the fire, bumping into each other, pushing the line back. One Eater turned around completely and stumbled toward the fuel shed.

Cuba only needed to hobble back to the engine. But he wouldn't.

Buck poked his head out of the cab. "That's it?"

Cuba sat up, grunted. "I thought it would blow

A mass of air punched him in the chest as a fireball erupted where the fuel shed used to be.

Eater parts and chunks of steel decorated the soot stained sky like tickertape. Pieces that didn't evaporate fell to the ground, flaming. Two hundred Eaters fell like trees around a meteor hole. They had trouble picking themselves up.

Cuba heard cheering from the train. He looked over and waved. *Damn, it feels good when*

A great weight slammed him to the ground.

He lay there, stunned. *Am I okay?* He didn't feel any pain.

A jagged pipe as thick as a cannon lay across both legs. He tried to raise his arms to move it. They didn't respond. He couldn't feel anything below his neck.

First he thought something held him down. His hands dangled limp and empty in the snow. Blood wept from a tear at the knee.

He couldn't feel any of it.

Claustrophobia set in as he realized what happened.

Trapped in my own body.

He saw Eaters pick through the wreckage, sniffing the air with decayed nostrils, headed right for him.

He struggled, tossed his head left and right. It made no difference. Immobile, helpless, cornered. His worst nightmare. He watched them come.

A pair of legs interrupted his view.

The Kid.

In shock, Cuba shouted at him, "Are you all right? Are you ok? Where's Mr. Crow? Give me Mr. Crow!"

The Kid looked torn between following instructions and inspecting Cuba's wounds. He dug around in the snow, found the crowbar, and placed it on his palm. The fingers didn't close. Cuba begged them to close with impotent willfulness. Angry, he lashed out, "What are you doing here? Get back to the train!"

The Kid wrestled with the pipe, jostling his body. Like Cuba, it would not move.

"Give up, Kid. You can't help me."

"I can try."

"You're not listening. Don't be a hero. Run."

The Kid glanced back at the approaching Eaters. "I have time."

He pulled on the pipe. Cuba heard fabric tear and watched a new spring of blood bubble upward. "You hit oil." His vision swam. He didn't feel well.

Eaters closed the gap. Twenty yards. The Kid put his back into it.

Cuba lost all strength. "Leave it," he said, more relaxed than he ever remembered. "Sit with me. You look sick. Are you okay?"

The Kid sat down. "No, I don't think so."

"You have to be careful out here. You'll get yourself killed."

The Kid wiped a tear off his cheek.

"How many," Cuba fought for breath. "How many you think I took out?"

He watched the young engineer's rational mind kick in to do the math. "They were all over that shed. Fifty, maybe sixty disappeared."

"I counted another thirty-eight during the shooting and fifteen back in town. Do me a favor, write that on my helmet."

The Kid reached for it.

"No, not here, when you get on the train."

"But, I can't..."

"I want Tara to have it. She earned it."

Eaters from the back of the crowd swarmed over the wreckage and wrecked bodies as if no explosion ever happened. His warm blood telegraphed his position. Ten yards.

"It isn't fair. I don't deserve to die like this. "

The Kid agreed. "No one does."

"No, I mean, like this. Painless. Peaceful. Those boys I killed, the women, the carnage and terror and pain. They deserve better. They deserve to see me suffer."

What responsibilities do the dying have? Bequeath a will. He had nothing in this world to give away. He thought of something.

"You take Mr. Crow. No, don't argue. He's got a lot more death dealing to do. Besides, you can't shoot for shit."

The Kid's mouth moved, but nothing came out.

"It's been a long day. Get back in the cab and get some rest."

The Kid didn't move.

"Get back on the train! Live! Let me think one person did."

The Kid ran, clutching his trophies, feet kicking up clouds of powder.

Cuba closed his eyes and held his breath, trying to pass out. A cold breeze brushed across his cheek. He heard the footsteps diminish, a shout, then the saddest sound of all. The hiss of brakes released on the train, the clack of steel rolling down the track, and the hush of blowing snow.

Cuba tilted his head back, watched the train go. North, to Churchill, maybe to a cure. He regretted he wouldn't see it through to the end, but he didn't regret the end. He had lived in pain as long as he could remember. The end is the end of pain.

He heard the wind blowing through distant trees, maybe palms.

"Is this okay, little brother? Is this enough?"

He felt delirious. Hot.

"I couldn't keep my promise. I couldn't. I tried." He began to cry, kept his lips tight, holding it back. "I tried."

For the first time in three months, the lump no longer pressed against his chest. The broken shin didn't trouble him. The half-healed wounds, the bruises, the scratches and scabs and hunger that make up the primary sensations of life on the road, all disappeared in a gray haze.

He didn't deserve this mercy. Not after what he'd done.

His body forced him to breathe. He inhaled a desecrating stench.

His eyes opened.

Every night he woke from nightmares, a thousand variations of this moment. Trapped, the blackened face of an Eater crawling up his legs, crooked fingers pulling on his flesh, perfect, unblinking orbs watching him for movement, dry teeth pulling back.

He never dreamt such a placid ending. Helpless, almost dead, beyond care, protected from corporeal horror, he could watch, a spectator, like an astral traveler, as they devoured a body, once his.

So he spectated. In fascination.

The first Eater found the blood on his knee appealing. It bent to taste it, exposing a patchy skull as grotesque as an eyeball. It drank deep.

A second Eater followed Mr. Crow's bite. Fingers reached in, widening the hole until the arm followed. The skin on Cuba's chest wriggled. The Eater drew out strands of intestine, bringing it to a blistered mouth. It proceeded to eat the steaming tube, swallowing in great, hungry, gulps.

For that brief moment, they were connected, a bridge between life and death, a digestive tract in place of an umbilical cord.

The Eater's stomach had rotted away long ago. Cuba's tripe, lightly chewed, dangled in the abyss that used to be an abdomen, then slithered into a coil on the ground.

Mercy intervened again, depriving Cuba of consciousness. Before a third set of teeth reached his jugular, he turned.

CHURCHILL

Fred Eggert found the body, behind the lone abandoned Hudson Bay Railway car.

Paul knew why. Only Fred hung around the station anymore. There hadn't been a train pull into Churchill in months, but he insisted on maintaining his rounds. Every day he puttered around, arranging and rearranging gear, greasing luggage cart wheels and fixing signals. After forty years on the line, it was inconceivable to him that the end of civilization also meant forced retirement.

When Paul arrived, Old Mike and Fred were standing over the body. It lay face up in the snow next to an overturned snowmobile. "Who is it?"

"Joel Mackie."

Joel. Paul's first thought was that somebody finally shot the poor kid. Joel didn't take isolation well. He was one of the few townsmen falling apart.

Paul heard a lot of versions of the tale, most of them unflattering. Joel had interests of some kind down south, and split loyalties tore him apart. Unable to settle his business, he self-destructed, getting drunk, starting fights, and taking pleasure in petty theft. Joel had a habit of stealing gas for hunting forays, and he never shared the meat.

He had no reason to steal. Most of the village worked on a sharing system now, but even before all this, if he needed something, someone would give it to him. It was that simple. In the old days, they would have bought him a train ticket and watched him go.

His train never came.

Joel's body was a mess. Something sharp slashed his neck. Immense pressure cracked his goggles and maybe his skull. Strong limbs ripped open his parka at the chest and stomach, tearing out everything underneath. Looked like a small bomb exploded somewhere inside his body. Most of the organs were missing, and he had long since frozen, snow drifting in the cavity. The setting sun washed the drifts in red.

Nobody shot Joel. Nobody ever got shot in Churchill, on purpose anyway. That was Paul's paranoia talking, too many years in dangerous places. Only one predator hunted man up here.

"Think it was them things from down south?" Fred speculated.

Paul shook his head. "Pretty clear what did this, though we haven't seen it in a long time." Paw prints the size of a human head tore up the snow, but the wind from last night covered any blood trail. "We'll have a hard time tracking him. I'll tell Wade we've got one in town. I want to see the look on his face."

"Weren't no polar bear." Old Mike inspected the tracks. "It was Paija."

"Who?" Fred asked.

Paul didn't have time for old myths. "It was a bear, Mike. It's been a while, but they're around."

Old Mike persisted. "Joel took more than his community had to give."

"Who's Paija?" Fred's wizened face looked frightened.

Paul tried to wave him off. "It's an Inuit myth. A woman, covered in black hair, one twisted leg protruding from her belly. She enforces tribal taboos. Supposed to... hunt in the cover of blizzards."

Fred's eyes widened. "Nobody's seen Joel since that blizzard two days ago."

Old Mike went on. "Sometimes a hunter will kill more deer than his family needs, or a village gives birth to more children than the winter can support. When this happens, there is no balance in the world. Paija brings the balance."

"How?" He had Fred's attention. "What does she do?"

"You find a man, frozen, in the snow, with a hole in his chest where she tore out his soul."

Paul had enough. "Let's not waste any more time. That bear knows where it can get food. It'll be back."

Fred tilted his head away from them. "Train coming. 400 cars out."

Two men came running up behind them. Paul filled them in. They helped Paul turn the snowmobile over. He hated being helped. He pushed hard with one arm and the stump of the other until the snowmobile rolled over. He pointed back at the station. "There's a sled over there; you can pull him back with this. We know it has gas."

One of them asked, "You want us to put him with that Japanese girl?"

"For now, that'll have to do. While you're at it, find Wade. Tell him to meet me out here, see if he can track this thing."

"No man can track Paija." Old Mike hopped on one foot. "She tracks you."

"Train coming. 300 cars out."

Paul wanted Mayor Fell to see this. Keep the rumors down. "See if Fell is over at the Lighthouse. Tell him... what did you say?"

Fred's eyes were on the southern horizon. "Eight, maybe ten minutes out." His voice took an air of curiosity. "Sounds like an engine, no cars."

Paul took a few steps forward. The rails were empty. No disturbance on the horizon except a low wind blowing dunes across the tracks.

But Fred was never wrong about the trains.

His stomach clenched with the thought of it. Not the train, no, what rode the train. What had eaten through everything south. For three months they'd been immune, forgotten, abandoned. Paul liked it that way. Sometimes he expected it to stay that way.

Like now. It looked like the same day it did five minutes ago. Not the last day. Not the end.

His head told him to run. *This is why you built a bunker. Get in it, and wait for news.* He could wait a long time. Years, if need be. He had the supplies, the air filters, water, septic, and plenty of entertainment. He didn't have to be up here, watching, waiting.

He looked at Old Mike and Fred. He thought about the rest of the town, waking up. He couldn't abandon them. If he were alone, he would have kicked up his heels, but now...

Thirty years living in this village made him soft. He'd come in middle age. That meant almost half his life spent with these people. They were as close to family as he ever had.

His gaze returned to Joel's remains. *That's where split loyalties get you.*

He shrugged it off. To the two men, he said, "Tell Fell a train is coming." He turned to Old Mike and Fred. "We better get inside."

The diesel skated across miles of ice covered plains like a coming storm. Plumes of snow blew up and away from it, obscuring the engine from view. The rails sang out a warning.

A month ago, against Fell's wishes, Paul stocked up a small arsenal in the station for such an occasion. "Time to form the welcoming committee." He didn't have to be paranoid, but it helped.

He'd imagined this scene a thousand times, rehearsed a hundred speeches to welcome or threaten away travelers. Now he felt them inadequate. One way or another, Death rode that train. What could he say to that?

What if they weren't travelers? What if they were... those things? Would they swarm the building like they did on the news before it went dark? He asked himself for the umpteenth time, *Why am I out of my bunker?*

"One hundred cars," Fred whispered, out of habit.

It blasted into a patch of rail scoured clean by the wind. An engine emerged from the white veil like an ugly bride. "One engine, no cars." Fred remarked, the mystery resolved.

"Less people to deal with." Paul reached out his one arm, hesitating between the binoculars and the rifle. He chose the field glasses. He focused on the cab. He couldn't see into the dark interior, but he could see a bullet hole in the window. "Or things," he added.

It slowed as it neared the station. Some form of intelligence managed to put on the brakes, and it came to a stop not fifty yards out.

Fred handed him the radio, keyed to the frequency of the train, or what they'd used back when the trains ran on a regular schedule. He spoke, "VF2312. Copy."

No response.

Fred rolled his eyes. "This is dumb. Those things don't know how to use a radio." He spoke into the mic, "Down and to your left."

Someone found it, keyed in. "What happened? You run out of fruit baskets?"

Paul felt some relief hearing the living, but this flippant attitude meant they weren't desperate refugees either. That cab carried someone dangerous. Probably lots of someones.

Paul started with the script: "Do not exit the vehicle or you will be put down."

The voice came back, "Why? Your hotels booked up?"

Until the rest of the town showed up, he couldn't back up any threats. Old Mike was a good shot, but slow. Fred didn't shoot. And Paul... he hated to admit it, but having only one arm made him a little slower on the reload. He didn't know how many people were in there, but if they made it this far, chances were they outgunned the three of them.

Where is everybody? We're two blocks from the Lighthouse.

When Paul asked her about it three months ago, the lone nurse remaining in the village, Sam, explained the protocol to follow when dealing with epidemics. Screen them with questions, then quarantine them. Paul stalled, starting with, "Have any of you been bitten?"

"No."

"Are you carrying any Infected?"

The leader hesitated before he said, "No."

Bad sign.

"Do any of you suffer from fever?"

"Does rice fever count?"

"How many people do you have?"

"Four."

Four against a town of two hundred. Paul liked those odds, but he hoped the odds would show up soon. He still didn't hear any snowmobiles or trucks outside.

"What are you doing here?"

The driver left the mic on before he answered, so Paul heard a woman say "This is a waste of time." Then the driver on the mic, "We were in the neighborhood; thought we might stop by."

Paul keyed off the mic. "A smart ass. You know what that means? We've got ourselves some very dangerous individuals." Fred and Old Mike nodded. He asked again, "Why did you come to Churchill?"

"Buy me a beer and I'll tell you."

"You can answer the question honestly or you can go back the way you came."

The man hesitated. Now Paul had a bargaining chip. This man didn't want to go back.

His crackling voice came through the speaker. "We've got four tickets for the boat off this island."

Something about the man's choice of words resonated with Paul. Dangerous they may be, but they were survivors who wanted to escape. Paul identified with that. "Wait there," he said.

A fleet of snowmobiles roared up to the station. So much for gasoline rationing. Seems everyone in town woke up to see this.

Four more black snowmobiles bypassed the station and skidded to a halt beside the train.

Paul recognized them. *Trouble.* He frowned and ran outside. "You monitoring the channel again, Wilson?"

Wilson didn't answer, unless you count jacking a round as conversation. He strode up to the iron beast with his shotgun aimed at the window and pounded the butt against the skin.

Light scissored across the steel as more snowmobiles arrived.

Paul caught sight of Mayor Fell. "Mayor, you gotta put Wilson on a leash!"

"Wilson!" the Mayor shouted. "Put the damn gun down. You don't know who's inside. Could be kids in there, or wounded."

"Could be them creatures!" the Captain strode up behind Fell. "They could take over our DNA and steal the town!"

Paul rolled his eyes, an automatic reaction when the Captain spoke.

Rifle barrels bristled as more people arrived. Funny how this show of arms didn't make Paul feel safer.

"Don't touch the train!" Someone shouted. "It might be contaminated!"

That made Wilson back off quick, but now he angled for the door. "Come out, come out, whoever you are!"

With an ear wrenching squeak the side door fell open. A man's head poked out into the glare of a hundred flashlights. He squinted. "Are you the welcoming committee?"

Wilson moved forward, but the Mayor shouted, "Don't touch him! We have a quarantine procedure."

"How 'bout if I shoot him?" Wilson asked. "Problem solved."

The stranger ignored Wilson. Instead, he called out, "Is this Churchill?"

Paul liked this guy. He kept his cool in front of a gun. A fellow adventurer, perhaps? A survivor at least. Maybe even a friend. "Yes!" He shouted.

"Great!" The man seemed genuinely elated. He climbed down the ladder and tossed Wilson the key. "Careful with her. She pulls to the left."

While Wilson fumbled with the key, the stranger turned back to say, "Come on out, kids. We're home."

First to emerge was not a child. A hulking dark giant, carrying an equally large rifle, stooped through the cab door. A petite but well-armed woman followed. Finally, hauling two backpacks, a young man.

That explained the stranger's nonchalance. The big man would have dropped Wilson before he got off a shot. And judging from the barrels protruding from the young man's pack, they could have held out against the whole town in that iron fort.

Wilson waved over his cronies who swarmed into the cab. A moment later, his head popped out again, angry. "The fuel's empty!"

The stranger laughed. "Yeah, just made it." Then he said to the approaching Mayor, "I need four

rooms, one with a king size bed, and cable if you
have it."

The mayor smiled. "We have the rooms, but we
have a decontamination protocol to follow. You'll
have to spend twenty four hours in quarantine."

"As long as it's warm and soft, I won't complain.
I'm Buck." He held out his hand.

The Mayor shivered away from it like roadkill.

Buck pulled it back, ran it through his hair.
"Right. Sorry. Quarantine before pleasantries.
Which way?"

The crowd parted. A tundra buggy, almost as big
as the train engine, backed up into the light.
Basically an elevated bus, it used to provide a safe
height for tourists to view polar bears. The Mayor
pointed at it. "You'll be comfortable. Folks used to
pay a fortune to spend the night in the Tundra
Buggy Hotel. Our rates are a bit lower now." He
pointed to the giant's long rifle. "We ask that you
leave your weapons outside."

Buck shifted his feet, looked down at the
ground. "Better quarantine them, too, don't you
think?"

"Town rules."

The man took a long look at the heavily armed
townspeople, then off into the distance at the lights
of Churchill. "Not too comfortable without something
to fight with."

"We'll give them back as soon as..."

"Oh we trust you. There are worse things in the
night." He jerked his thumb into the darkness
behind him. The crowd responded as one, muttering,
retreating, stabbing the horizon with pins of light as
if this stranger brought Hell on his heels.

Even Mayor Fell took a step back. "Are they... close?"

Buck paused a moment before he said, "Let us keep the blunt instruments." He pulled a crowbar from his pack. A black feather tumbled around it.

Paul sensed a bluff. They didn't seem in a hurry, and even surrendered their firearms. Whatever chased them did so at a fair distance. Relief and disappointment fought for control of Paul's emotions. When you can't avoid a fight, you want it to come sooner than later.

The Mayor kept his eyes on the darkness. "It's a deal. Crawl into the Buggy and we'll take you in. Paul, you drive."

Paul walked past tires high as his head and opened the rear door for his guests. "You'll be safe in here. The steel's so think a polar bear couldn't get through it. And the windows are too high for anything to get in. I imagine those things we've heard about aren't taller than a polar bear?"

"They're about as tall as you," Buck said. As Paul watched, Buck helped the woman in first, then the boy, then got out of the way for the giant. The big man stood tall as a polar bear on its hind legs. Paul felt safer when the door closed.

Paul hit a trigger, locking them in from the outside.

The show over, most of the snowmobiles headed home. Wilson and his boys lingered, but Fell pushed them on. "Nothing more to see here. Nothing to do but wait till tomorrow. We've got nothing but time."

When the area cleared, Fell pulled Paul aside. "What happened with Joel?"

"Bear. Tell folks to keep an eye out. It'll be back."

"Right." He looked up at the bus. "Take them out to the edge of town. Someone will follow you and bring you back."

Paul climbed into the cab. Old Mike waited in the passenger seat. Paul looked at him with surprise, but Old Mike only shrugged, cranked up the heater, and threw a look over his shoulder at the four huddled in the back. "Not many tourists this year."

Paul knocked the bus into gear. "I blame the economy."

An intercom connected him to his restless cargo. He used his stump to steer while he pressed the intercom button. "Hello folks. Welcome to Churchill Tours. I'm Paul. I'll be your guide today. Please excuse the welcome. We're a little crazy up here, but safe. We haven't seen one case of the living dead, and we don't want to. You'll notice there are beds, a washroom, and some outdated reading material. If you're alive in the morning and not craving brains, we'll let you out.

"If you look to your left you'll see the wasteland that protects us from the outside world. And on your right is the emptiness that prevents us from leaving. If you look behind you... it's dark.

Buck got up next to the glass to ask him something, but he couldn't hear a word. No one thought to put a microphone in the back. The only way for Paul to talk to the strangers was to get in the box with them.

Roaring back on a Ski-Doo, his ride dropped them off at the Lighthouse. The only bar in town, it doubled as a community center. With the bar, a restaurant, and an event space known as the Dark

Room, it could hold most of the remaining inhabitants, the majority of whom now stood outside on the street, gossiping. Mayor Fell tried to disperse the crowd, shooing them away. After half an hour in the cold, they chose to continue their conversations at home.

Except Wilson and his three ardent followers. They tended toward unruly, and the magnetism of the only bar in town kept them in a close orbit. "We better go out and stand guard, make sure none of them tries to get out."

"What you need to do is go home and sleep it off." Mayor Fell held a trump card over Wilson and his men. He *owned* the only bar in town. With hunting and drinking their principal hobbies, the threat of banishment had an impact on both. "There won't be any new information until morning, so get, and leave our guests alone!"

They shuffled off, grumbling and spitting in the snow.

That left Paul alone with Mayor Fell and the Captain. With the coast clear, Fell waved them inside.

Taking a table close to the bar, Fell didn't offer them anything. Instead, he settled into a chair and did what everyone else was doing. "What do you think?"

"I want to get in there and talk to them." Paul fought an internal war between his burning curiosity and his desire to stay away from any disease. He wasn't a doctor. What did he know about what they might or might not have? But he couldn't leave it alone. They knew. They'd seen the outside world. They had information that this town didn't have. If information is a weapon, Paul was unarmed.

"We can't wait twenty-four hours. There might be a security issue."

The Captain's leg bounced so hard it threatened to tip his chair over. "This is huge! I need to get in there. My audience deserves to know."

Mayor Fell paced, waving his arms. "We don't know how this is transmitted. I'm not taking any risks."

Paul tried for the paranoia angle. It worked before. "What if they were followed? What if those things are out there on the tracks right now?" He pictured Buck speaking through the glass. Was it important? Was it urgent?

"It's a conspiracy, man." The Captain's excitement blocked his reason. "First they send in a scouting party to test our strength. Then they invade."

"That's plausible," Paul added. It wasn't plausible, but Paul accepted any argument that got him in there.

"Look guys. It's my ass on the line. This is a public health issue. Wait twenty-four hours and then, maybe..."

Paul pulled the hard line. "I'm calling in my favor."

"What favor?"

"You know what I did for you."

"Shit, Paul, this isn't worth..."

"Captain, I got a good story for you..."

"All right, dammit, you're in."

"What story?"

The Mayor cast Paul an evil eye. "On one condition. You go in there with them, but you don't come out until the quarantine ends."

That put a different spin on it. Paul wanted twenty minutes, hopefully not long enough to contract anything. What if they turned overnight? Stuck in a twenty foot steel can with four undead candidates violated his prime directive. Still. He had to know. "Deal. But I want a radio. Something goes wrong, you come in shooting." Saying this, Paul realized he put himself in a disposable position. Did he trust everyone involved? After living in Churchill this long, yes, he did.

The buggy stood at the edge of town, engine purring away irreplaceable fuel. Crunching through the -40 wind chill, Paul had second thoughts. And third thoughts. What if he hadn't read this Buck correctly? What if the strangers mugged him, tried to bargain with his life to be set free? What if the Mayor didn't accept? The radio in his hand felt as reassuring as a paperweight.

Curiosity goaded him beyond fear. Whoever they were, they knew more than he did. And they were alive. He'd take his chances with the plague, or whatever it was. He had to know the truth about what killed the world.

"Whether you live or not," the Mayor started, "I need a hero. You're it. If anyone asks, this was your idea. Bravo."

Which left Paul's ass on the line, not Fell's. *He should have run for a higher office.*

The Captain bounced around like a puppy. "I want a full report when you get out, you lucky bastard." Then he whispered, "What do you know about the Mayor?"

"I don't know what you're talking about."

Wearing a respirator, gloves, and goggles, Paul reached for the door handle, paused to catch his breath, and opened the door. When no one flew out, he pulled himself inside. The door thudded behind him like the lid of a coffin. Even with the heater running, his blood ran cold. "Hi," he said.

They were asleep. Two of them raised a head when he entered, grunted when he posed no threat, then passed out again.

A flood of disappointment washed over him. This anticlimactic response was in none of the scenarios that crowded the last hour. He wanted to kick them, shout at them to wake up and answer his damn questions.

He paused. His skin puckered. He imagined a million tiny legs crawling up his arms like spiders. He knew viruses don't spread that way, but his skin wasn't convinced.

Maybe these people were infected. Maybe they were already dead, moments from rising to maul him in a frenzy of blood and grey matter.

Tomorrow's big news: Paul emerges a zombie, shot by Wilson, the new town hero. The thought was almost as repulsive as the disease itself. Wilson lounging in Paul's bunker, gorging himself on a lifetime supply of painstakingly preserved salting crackers, burning his books for fuel. Paul pushed the thought away.

The big one let out a tenorous snort. The woman whimpered. They must have been exhausted.

Paul sat down near the door and waited. And waited. His thoughts turned to nightmares, drifting from dream to dream, and he almost fell over when the radio erupted in his headphone.

"How'd they sleep, Paul?" Mayor Fell stood outside. Morning light slid across the snow.

"Like the dead," he whispered into the radio.

"I hope not."

"They're asleep. You want me to wake them up for you?"

The Mayor peeked in the window. "Yeah. Wake 'em up. Let 'em out. They have something they need to do."

"It hasn't been twenty four..."

"C'mon Paul. I'm looking at four healthy people, and I've got two hundred more in the Lighthouse waiting for news. I hope these aren't the type for stage fright."

"You're going to expose –"

"Expose? Paul, let me lay it out for you. I know you have a bunker full of food, but even you can't feed the whole town. We're dying up here, with or without the plague. Three more months without resupply and we'll either go native or starve. If the bears don't get us first. These four are a diversion and, let me tell you, I could use a diversion."

Politics before plagues. *He could have been Prime Minister.*

The door squeaked and grated as Paul opened it. That woke them up. The two men and the woman were on their feet in an instant. *These are the warriors*, he thought. The young one took his time. *And that's the tourist.*

The Mayor entered first, shaking hands with gloves on, all smiles. "Hi. Welcome to Churchill. Hello! Nice to meet you."

The skinny one, Buck, ran through the names of the others with a pointed index finger. "Tara. Fifty.

The Kid. What do you eat for breakfast up here? You got a Tim Horton's?"

"I wish! No, but I'm sure we can rustle up something for you."

The woman, Tara, remembering what she heard last night, asked, "You haven't had any cases? The town is Eater free?" She looked disappointed

"That's right. We're pretty isolated up here. The trains and planes stopped running after it hit, and no one else comes up here in the winter. The plague never reached us. You're the first visitors we've had in months. I hope you'll excuse our caution."

Buck smiled. "We're not here to make trouble. I'm just glad to be here."

"Sure, but why Churchill? You don't sound Canadian."

"I'll tell you over a beer."

"It's never too early for a beer. It's the one thing we stocked up on."

Everyone congregated at the Lighthouse. The bar had chairs enough for a hundred people, but at least a hundred more packed themselves in around the pool table and the poker machines, well over capacity.

That many bodies heated up the space, most too distracted to take off their parkas. Toddlers in the back couldn't sit still. Perennial drunks like Wilson's crowd leaned against the bar. A controlled pandemonium reigned.

Boot scuffs and coughs replaced conversation as a hole opened up for the newcomers. All eyes watched them.

The mayor stopped in a square space reserved for dancing and bands. A low railing separated him from the crowd, enough to buy a second or two if his guests needed to duck behind the bar and get out the back door. These were good people, but they were scared. Frightened people do dumb things.

Paul took a spot in the opposite direction, near the door. If anything went wrong, he had his escape route planned out.

The Mayor held out both hands with the mic. "All right. By now you've heard the news. Yes, we have visitors. Let's give them a warm welcome as I introduce...."

"How's Winnipeg?" Someone shouted, which set off an avalanche of questions, desperate to be heard over one another. People stood up. The crowd in the back inched forward.

"Hold on, now. They're not going anywhere. We got plenty of time for your questions. First, let them have their say."

Buck stepped forward, not shy at all. In fact, he had a smile from ear to ear. "Hi, y'all. I can't say how good it is to see so many living faces." He got dead silence in return. "We've been working our way up here for months. Seen a lot of carnage in that time, so your hospitality is much appreciated."

In a room full of hope, his words fell like a lead blanket. That's not what they wanted to hear. They wanted: the plague is over, the government sent us to check on you, it's ok to come out now, everything's fine.

Buck's happiness was the worst possible news. Effectively, he told them: this is as good as it gets.

Leave it to Wilson to pick a fight. "You come with any good news? Otherwise go back the way you came."

That caused a commotion. Shouts in agreement. Arguments back and forth in the crowd. These people knew each other. An event like this opened wounds, new and old. They squabbled like a family barbeque when the bad son comes home.

Buck's voice, drowned out, faltered. "I wish I did have good news for you. I wish I could...

The Mayor took over the microphone. "Our guests have come a long way, and as you can see," he untangled his foot from a chord, "they are healthy and disease free. That's good news to me. Somewhere out there people are still alive, and that's how we start over. Now, I know you have a lot of questions, so let's get this started proper, one at a time."

"How many of them things have you killed?" Someone shouted out.

"If you have a question, come to the front," the Mayor instructed. Chairs scraped as half the room stood up. "One at a time. C'mon folks. We have all year." Most sat back down.

An ancient Dene woman remained standing. She gave Buck a good once-over from head to toe, then asked. "How do we know if someone is one of them things?"

Buck looked relieved to be on solid ground again. "It isn't easy, right after someone turns. Except for the wound that killed them, they'll look the same. Not like in the movies. No bloodshot eyes or black drool. No growling except for this noise they make at the back of the throat." He imitated it.

Paul's hair stood on end.

"We call it The Purr. When you hear it, you either kill it or run."

"So they could look like you," she went on.

He shuffled a little. "But Eaters don't talk. They just come after you. They're hungry. We don't call them Eaters for nothing."

Wilson shouted, "I don't hear the big one talking! We need to kill him or run?" Laughter from his little crowd, with nervous shuffling.

Paul expected the warriors to shout back. They tensed up, their eyes on the exits, looking like they didn't want to be here.

Buck hurried on, "Later, it gets easier. The body starts to decompose. Fat disappears. The skin sags. Looks like a body suit on the wrong person. Sometimes it falls off. Up here, frostbite hits fast. Skin turns black with boils. Hair, nose, and ears break off. Internal organs rot out. It'll stink like nothing you've ever smelled. And it can't digest, so anything it eats sits in the stomach and rots. It rots instead of freezing because their bodies are warm."

"Why is that?" someone shouted. No one asked him to stand up because everyone wanted to know.

"No clue. But I can tell you how to kill it. Destroy the brain and it won't get up."

"Everyone knows what causes it!" The Captain stood up, laughing, addressing the room. "It's the alien DNA. They were injecting US soldiers down in Venezuela with it."

The room erupted again, some shouting him down, the rest agreeing with him.

"They ain't dead," he went on, encouraged. "They're human-alien hybrids bent on world domination and a One World government."

The Mayor waded over to him and cajoled him to sit down. "Let's hear their version." The crowd eased.

Somehow, the Mayor got them to come up, one by one. How many did you kill? How did you survive? What do you know about what happened? Have you heard from this town or that one?

The Captain laughed at most of the answers, corroborated some, like the news that the nuclear reactors went down at the same time.

Paul didn't know how much of it he believed, but it scared him. He wondered if he should hole up in his bunker now. Get it over with.

He looked across the room at the frightened faces, the hopeful faces, even the bored ones. He knew them, the way parents know the faces of offspring. He couldn't leave them to this fate. He had to be a part of it, whatever "it" was.

Some of the crowd grew restless at too much detail. They walked out, in twos and threes, to go home and distill it in their own conversations. The crowd thinned.

Finally, someone asked the big question.

"Why did you come to Churchill?"

It was Paul. He heard the answer when they got off the train, but he needed more.

Buck scraped his boot against the stage. "To escape the island of North America. On the Pegasus."

General laughter. They thought it was a joke. The room went silent as they waited for the punchline.

Buck's swagger wilted. "It's here, right? It winters here?"

Wilson answered. "It winters here, it summers here. It'll be here till doomsday."

One of his crew chimed in. "That rust bucket isn't good for scraps."

The Captain stood up. "You don't talk about her that way! None of you!"

Wilson kicked back his chair and stood up. "You got a problem? Huh? Let's take care of it."

"C'mon, don't...." the Mayor waved a few of his friends to intervene while he took the mic. "I think we've got more than enough information for one morning. Let's give our guests a break and talk about it again later."

A sick expression stretched across Buck's pale face.

Chairs squeaked, as the Mayor gave out a cheerful, "Thank you for coming!"

After the meeting broke up and Lighthouse staff herded most of them out of the room, Paul ventured to where Buck and his crew stood hunched over the rail. Mayor Fell and the Captain joined him. "How about that beer?"

Paul wanted to understand what drove these strangers thousands of miles into the northern wastes. Not the superficial answers, the real ones. Their hopes, their fears, justified or otherwise. He needed to know what he was up against. He figured alcohol would loosen them up.

Buck held up the beer offered him, squinting at the label. "What is this?"

"'La Fin du Monde'. Made in Quebec."

Buck looked suspicious. "Don't drink beer with French names. Mine usually have the word 'Lite' at the end."

"Means 'End of the World'."

"How appropriate." Buck took a sip. Something about the meeting kicked the fight out of him. Foam coated an upper lip as it stretched into a weak smile.

He held it aloft. "I have tasted The End of the World, and it is sweet!"

The Kid choked on his beer. "You seem pretty safe up here."

"For now. We're far from self-sufficient. If the world doesn't collect itself by the summer we'll have to head south."

"There's nothing for you south." Buck wasn't smiling now. "I lost a lot of people getting up here."

The Mayor chimed in. "There's only two directions out of here. There's south and, uh, south."

Buck hung his head. "The Pegasus. It won't sail?"

"You want to talk to the Captain."

The Captain jerked his head up, his eyes on Tara, expectant. "You need me?"

Buck waved a hand in front of the Captain's face. "North America is an island. We want off."

That line again. He must have practiced it on the way up.

"Oh, yeah!" The Captain lived for this. "Yeah. We're out of here! China, baby!"

Paul scoffed. "Why the hell would we want to go to China? Lower quality zombies?"

"No, man, doesn't anyone listen to my show?" They sat back, avoiding eye contact, looking uncomfortable. "Oh, this is embarrassing. If I can't get my own town to listen, who can I get?"

"You're a hero in Hudson Bay," the Kid offered. "They listen religiously. Told us to get your autograph."

The Captain made a little bow. "Thank you. And thank you for the letters. We found them on the train. They were...encouraging."

The Kid smirked. "They told us you intercepted Chinese radio traffic. Something about a cure?"

Tara leaned forward. "Is it real?"

"Not just a band, baby." He reveled in their attention.

"What do you know about it?"

"You're interested?"

Paul hated when he did this.

"We're interested."

A broad grin stretched under his half-closed eyes. He stood up, leaning against the table. "You see?" He waved his arms and addressed the empty room. "The Outside World is interested in what I have to say. Not like you uneducated Philistines." He crashed back into his seat. Glassy eyes stared contentedly at his new audience.

They waited.

"The cure?" Paul prodded. He dreaded another half hour wasted listening to The Captain's wild theories, but he played host to their guests. They might as well see for themselves.

"I have a theory," The Captain started.

Here we go.

"The Americans. They invented this plague, something to help them win small wars, wars like the one in Venezuela.

"They faced stiff resistance from the locals, villagers, civilians who sometimes pick up guns to shoot back. Pacify the people with a simple disease and they're too tired to fight back. Rockefeller funded the initial research back in 1910. Hookworms. They wondered why the Southern economy never recovered from the Civil War, why Southerners were so lazy. Turned out to be hookworms. Rockefeller sold that knowledge to the Army. And here we are."

"You're saying these creatures are caused by hookworms?" Tara struggled to control her anger.

Paul interrupted. "Hookworms. Rockefeller. American health care is next. Then he gets into the thirty seven species of aliens. Let me save you a day of crazy talk. Tell them about the Pegasus."

"Eighty-two species," the Captain corrected him. "It's eighty-two."

"No, no, I know what he's talking about." Buck brightened, like a kid on a scavenger hunt who found the first clue. "Back in 1910, Rockefeller funded a study that proved hookworms caused Southerners to be susceptible to multiple diseases. With their bodies wasting calories on parasites, they didn't have energy to work. Once Rockefeller's people removed the hookworm, the South flourished. Many believe that's why Africa remains the third world."

Tara wrinkled her brow. "How do you know this?"

"We have books in Oklahoma."

The Captain gave Buck a knowing look and tapped an index finger to his temple. Thus encouraged, Buck said, "Go on. I'll translate."

"You speak Crazy?"

"It takes one to know one."

"As I was saying," The Captain huffed. "It's because of the American health care system."

Paul rolled his eyes at his guests. *See?*

"If the insurance companies had funded operations instead of denying coverage, the contagion may have been controlled. Sick people, too afraid to lose their homes or college tuition to medical bills, refused to report the disease. That delay turned family members into meat eating, flesh deprived somnambulists. No! Health care costs an arm and a leg, literally! Better to keep grandma locked in the basement, toss her a rabbit now and then."

"So it was a virus."

"A virus!? You think a virus caused this? Man, you guys are something. You ever wonder why the nuclear plants started to go down, all of them, at the same time?"

When no one responded, he went on, "Nuclear facilities are designed to withstand direct nuclear blasts. They can run on reserve generators for days in the event of a power failure, and even longer if they get diesel fuel supplied. If they have to shut down, they do it fast, safely, without a failure. No, there's only one thing that can kill a nuclear plant — lack of equipment. See, everything in the plant runs on electricity. All that redundancy, all those backup systems, all that backup power, don't mean shit if that equipment is destroyed. That's how it happened."

The Kid didn't follow, "So, how did it happen?"

"That's what I don't know. I can't figure it out."

Paul's eyes hurt. He closed them. "So, can you get around to the Pegasus or the cure? Either one is fine with me at this point."

"I'm getting to that. I had a friend, in DC, a ham operator like myself. Before DC went dark, he fed me the military chatter, the martial law in Texas, the riots in Chicago and LA, the silence of Philadelphia. He heard about the man who started it."

Tara regained interest. "Who? Who was it?"

"A scientist. Did work in Venezuela at the start of the war. Said he was a traitor, sold the secrets of his work to the Chinese, defected even!"

"So there is a Chinese connection." It gave Paul a headache, trying to piece together the Captain's theories.

"Do you think he came up with the cure?" The Captain had Tara's full attention, now.

"The cure? Man he started this whole thing! The government was in on it! Hell, they probably sold him to the Chinese to infect them, too!"

Tara had a look of laser focus, barely containing her anxiety. "What was his name?"

"I don't know. It was a long time..."

"His name!"

"I don't know. John Something."

"John Something," Buck repeated. "Middle name 'Some' last name 'Thing'? Or.."

Paul just about had it. "For Christ's sake, tell them about the cure!"

The Captain paused, organizing his thoughts. He tilted his head back, fingers touching the air. Seconds ticked by as his eyes crossed. "So the Chinese have a repeating broadcast. It's been playing non-stop for the last month."

"You speak Chinese?"

"No. But he does." The Captain pointed at a slight Asian man standing over a broom, texting someone. The man looked up, like an actor waiting for his cue. The Captain waved him over.

Young, thin, and healthy, anyone could see this guy wasn't from around here. Paul introduced him. "This is Ando, one of the few tourists trapped here when transportation shut down. Fell found him work at the Lighthouse to pay for his room and board."

"Ohio," the young man said as he bowed to them.

"You're Chinese?" Tara asked.

"Japanese. But, like most Japanese after China became the dominant global economic power, I learned to speak Mandarin in business school."

The Captain slapped his arm. "Tell them what the broadcast said."

Ando looked up, remembering. "'Attention survivors, the strong country of China, beautiful country of plentiful natural bounty, smart country of...'"

"Skip the propaganda part," The Captain hung his head and waved his hand. "The message."

"Uh." his lips moved as he fast-forwarded through what must be a long preamble. "Yes. 'Come to Shanghai, Hu, Shen, China's Excellent Tourism City, Most Revered...'"

"Skip!"

"Uh, 'come for The Clear Brightness Festival. The light will make you whole. The dead will fall as you rise. We have the solution.' Then it repeats."

"That's it?" Tara looked angry. "They didn't say anything about a cure."

The Captain nearly jumped off his stool. "The solution is the cure! It translates both ways!"

"Technically," Ando corrected him, "it is translated as 'the solution'."

"Whatever. It's a cure. Tell her the cultural meaning."

"The Clear Brightness Festival, Qingming, is a day to honor the dead. On that day, the Chinese sweep the graves of their ancestors."

"We think it's the time China will make the dead stay dead."

"Qingming marks the beginning of spring. New life emerging."

Tara tried to follow. "So it's about regeneration. Life from death."

"Once the Plague ends, humanity can rise from the ashes."

The Kid, skeptical, chimed in "Or, once the dead fall, they rise as Eaters. Life from death. Does this not sound ominous to anyone else?"

The Captain worked himself up into a frenzy. "They must have the cure! A new beginning for mankind! Or, at least, for those who arrive in Shanghai in time for the Festival."

Buck leaned forward. "When is this Festival?"

Ando answered. "According to the lunar calendar, April 5th this year."

"That's in four weeks! How long will it take to get there?"

"Three and a half." The Captain answered. "I've made the trip before."

Buck sat back. "That gives us two days to prepare. Can we outfit the ship in that amount of time?"

The Captain dissented. "No way. Takes two weeks to load a ship. Then there's the problem of supply, maintenance, fueling. And the shipping season doesn't start until..."

"Shipping season?" Buck laughed. "Are you kidding me? There are no shipping seasons anymore. The world is dead."

The Captain scoffed. "We're in the Arctic. We wait until the winter sea ice melts and storms..."

"Did you see ice last year?"

"No, but the insurance company mandates..."

"Well I hope *they* were insured because they're..."

"Gone." Paul started to get the picture. Buck might be on to something, but, "We have no reason to go to China. We're not infected. We don't need a cure."

Mayor Fell jumped in. "We have something worse. It's called starvation."

Buck clapped. "I knew it. I knew it. I knew we'd come up with a plan when we got here. 'Go East young man'. We're going to China!"

"I came up here for a reason." Paul tried to temper their excitement with a calm voice. "I studied the world for the safest place, and this is it. Churchill is the farthest point from civilization in the civilized world. Pick a catastrophe: climate change, nuclear war, asteroids, this is the best place to live outside of Russia. Right now, right here, you are at the edge of civilization. And that's the problem with your plan.

"Humans are everywhere on this planet. If it's hospitable, if it can grow food, if there's water, if there are resources of any value, we're there. We've spread across the earth like termites. Now, thanks to the Plague, anywhere that's 'safe' for humans to live on a subsistence level is swarming with former humans. There are only two places left on earth. Places that will get you killed, and places where nothing lives. Go to China? Land of a billion people now turned into ravenous monsters? No thank you. I'm fine right here."

"Not everybody has a bunker, Paul." Fell gave him a withering look. "The world isn't civilized anymore. There's no resupply. The way we live now, hell, even the Dene have snowmobiles and rifles. They couldn't go back to living off the land any more than we could. It won't be long before our fuel runs out, our gunpowder, our food, and this place becomes very, very cold. I've seen the Eskimo Museum. I don't even want to try to live that way. Now, I don't think we can do it in two days, but Buck's right. We need to go."

Buck joined in. "If the Chinese say they have a solution, we don't ask questions. We go for it. If we're wrong, worst case scenario, we die a little sooner with a white shred of hope in our hearts."

"Despite the machines in my bar," Fell pointed toward the video poker and slot machines in the back, "I'm not a betting man, but odds this bad make it irrelevant."

"Speaking of odds," Buck smiled, "Fifty, what are our odds of surviving a trip to China?"

"Fifty/Fifty."

"Damn straight. Good enough for me."

Paul didn't understand the math. Must be an inside joke. The general opinion swayed against him. Paul understood why people followed Buck. He had a certain charisma. He kept using the word 'hope'.

But what happened to the rest of his followers?

"Two days?" *Impossible,* Paul thought. "Good luck."

The Mayor clapped him on the back. "I know I can count on you to collect supplies."

That was Fell's way of asking for donations.

Fell made arrangements for the strangers to stay in his hotel. It wasn't hard. He only had one guest at the moment.

After they dropped their gear in the rooms, Paul found Buck and beckoned him aside.

Buck was jubilant. "I appreciate the hospitality this town has..."

"Before you thank me, maybe you better take a look at what you're up against."

"What do you mean?"

"Let's go take a look at the Pegasus."

Paul led him to his snowmobile and indicated he take a seat behind him. It was a short walk to the Port, and fuel was precious, but Buck needed to see this sooner rather than later.

They followed the road out of town where grain silos dominated the horizon. Even from a distance, the decay was evident. A paint job would have gone a long way.

"Used to be 10,000 people up here," Paul shouted back over the noise of the engine and the wind. "Over the years the army left, the port almost closed. Down to 800 people we did okay with polar bear tourism. Then the ice melted, the bears either left or died. Not many people stayed after that. Mostly indigenous people, but even they're accustomed to heated homes and running water. You're seeing the town at its worst."

He pulled through a chain link fence and roared around the silos. A hulking cargo ship lurched into view, blurring into dark silhouette against the low sun.

The Captain waited for them on the dock. Paul had asked him to walk the ship with Buck. Two dreamers, they both needed a wake-up call.

Paul pulled up beside the Captain.

As soon as Buck alighted, the Captain launched into it.

"I present to you, the Pegasus, sister ship of the Nunavik and Umiak. Built in Tsu shipyard, Japan. 188 meters of pure Polar Class. A twenty-two ton Handysize bulk carrier with an ice-strengthened hull, 47 millimeters of high-tensile steel on the bow with a 33 millimeter ice belt around the sides. We 'aint afraid o' no ice. She can run 13 knots on one third of her seven cylinder cross-head diesel engine, more if we're in a hurry. In fact, with no cargo and enough fuel, she'll give me double that. This is going to be fun!"

She was big, but she wasn't much to look at. Little more than a hull with a flat deck punctuated by a wheelhouse at the back. Four cranes protruded across the top. Rust and decay covered every surface.

"Does the rust slow her down?" Paul couldn't help it. It looked like a tetanus shot waiting to happen.

"Blasphemer. A little skin of rust is good for her. Keeps her warm."

"Like hell it does. Tell him the bad news."

"Don't worry about bad news. This is our only option."

"He needs to know."

Buck smiled. "What's the bad news?"

The Captain denied it. "I can navigate this ship through any waters on my own. I don't need help from anyone. I've been..."

The Captain would never fess up, so Paul said, "It uses satellite feeds for navigation. Not a lot of that going around these days."

Indignant the Captain said, "I know these waters like the back of my..." he pulled off his mitten, palm up. He turned it over. ".. the back of my hand. I can pull this route with my eyes closed."

"Really?" Paul had too much fun goading him. "When was the last time you took her out?"

Now the Captain was coy. "It's... been a while."

"Ten years. And when you did..."

"That was a long time ago. People change. I've changed."

"What happened?"

"That's in the past. He doesn't need to know..."

"He hit a growler. Had to be towed back in. After they patched her up they took her out of service. Been sitting here ever since."

Buck wasn't impressed. "What's a growler?"

Paul laughed. "You'll see."

The Captain launched into a tirade about what's fair or not, going on about his personal history, but Buck walked away.

Even though he orchestrated this, Paul felt bad for Buck, crushing his dream, his hope. What would he do now, stuck in Churchill, waiting to die like the rest of them? What would he tell his little crew?

Buck stopped next to a massive chain holding the ship to the dock. With one gloved hand, he reached out and leaned on the chain. His head fell, and a moment later he wiped his eyes on a sleeve.

Nice work, Paul. You made a grown man cry.

Paul walked up behind him, patted him on the shoulder. "I know how you're feeling right now. I've been there. You feel trapped. All your plans for nothing. But Churchill isn't a bad place for the journey to end."

Buck struggled to control his voice. "I've been looking for this so long. It's hard to believe I'm here. Touching it. It's real."

"It's an emotional time for all of us. You came a long way. I'd be upset, too."

"I'm not upset." Buck raised his head. Tears froze on his eyelashes. "I've never been happier! My last mode of transportation showed up on fire! At least this one floats! My luck keeps improving!"

Paul's plan backfired. Showing him the Pegasus strengthened his hope. Even now, Buck rejoined the Captain in an excited conversation.

They're doomed, Paul thought. *They're all doomed.*

Somehow, Mayor Fell managed to get the town on board. Maybe it was the shock of these strangers and their bad news. Maybe it was the fear that more might follow. Paul was surprised so many would leave town. They were born here, used to privation and hard winters. This thing down south scared them, made them do irrational things, like pinning their hopes on a country they'd never seen. Paul played along, outnumbered.

But when he talked to people, he realized he was wrong, in many ways. They were a community of giving. They didn't work out of fear for themselves. They worked to be useful to others. When strangers needed help, they found a way to help. If that meant outfitting the ship to travel, so be it.

As for leaving, the Dene had always been a nomadic people. They followed the seasons, followed the herd, followed the resources. For generations, those resources were in Churchill, either jobs or government help. Now, they could move on.

Fear didn't drive them out any more than laziness made them stay. They had a talent to recognize opportunity, borne of millennia in a harsh climate. Buck's plan aligned with their interests, a natural fit.

Paul volunteered to organize a committee to collect foodstuffs, but the town buzzed with activity. Even the few people who wanted to stay gave up their meagre supplies to the ship. Happily.

Out of 200 people, only ten families opted to stay. They had their reasons. Elders who wouldn't survive the journey. Roots that ran too deep.

But they still did their part to help.

Long after nightfall, the Lighthouse pulled the town in. They arrived in twos and threes, tired but cheerful. Round and bundled, playful even, the townsfolk made this look like a sport.

Survival isn't recreation.

This is how they look before the horror starts.

He remembered a quote by Gaugin, the painter, describing a walk among the natives of Fiji. "I alone carried the burden of an evil thought, a whole civilization had been before me in evil and had educated me." They were an island of innocents in a world of devils. They didn't know the horrors residing in Paul's Western mind, both seen and imagined. How would his neighbors treat him if they knew what he'd seen, what he'd done, in Africa?

The word, Africa, and the stump of his left arm pulsed. His eyelids flickered with the image of a young woman roasting in a shipping container. His stomach churned as his airplane wheeled wing over wing across a beach. His toes curled, recoiling from red sand. His forehead ached from years of homeless wandering under a merciless sun. His ears shut out the chatter of automatic gunfire.

He felt shame, not just for himself but for all the civilizations behind him. Somewhere in time, they'd given up or sold out the innocence these people take for granted. They let the devil in, and it lived inside them ever since.

He wished he could see the world as they did. With trust and love and hope and joy. They hunted for food, and when it came time to kill, they did so without damaging their hearts.

What was Paul's excuse?

He shrugged it off and took a seat beside Old Mike. Paul found comfort in his company. Even-keeled and patient, they shared a calm that comes from outliving old mistakes.

Old Mike smiled. "Did your bear eat anyone today?" Pillows of skin hid his eyes, his cheeks, his chin. A fractal network of wrinkles took root in age spots and scars. Winter stole from him what time did not, but Old Mike had seen enough of each.

"Not today."

Buck and his crew came in last, exhausted. They'd been the center of attention all day. With the other tables filled, Old Mike offered, in a soft voice which never hardened, "Sit with us."

As they gathered around, his wrinkles deepened, smiling at Tara. "My people always welcome strangers. We share what we have, even when we have little for ourselves."

Old Mike's habits rose from a deep well. He was the product of thousands of years of human cooperation in a harsh climate. Modern man reacted out of selfish concern because he could, because resources were more plentiful with every decade of added prosperity. Yet every decade they forgot that community is the foundation of society. When individual rivers erode those stones, society crumbles.

"When we starve, we share our sled dogs with the stranger, equally. When there is no food, the old and sick die first so that the young may survive and have families and grow old themselves. It is as it should be."

That could be him, in this case. Seeing him accept death as a way of nature gave Paul comfort and lent great credibility to his words. His interests were not served by keeping strangers alienated.

He chose to embrace them.

He wasn't the only one. Tara's presence attracted the Captain to the table. He squeezed his chair in beside her, leering. "You know why you get horny when you drink?"

Mood broken.

She gave him a withering look. "I'll bet you have a theory."

"I do. Yes. See, alcohol is a poison. It depletes the oxygen in your bloodstream. Without oxygen, the cells of your body start to die, like drowning. Your body, thinking it's dying, makes one last attempt toward its evolutionary prerogative, tries to pass on its genes to the nearest available mate."

Paul smiled. "That's a pretty good theory. I never heard you mention that one before."

"Tara inspired it."

"Touch me and you'll wish you were drowning," Tara growled.

"Oh! Grrr. You're as tough as a polar bear."

Tara looked ready to punch the Captain, so Paul said, "That reminds me of a joke!" The situation needed a little levity. He stood up, positioning himself between the Captain and Tara. "When

Alaska became a state, the Texans weren't happy, one Texan in particular. So he heads up to Alaska, walks into the first bar he finds and says, 'I've got the biggest house and the biggest cows on the biggest ranch in the country and dogonnit if I'll hail from anywhere but the biggest state. How do I become an Alaskan?

"An old native tells him. 'Simple. Kill a polar bear and sleep with an Inuit woman.'

"Without a word, the Texan leaves. Weeks go by, and they don't hear from him. In the middle of a violent snowstorm, they'd given him up for dead, when the door to the bar slams open and there stands the Texan, scratched and cut and bruised and bloody, with a big smile on his face. 'All righty!' he says. "Now where's the Inuit woman I have to kill?"

The Kid released a giant belch. "That's my opinion. Anyone want a second opinion?"

"What's this about a bunker?" Buck asked.

The Captain laughed. "We built his coffin!"

Paul shrugged. "I... have a bunker. Underneath my house. I built it thirty years ago." He didn't like to talk about it. It wasn't a secret, but you don't store a cache and then tell everyone where it is.

"Took us three weeks to thaw the ground enough to dig it up." The Captain bored his finger into the table. "The whole damn thing is built under six feet of permafrost."

Buck looked impressed. "You're a survivalist?"

"I'm a survivor. I used to be a pilot in the war."

"Which war?"

"Pick one. Plenty of wars."

The Captain delighted in giving away Paul's secrets. "He fought in Africa."

"That was a long time ago."

"So how'd you lose your arm?" The Kid asked.

Buck scolded him, "A little tact, Kid."

Paul put on his most serious face. He leaned in close to the Kid. "They told you about the polar bears up here, right?"

The Kid's eyes went wide with respect.

"Wasn't no polar bear!" the Captain laughed.

"Captain, don't." Paul wasn't quick enough.

"It was cannibals!"

The table went silent. Even Old Mike didn't know this story. Paul wished he'd never told anyone, least of all the Captain. Hard to keep secrets for thirty years. Drinking loosens the tongue.

"It's not something I like to talk about," Paul said.

"Bet you're going to miss that bunker," Tara said.

"Oh, I'm not leaving." Paul tried not to meet their eyes. "Old Mike will keep me company."

Shocked, Buck glanced between Old Mike and Paul. "You're not coming?"

"I am an old man." Old Mike smiled, most teeth missing. "I will wait where the Snow Walker can find me."

"The Snow Walker?"

"He will come to reunite me with my ancestors. I welcome that day."

Buck looked frantic. "It's not safe for you here. Either of you. Those things..."

Old Mike patted him on the hand. "I have not seen them, but I know them. They are the *kadzait*. Mad wolves." His smile faded. He grimaced. "They have forgotten why they kill, only that they must kill." His hand moved up his left arm. "The Snow

Walker led them away, but they came back. Paija, she hunts them now."

Paul stood up. "Are you ok?"

Old Mike slumped in his seat. He held his arm and rocked back and forth, brow furrowed. Sweat broke out on his forehead. Paul had never seen him act this way. "I need help! Call Sam!"

Old Mike stared at Tara, eyes wide with horror. "Three footsteps in the snow! She walks with you!"

Tara rose and backed away. "What's that supposed to mean?"

Old Mike coughed. His face convulsed. He hugged his chest, bent over the table, then tried to rise. He tripped over the chair, sent it clattering across the floor. The room went silent as everyone turned to see Tara standing opposite Old Mike. His body fell like a stone in water, setting off a ripple through the crowd that pulled back as a human wave. It crested over him, a hundred panicked eyes staring at two that saw no more.

Someone screamed.

Paul rushed to his side as a torrent of voices crashed in. "Give him something to bite on, damn it. I don't want him to bite off his tongue."

He pulled up Old Mike's coat sleeve, felt for a pulse. Nothing.

Training kicked in. He pumped Mike's chest before he realized what he was doing. He blew into the old man's mouth. One-two-three. "Come on, Mike. Come on. Not now." Seven-eight-nine-blow. "I need your company old man." Seven-eight-nine-blow.

A subconscious dialogue erupted into spoken words. "I need your company. I can't die here alone."

Mike's upper lip twitched.

"That's right, old man. You tell that Snow Walker to wait. You tell him..."

A long, slow hiss wheezed out of Old Mike's windpipe, terminating in a low growl.

He'd seen it in videos, heard about it on the news, but he'd never seen it in person. None of them had. He'd never realized how normal they looked right after they turned - no blood, no sharp teeth, no black bile, just like Buck said. That frightened him even more. It was still Old Mike lying there. This was impossible. The gurgling was a practical joke. It had to be.

Someone even laughed.

At the same moment he felt Buck's hand on his shoulder. That hand shoved Paul back across the floor.

Buck shouted. "Stand back! Fast!" His arms out like a goalie, he pushed against the crowd.

Old Mike opened one hooded eye in time for Tara to plunge a pool cue through it.

Now there was blood.

That set off a violent reaction as someone pulled Tara off the body and Buck intervened on Tara's behalf. Within seconds a bar fight backed the four newcomers into the corner. Buck held out his hands.

Mayor Fell jumped in between the two parties.

"Stop! Stop! You know what this is! She did the right thing. Maybe saved us all!"

Paul watched, stunned, holding Old Mike's bleeding head.

Wilson shouted, "She killed Old Mike!"

Buck jumped in, "It's not her fault. It was instinctive."

"The hell it's not her fault! We never had the Plague until you showed up!"

The shouting renewed and the crowd turned ugly. Even Fell didn't have an answer.

Buck and his crew formed a defensive semicircle in front of the bar.

The North attracts a fair amount of brawlers, but they don't winter. That type don't have the temper for the long, dark, cold days. So the crowd that faced down Buck's crew, though indignant, also sensed a mismatch between themselves and these hardened killers. Even the Kid looked resigned enough to take them on alone. A moment of indecision quieted the crowd.

Buck spoke. "We have a rule we have never broken. We don't kill the living. Now I haven't known Old Mike that long, but I liked him. He seemed like a good guy. But that growl you heard wasn't something he made. I've heard that sound so many times, I am one hundred percent sure. That's the sound my girlfriend made when she turned. That's the sound that wakes me up every night. And Old Mike, when he made that sound, he turned.

"All four of us lost loved ones out there. The Kid here lost his whole family in Winnipeg. We may not know exactly what you're going through right now, but we do know it's scary as hell. I want to know how this happened as much as you do, but until then let's give Old Mike there the last rights he deserves."

It was a good speech, and the length of it had the same effect as counting to ten.

Paul knew what had to be done to the body. Take it outside to the shed to freeze until the funeral. He looped his arms under Old Mike's shoulders, his hands slick with blood, not looking down at the mess of that beautiful face. "Help me carry him," he told the crowd, not looking up.

No one moved.

"Help me carry him, damn it! He's Old Mike! Our Old Mike! Give him the dignity to get him out of here. "

Fear of the Plague kept them away.

Then Buck reached for a leg.

"Not you!" Paul shouted with a vehemence that surprised him.

He searched the frozen eyes of each statue around him and saw horror and fear.

"Someone help me move him," he repeated.

Most of them backed away. No one offered. Even the Mayor, who should have stepped up. Not even the Captain, who counted Old Mike as his friend.

That old sense of resentment in the human race flooded Paul, those feelings that drove him north in the first place. They would save themselves. They were animals, all of them. He knew where he stood. If it were him on the floor...

Alone in the company of man. As alone as he always wanted to be. The closest thing to a friend lay dead in his arms.

He pulled that awkward body and its unnatural weight across the smooth wooden floor. No one stood in his way. When he reached the door, he fumbled for the knob, his stump holding Old Mike, his bloody hand slipping on the handle.

Buck took up Mike's legs, innocent emotion raw on his face.

Paul growled, "Fuck," and relented. If his heart hadn't been cast in lead years ago he would have broken down crying on the threshold.

They crab walked Old Mike to a small metal shed near the train station. Paul banged on the door with his fist. Rime shivered off, exposing a latch with a heavy padlock. He fumbled with a key around his neck, then kicked away the snow that drifted against the door. The door opened sideways.

Inside, silence reigned. There wasn't much inside but a backhoe, a few folding tables, and, on top of them, three bodies. They lifted Old Mike up on a table.

Paul pulled a blue tarp over the old man's body. He couldn't bear the sight of that horrible wound. He remained there, hunched, both hands in fists, silent. Finally he said, "Second one today."

Buck stepped away from the table and looked at the other bodies. They lay uncovered, frozen. He reached an unsteady hand toward the face of Joel Mackie. His fingers stopped before they touched the head.

And for the second time today, Paul saw this man crying.

"You don't how long it's been since I saw someone like this." Buck bowed his head over the table. When he came back up, he had tears on his face. "Whole." He wiped his face. "They look so peaceful."

Paul's anger faded. This man carried his own burdens, his own litany of lost friends. He pulled himself from his grief long enough to attempt, "Thanks for…"

"It was the least I could do."

"They're afraid," Paul apologized for the others. "This is the first time they've seen…"

"The first time is always the worst."

Buck moved around to the side of another body. A young woman, barely more than a girl, lay wrapped in what looked like a kimono but on closer inspection proved to be a white bath robe. A knife lay on her chest. Cotton balls filled her ears. On a small table beside her lay dried grass, a candle, and coins.

"That's Ando's wife, Tomoko. She passed away from a fever."

"Did she..."

"No, no. It was peaceful. She slipped away. A real shame. They were newlyweds. Came up here for the honeymoon. Japanese believe the northern lights are good for fecundity."

"Fecun..."

"Baby-making."

"Oh."

"He made us prepare her in the traditional way. Made us cover that window with white paper to drive away 'evil spirits'."

"Guess it's working."

"We're breaking every custom of our own. We don't usually hold the bodies. Years ago we used to have a hospital here, but they tore that down when the population sank. We can dig through permafrost with the backhoe, but fuel is low. And that one over there, the first one, is from Thompson. Snowmobile accident the first week after the trains stopped. Thought we'd hold him until the next train, let his folks bury him at home. Train never came."

They stood in the semi-darkness of the shed, thinking their individual thoughts, remembering their individual horrors. Breath steamed the air in front of them, a timorous reminder that they were the lucky ones.

"The truth is, we were scared. With talk of the dead rising, we didn't know what to do. What if we buried them, but they crawled out in the middle of the night, like the movies? No one could sleep with that in the back of their mind.

"Ando wanted Tomoko cremated, but we wondered. Would the ashes drift over our town, infecting everyone? Back then we had a lot of ideas, a lot of fear. Still do.

"We compromised, kept them here, locked up. Waited for the outside world to go back to normal or wait for an official notice. I don't know. I think the natural human reaction to indecision is to wait it out.

"So we waited. They never rose. We left them here and forgot. When spring comes, I'll do the right thing."

Buck stood still, watching Tomoko's beautiful, innocent face. But for the crystals on her cheeks, she could have been sleeping.

"They're going to blame you," Paul said.

Buck didn't look at him, his attention on the woman. "Yeah," was all he said.

Paul wanted to get home. He even considered crawling into that bunker, sealing the door, and never coming back out. Let the town figure it out for themselves.

Thirty years he'd been here, but he felt like a stranger. It was his fault, not theirs. He never let them in, hid his past, the past that defined him. He kept his thoughts private. He was a part of the community, but at the end of the day he knew them better than they knew him.

He had trouble trusting others, he knew this. Their responses were so predictable – fear, indignation, self-protection. He wanted to see the best in humanity, but humanity showed him an ugly face. Even now, with almost no one left, Paul wished for fewer. He looked forward to the ship leaving, looked forward to having the world to himself.

Quiet.

Peaceful.

Uncomplicated.

And if not having the support of others killed him, he'd die a happy man.

Paul slowed when he spotted a figure seated on his front steps.

Tara.

He didn't know what to say to her. He had raw feelings about what he'd seen her do. Maybe it was the right thing. Maybe Old Mike had turned. Or maybe he'd had a heart attack and could have been saved. They'd never know, would they? She'd rammed a pool cue into his best friend's eye socket. The blood... Paul still wore it on his coat.

But here she was, on his doorstep, head in her hands, shoulders shaking. She was crying. Paul had a soft spot for women's tears. They melted anger like a laser. He managed to ask, "Are you all right?"

She looked up at him, but her grief prevented an answer.

He didn't know what to do. He reached out and patted her on the head. *Awkward.*

She found her words. "I'm so sorry!" This gave rise to another round of tears.

Paul took a step toward the door, but she took his hand and held it to her cheek. He felt trapped. Even though he wore gloves, he tensed at the possibility that her tears carried the Plague.

Her voice cracked when she spoke. "I was never safe enough to think about it until we got here." She took a breath and wiped her eyes. "Being here, where everything is normal, I realize... they're gone. My family. My daughter. My parents. All of them. My daughter's friends. Their parents. Her teachers. My friends in New York. The people I grew up with, went to school with, went to college with, worked with... Not one of them survived. I know that now, and I have to ask myself, 'Why me?' Why am I alive while they're dead? I'm not special. I'm not better. I'd give anything; I'd give my life, if I could bring one person back."

"Even Old Mike?"

"Especially Old Mike. He didn't deserve it. I don't deserve it. I'm not a killer. Why do I have to be a killer?" She broke down again.

She was a tiger, but even tigers have cubs. How many times had he seen survivor's guilt? How many times had he felt it? This he understood.

He slid down the wall to sit beside her, put his arm around her shoulders. "I know how you feel, but you can't trade places with them and you can't bring them back." He knew she was too deep in her own thoughts to listen to platitudes, but perhaps his voice would calm her. "Before this began, I had already lost everyone close to me. I've seen my share of catastrophe and death. There are no reasons why one person lives and another dies. It has nothing to do with purpose or merit." He felt so old, like a vampire who lives too long and sees one too many kingdoms fall. "I find some comfort in the Eastern philosophy that we are part of something infinite. We have our time, and then we yield it to those who come after, just as those who came before us. The length of time we get, no matter how short or long, is infinitesimal on the whole. We're not special, not as individuals, but we're part of something special.

Something bigger than us, something that survives when we die, something perhaps unique in the entire universe. We're alive. Right now. That's the part we play in the history of time."

She stopped sobbing. Her breathing became more regular.

Paul went on. "I'm glad every day that I wake up. I'll play my part as long as possible. When the end comes, my work is done. Be grateful for the chance to continue. Live not for those you've lost but for those yet to come."

"Paul, I didn't know you were such a philosopher." Her eyes challenged him. Then she started laughing, wiping her nose.

"Are you making fun of me? I'm serious. I live that way. It helps."

"I'm not making fun of you. Maybe someday I'll see it that way." Her lip curled as she tried to stop the tears. "Not right now."

He sat with her in silence as she recovered. She reminded him, somehow, of himself, long ago, walking the same path.

He pitied her for all the horror to come.

She turned toward him, calm and earnest. "Thank you Paul." She laid a gloved hand on his. "I appreciate your help. I'll be all right now."

"Don't go it alone. You came here with friends. They care about you. Stay with them. Let them know what you're feeling. Chances are they feel the same way."

She smiled, shy.

"It's not your fault," he said. "You have to go on."

"I'm starting to understand that. It isn't easy."

"Eleonor Roosevelt said, 'Life doesn't get easier. You get better.' You're better already."

"Wow," she said, wiping her eyes. "Eleanor Roosevelt and Buddhist philosophy. You're a deep guy, Paul." She took a deep breath, and stood up. "Thank you. And I'm very sorry about your friend." With that, she walked away.

Even as she went, he saw her straightening, tensing, transforming into something fierce, ready to stalk the night. He started to believe in Paija.

He went into the house and closed the door.

He never made it down into the bunker. He fell asleep on the couch.

Paul woke late, but he wasn't concerned. After last night's events, there was no way the town would follow Buck on a wild goose chase into China. More likely they'd chain Buck and his team onto the ship and set it adrift, banishing them from Churchill. Maybe they already had, and he could get back to having coffee in the morning at the Lighthouse like he did every day.

But when he entered that singular establishment, dozens of volunteers bustled about, arranging supplies, boxing up cans and foodstuffs, and carting them out the door. The pace of activity doubled, like a stirred up hornet's nest. They moved with twice the energy they did the day before.

Fear and excitement surrounded him. Every now and then he caught the word 'cure'. They'd seen it. They knew what they were up against. The Plague had reached the village. There was no fighting it, no denying it. It was time to flee. They had their hopes pinned on China.

Buck and his crew whirled in the middle of it, helping out. Buck's determination informed his decisions, calling out orders like a gentle commander. Tara's grim defiance had returned. Fifty, silent as ever, busied himself with medical supplies. The Kid chatted with one of the young females of the Lighthouse staff while they boxed cans together.

For a moment, Paul felt like the outsider. No one fetched him for the party. No one seemed to notice his absence. The strangers were taking away his town. It hurt a little.

Mayor Fell waved him over. "They started refueling the ship this morning. Sounds like we have just enough in the reserves. We might make it."

"That's great," he said without enthusiasm.

The door opened, and Fred Eggert stepped in, stomping his boots.

The Mayor clapped his arm around Paul's shoulders. "You sure you won't come with us? It's gonna get lonely around here."

"I'll manage."

Fred stood behind the Mayor, trying to get his attention.

"Wait a minute, Fred. Paul, I'd feel better with you on board. With your survival skills…"

"You mean with my year's supply of food in the bunker."

"Mayor?" Fred tapped him on the shoulder.

"I wouldn't lie to you. Those supplies will come in handy. So would you. You have instincts the rest of us don't have. We're going to need those when we're out in…"

"Mayor, Old Mike's gone."

"…the wild ocean… what?"

"Old Mike. He's gone. I checked the shed. He's not there."

Paul's chest froze. "I thought he couldn't... I mean, didn't she hit his brain with..." He realized he was pointing at Tara.

All chatter ceased.

"I don't think he wandered off," Fred added, calmly. "He was taken."

It wasn't bad enough that the strangers killed Old Mike, now they were body snatchers, too? A new cloud of menace gathered in the room.

Tara shook her head with confusion.

The Mayor intervened. "Let's not jump to conclusions. We'll go take a look." The crowd followed, including the newcomers. He turned, "No, you lot stay here. You have a lot of work to do. I'm sure we'll sort this out."

It turned out not to be a mystery. The door to the shed curled outward like the lid of a mackerel tin. Blood stained the snow. Paul inspected it, prospecting for prints. He found them. Too big for a man, five toed, with claws.

The Mayor saw it, too. "It's that damn bear. It came right into the village!"

Only Old Mike's body was missing. The others lay *in situ*, calm as statues.

"Why did they take Old Mike?"

"He wasn't frozen yet. Guess he smelled like meat." Paul regretted putting it that way, and old associations brought bile up his esophagus.

"But... how did they get in?" The Mayor ran his glove along scratches on the door. "They've never been able to get in before."

Paul inspected the padlock. It gleamed silver in the snow, cocked open. Paul felt a sickening sense of shame. He looked up at the stars, then back at the ground. This was going to be hard to say. *Sorry Old Mike.* "I forgot to lock it."

"You what?"

"I got caught up in conversation with Buck and forgot to lock the shed on my way out."

The Mayor said nothing, gave him a hard stare. "You know, one of these days your mistakes will come up and bite you in the ass."

The Captain spoke up. "It has a taste for man. We have to put it down."

Paul laughed. "What difference does it make? Everyone will be gone."

"You won't."

And just like that, he belonged again. They would drop everything, even risk missing the cure in China, to make sure they didn't leave a man-eating bear in Churchill for Paul to deal with. That made Paul feel good.

Then the Mayor spoke. "Paul, everyone's too busy with preparations to hunt down a bear. It's something you have to do." Then, as a consolation prize, "You can take the strangers. Good to get them out of town until this blows over."

"Haven't hunted a bear in years." Wade, from Manitoba Conservation, took the lead on the hunt, his boots squeaking across the tundra toward the coast. "Back then, the bears liked to stay near the coast."

"I'm feeling rusty myself," Paul admitted. Every snow-capped rock looked like a bear to him.

Buck and Fifty lagged behind, but Paul couldn't figure out why. They weren't tired. It wasn't hard to keep up with a one-armed septuagenarian. It wasn't fear, either. Fifty's rifle could tear through three bears.

"Do we have to kill it?" Buck asked.

It was sympathy, for the bear.

"Once he knows where to find food, he'll keep coming back for more. It's us or him."

"Aren't they an endangered species, almost extinct?"

"Aren't we?"

That kept him quiet for a while.

"We used to tranquilize them," Wade joined in. We had a 'polar bear jail' where we held them for a few weeks without food. Then we'd carry them by helicopter 100 kilometers from town. We had repeat offenders now and then, but it worked. A few overdosed on tranqs, but most lived. We removed the threat. We only put them down if they mauled someone. Unfortunately, that got to be pretty often when the ice disappeared. Without seals, humans became a food source. Then they went on the endangered list and we compromised with the environmentalists. Set up feeding stations outside of town. That kept the bears alive, kept the tourists in town, but over time even that wasn't enough."

"Why? If they had food, what was the problem?"

"Permafrost melted. Dens collapsed. The females had to raise their cubs in the open. A male bear will eat a cub when it's hungry enough."

Paul's arm throbbed at the thought of cannibalism.

"Weren't enough cubs surviving year on year to support the population. We tried artificial dens, but couldn't find the magic formula. After a while, the bears stopped coming. This is the first bear I've seen in years."

"So it might be the last one."

Wade didn't answer, his gaze fixed on the ridge. Humped boulders made up a low rise before falling down to a pebble beach and the ocean.

Paul saw it, a flicker of movement behind a rock. A nose up in the air. "He knows we're here."

Wade unslung his rifle. "Can't get a shot at him from here. We're going to have to get closer." He waved to Fifty and Buck. "You two stay here. Set up that beast in case he gets too..."

A second pair of ears poked over bedrock to the right.

"He's not the last one. There's a female."

Two heads protruded from behind the rocks, eyes locked on Wade. He hesitated. Paul knew even Wade didn't want to shoot a female, but there was no telling which of them got Old Mike, or if they did it together.

"What do we do if they..."

"Don't run. Stay calm. Stand your ground. Take your shot. They're fast. They cover a meter with every step."

The male reared up on its hind legs, sniffing the air. Paul couldn't believe how thin it was, ribs visible through the thin fur, arms like sticks, neck more like a bird than a bear.

"Jeez," Wade cursed under his breath. "This bear hasn't eaten in nine, twelve months."

Paul felt a twinge of regret. Maybe the world ended long before the Plague. If the bears starved and went extinct up here, what chance did humans have? Was it only a matter of time before the whole food chain broke down? And he was electing to stay?

A rifle shot crackled through the cold air. In front of the bear, a chip ricocheted off a boulder, singing across the shore.

The bear ducked down and ran. Glimpses of fur appeared behind rocks and snow before they both disappeared.

"Did I hit him?" It was Buck. "I... I wanted to put him out of his misery."

"You missed." Wade looked concerned. "The thin ones are the most dangerous. He'll be hunting us now."

"Hunting us?"

"Bears are the only mammal that thinks of humans as food. A true predator. A land shark. I need everyone to keep sharp. When they come, they'll come where we can't see them." Wade moved forward and waved them on. He'll conserve his energy until we're closer, but when he comes he'll be desperate Don't be conservative. Shoot, and shoot often."

They moved off the tundra and onto the rocks lining the ocean. The jagged boulders slowed them down. Windblown snow lay on a thick layer of ice, making every rock slippery. One moment Paul was on top of the snow, the next he was hip deep in a granite cleft. He kept one eye on his footing and the other eye out for bears. His good arm carried the rifle. His stump he used for balance. He felt disadvantaged. His body heated with exertion. He wanted to unzip his jacket, but that meant putting down the rifle. Sweat ran down his back. Any moment he expected to see a white blur burrow into his side, rip into his throat, plunge into his belly.

Wade whispered to him. "We should be able to hit them from that rise." An escarpment of rock overlooked the beach near where the bears had disappeared. "Hustle."

Wade didn't need to whisper. The gear creaked and boots squeaked and leather rifle straps slapped against wood stocks. Stealth was impossible.

Paul crawled over the final ridge, barrel first. The tussock crumbled beneath his gloves and knees, brittle in the cold. Peering over the edge, he didn't see the bears. "Where are they?"

Wade had his eye to the scope, scanning the beach. "I don't see them."

A single stalk of grass stabbed his cheek as he leveled his own rifle on the rock and peered through the scope. "Maybe they're over the next ridge, or..."

The scope blurred to white as something big roared up in front of him. Startled, his finger missed the trigger. A hot breath warmed his neck before a sledgehammer crashed into his shoulder. The blow knocked him off the hill, rolled him onto the beach. He heard a shot go off and, in the confusion, worried his rifle discharged toward his companions. Realizing he'd lost the rifle altogether, he bounded back to his feet, ready to run but unsure of the direction. Several more gunshots rang out.

One bear, the female, lay dead on the beach not three meters from where Paul stood, but the men on the ridge had their rifles up, aimed behind him. He swiveled.

The male limped off down to the beach. A glossy smear stained its right front shoulder.

Buck was first down to the beach. "I call it a draw," Buck smiled, offering Paul a hand.

"What happened?" Paul watched the white bulk barrel into the surf. It leaned to the left side, head kicking up for air.

"You two exchanged blows. He walloped you pretty good in the shoulder."

Paul looked down. The fabric of his coat was intact. There was no blood. The beast had cuffed him. "Who shot it?"

"You did, technically."

"Not a very good shot."

Buck chuckled. "Tough to aim when you're not holding the rifle. Lucky for you, it went off when it hit the ground."

Paul cursed his poor reflexes and worse gun etiquette. Guns rarely go off when dropped, but he could have killed somebody.

Buck shrugged. "Looks like it's true what they say. He's more scared of us than..."

"He's dying." Wade watched the bear run.

"How do you know?"

"The shock of the bullet collapsed a lung."

Paul shook his head. "So why's he going out to sea? He'll drown."

"He's looking for ice to die on. It's instinct."

Buck nodded, "But there isn't any."

The bear paddled out, massive paws pumping, graceful as a seal in the water, but struggling to stay above the waves. Blood stained foam broke over its hide. Any minute, Paul expected an orca fin and a bloody explosion, but instead the beast suffered, struggling farther out.

Buck shifted from foot to foot. "It's kinda sad. Can we shoot it again?"

"Too far. Can't help him."

Fifty leveled the Barrett. Paul covered his ears, waiting for it to bark. For a full minute, nothing happened. Fifty wiped his eyes, raised the barrel. No one spoke. They watched the bear swim out until darkness obliterated him.

The female lay on the beach, eyes open, tongue lapped over her jaw. Blood bubbled from a hole behind her eye. Even emaciated, she weighed a good 200 kilos.

Wade bent over and ran his hand through the fur. "We can butcher it. Not a lot of meat, but she won't be wasted."

"I wouldn't do that." Buck adopted a low, serious tone. "It might be infected."

"You mean, like Old Mike?" Paul sensed something wrong.

Wade jerked back. "Should we be touching it?"

Buck shook his head. "I don't know."

Paul caught a flicker of emotion. He did know, or at least suspect. So why the expression of weary regret? Alarm bells went off in Paul's head. "There's something you're not telling us."

Buck shrugged. "There's a lot I don't know."

"It's asymptomatic isn't it?" Paul cursed himself. He should have seen it sooner, should have never let them out of isolation. God damn it! Why didn't he think of it sooner? "You've got it, and you can spread it!"

"We don't even know what 'it' is."

Wade started to catch on. Panicking, he raised his rifle. "I have an obligation to everyone in Churchill to make damn sure you don't go back to the village."

"So you're going to shoot us, in cold blood? Then what? You're going to shoot Tara and the Kid? Then you're going to shoot yourself?"

Wade wavered. "Myself? Why..." He steeled himself. "If I have to."

Paul noticed Fifty and Buck both curl their gloves around a trigger, barrels ready. These two had fought a long way to survive. Even with Buck's mantra, Paul couldn't be sure there weren't a few 'hunting accidents' along that trail.

There was a time he might have taken his chances, test who had the fastest draw. Those days were gone. "Hold on, Wade. Slow down. Mexican standoff won't solve anything. We'll go back to town and talk about it."

"Take them back to town? That's what they want!"

"Wade, in your scenario only two men walk back. I'm not so sure it'll be us."

Buck and Fifty maintained silence.

Wade's rifle shook a bit. He was a good man. Killing humans wasn't part of his hunt. Paul placed a hand on his arm with gentle pressure. Wade shrugged him off. "All right! Damn it!" He let the barrel fall.

"Now give him your rifle." Paul held out his own.

"I don't want to carry your rifles," Buck said, relaxed. "But you can walk in front."

They walked in silence. The tension eased. Paul and Wade kept their distance, Paul out of respect, Wade out of fear. Paul took the opportunity to drop back within earshot of Buck.

"God damn it, Buck. I trusted you."

"I'm sorry Paul. I wasn't lying. There's a lot I don't know."

"Well what do you know?"

"I know you don't turn Eater until you die."

"Small comfort. But is it contagious?"

"I never met someone who didn't have it."

"We didn't have it! Not until you came into town. We've got three dead bodies on ice to prove it. I showed them to you."

"Yeah, we'll, that's when I realized...."

"Realized that you fucked us."

"Pretty much, yeah."

Paul remembered the tears on Buck's face when he saw the bodies. He softened. Buck was telling the truth. "You really didn't know."

"I'm so sorry, Paul."

Paul thought about Old Mike. So he really did have a heart attack and died of it. He wouldn't have turned otherwise. Tara didn't kill his friend. Nature did. She did the right thing, under the circumstances, but her reaction time... "You didn't know, but you suspected."

"Suspected? After all I've seen, I've got a lot of suspicions. Yeah I suspected. But everything south of here is burned. Churchill's the end of the line. What would you have done?"

"I'd have said something in quarantine."

Buck was silent for a moment. "Why do you live here, Paul? You could have set up your bunker anywhere, in the middle of a mountain range, and had supplies air dropped to you. You could have lived the rest of your life without seeing another soul. But you didn't. You moved into a town. A small one, at the end of the earth, I'll grant you that, but a town nonetheless."

Paul had a sick sense he knew where this was going.

"You need people. Everyone does. I want to get off this island, find someplace safe, but I don't want to do it alone."

Those words hit home. He'd survived an island alone. It wasn't any fun.

"I get it Buck, but it's gonna be a damn hard sell back in town. When they hear you're the Masque of the Red Death, they're going to break out the pitchforks and torches, with Wilson at the head. I can't help you then."

Buck shook his head. "They won't do that. They're good folks." He thought a moment. "That's something you and I would do."

They had more in common than Paul wanted to admit.

Buck smiled. "I've learned something about people on the way here. They've got something in them more powerful than fear. You feed it, and they can overcome anything."

Paul knew the answer. Buck said it all the time. "Hope."

"Maybe we are infected. So what? The infection doesn't kill us. That means this doesn't end until we find a cure or die. How is that any different than life before? We might as well focus on the positive."

"Your Pegasus."

"The only option without a pre-defined ending."

Paul pulled his truck onto the dock with the last load of supplies to watch them go.

The ship loomed large in the grey twilight of a growing dawn.

Work continued deep into the night as time ticked by, time they didn't have.

From the exterior, there wasn't much to see. The hull lay lower in the water, no longer a dormant beast of burden. Rime and frost covered the antennae and guy wires. The cranes hoisted containers and snowmobiles into the hold. People shuttled up and down the gangplank with boxes spilling over. Clothes, food, tools, everything they needed to set up life on the ship or in a new world.

Someone repainted the word Pegasus, shiny and white, the only cosmetic improvement. Rust dominated the rest, a massive hulk of steel held together by ambition.

It was a big ship. They took almost everything.

The last thing they took was Tomoko's body, lying in a crate someone had in storage. Ando insisted he take her home. If they were going to China, maybe he could find a way to get to Japan.

Paul watched the loading and thought again about being left alone in Churchill. He dreamt of it for so long. He couldn't let it go now.

He knew it was only a matter of time before the food ran out, until his neighbors pounded on the bunker door to find a moment of safety. And when they did, he'd let them in, share what he had, welcome the company. Or, more likely, a week later he'd come back out, start checking on the remaining families, see if they needed anything.

Who was he kidding? If he couldn't go it alone in the village, why not go on the ship?

His days of adventure were over. He wanted it that way.

Didn't he?

Early the next morning, before daylight, the Pegasus blew its horn three times, the signal to board.

Ropes held up wooden gangways, one for families to board and one for crew. Happy clusters lined up in the cold morning. Adults carried duffels and suitcases. Children cuddled toys and stuffed animals, all smiles and excitement.

In those faces, he didn't see a flicker of fear. No resistance, no second thoughts, no remorse. This wasn't an evacuation. It was a cruise.

Paul stood near the gangplank with the few families staying behind. As the line boarded, they shook hands, hugged, said their goodbyes. He never liked goodbyes. They seemed unnecessary. Life is long. You can always pick up where you left off. This time, though, he knew he would never see any of them again. They would die, or he would.

He had no doubt they would die. A plague sailed with them. That old man, Death, had passed Paul often enough for him to know the knock at the door.

But this time it wasn't his door.

He spotted Mayor Fell, Buck, and the others at the end of the line, last to board.

He knew what he had to do.

When they approached, Paul stepped forward, stood in their path. He held up his arm, palm out. "I can't let you get on that ship."

The Mayor laughed. "C'mon Paul. Let's not get sentimental."

"I've been thinking about this all night. Some of those people might not be infected yet."

Buck moved forward. "I told you. We don't know enough about..."

"You said you don't know how it's transmitted. Well, just before Old Mike died, he touched your hand. I've replayed that scene over and over again, and now I see it clearly. He touched your hand. That's how it spreads."

Fell turned his head back and forth, unsure who to defend. "Is that true?"

Buck lowered his head. "We don't know."

"Most of us haven't touched you, any of you. We've got gloves and coats."

The Kid looked away.

"It's possible that most of those people aren't infected, and I can't let you on board for three weeks sitting with them, eating with them, infecting them. I can't let you do that. Those are good people. They have no idea what you're bringing on board!"

"It doesn't matter."   Buck's voice flattened. "We're going to find the cure, for everyone."

"You don't believe that, Buck. You want to get on that ship the same way I want to get in my bunker. You're selfish, stubborn, and wrong!"

"You can't stop us from getting on that ship!" Tara raised her voice.

"Not the living. That's your rule, right? There are two hundred living on that ship. Get on board, and you're killing them. All of them. Do you want that on your conscience?"

It was a poor argument, and Paul knew it. He could imagine what was on Buck's conscience already.

The horn blew again.

The Mayor danced from foot to foot. "Paul, let's be…"

"You're right." Buck said. "You're right, Paul. It's on us. It's on *me*." He pushed a finger in his own chest. "The safety of everyone on board is on me. I take that responsibility. They won't die from the infection. I'll take them through to the end."

A young woman on deck waved and called down to the Kid. He waved back.

Paul wouldn't let Buck go. "Really? How many people did you start with, Buck? Did you start with two hundred? Because I only see four of you left."

Tara started shouting, the Kid joined in. Buck gritted his teeth and clenched his fists.

"You'll kill them, Buck! It's what you do. It's what hope does."

Fifty, calm as ever, stepped forward, brushing Paul aside like lint from a coat. Tara and the Kid followed in his wake. Tara pulled Buck along. The Mayor followed.

Paul stood helpless, frustration and anger welling up in him. It wasn't right. These were his people. It wasn't right.

"We'll come back," the Mayor said, "with the cure."

Paul rushed back to his truck, pulled an axe from behind the seat.

He overtook Buck's crew, axe raised. They backed up. He strode past them, straight for the gangway. He hacked at the rope that held it in place. Two strokes and it snapped. The ropes flipped upward toward the cranes as the planks swung back against the ship like a gong.

Out of the corner of his eye, he saw the Kid rush him. He turned too slow. The Kid's shoulder slammed into his chest, sending him sailing out over the water. He plunged in backward, water closing over him. The cold shock knocked the wind out of him. His arms and legs cramped, wouldn't move. He panicked, tried to breathe, sucking in water and coughing out air. The ship loomed over him. One wave would send it his way, crushing him against the dock.

Darkness descended as the surface closed over him. A tug on his hood, and he felt himself pulled upward. He dripped over the concrete dock, flopping down like a fish. His lungs begged for air, coughed out salt water. Frigid air stabbed his throat as it crawled in. Sopping wet, he controlled his breathing long enough to look up.

From his prone position, he could make out Buck's crew running for the second gangplank.

It had been for nothing, then, and the only person to suffer for it was the hero himself. *Idiot*, he thought.

Alone on the dock, he stripped off the wet coat and beat his arms and legs against the ground to get the blood flowing again. His warm little bunker seemed miles away. If he could get to the truck, he might survive. The cab was probably still warm.

He hobbled across the dock as the ship groaned out of its mooring, gliding past him toward the sea. He made out Buck and the crew at the rail, watching him. It was the giant that saved him. They cared. They wanted him to live. Bastards!

He made the truck and crawled inside. He stripped off everything, reaching for a spare parka wedged behind the seat. The plastic seats stuck to his wet skin, already cold. He couldn't uncurl his fingers. He cranked up the diesel and let the warm air dry him out. Even as the cab heated up, he shivered.

The boat cleared the dock.

He felt an unexpected wave of isolation. Panic rose in him. *Alone.*

He blew on his fingers, alternating between holding them under his armpit and fanning them in front of the vent. He could feel them again. The panic passed.

He wanted this, right? He was ready.

He threw on the spare parka, nude otherwise. It felt odd to press the gas pedal without boots. The truck lurched forward and braked hard as he got used to the pressure of the hard rubber beneath his toes.

He drove through town toward his house. Home after home, windows once glowing, now lay dark and cold. He eulogized them as he passed each empty shell, like shrines erected for those lost at sea. Only wind and snow would ever live there now.

Paul's bulwark against society became a prison.

He realized it too late. At his age, he thought it couldn't happen.

He was in love with all humanity.

But humanity would never return.

As it floated away without him, he felt lovesick. This loss would never heal. The hole would never fill on its own. It started in his stomach and moved up to his heart, akin to fear.

Where there had been chatter and ideas and games to play and nights of anticipation, where there had been both certainty and uncertainty in human behavior, now there was only emptiness.

Leaving is the same as dying. Each party moves on, secure in their leading role, as the other disappears into oblivion.

He wanted to run, to chase the ship, to have that argument again. He wouldn't change his mind, they wouldn't change theirs, but it wouldn't be goodbye. As long as they fought, they were still together.

You can't fight alone.

He parked the truck in front of his house. He winced as he pulled his soggy boots back on. Better than walking barefoot through the snow. The rest of his clothes he laid out in the truck to freeze dry. He would survive the ten steps to the door, even half naked. Who cares? No one left to see him.

His boots squelched and crunched as he stepped out. The door thunked closed. But for the ever present breeze, silence filled the rest of the village. Despite his shivering nudity, he stood still to enjoy the unusual sound. *That's a sound I could get used to!*

The presence of nature calmed him. Vast. Everlasting. His.

He took a deep breath of arctic air. *This is what freedom smells like.* After a lifetime enduring the presence of others, he had most of the North American continent to himself. He had lied to them about his supplies. He had at last three years' worth, and plenty of time. If he ever did want to leave, he had his own personal train. Right now he needed warm clothes and a nice, long nap.

He decided on the first book he'd read downstairs. *100 Years of Solitude.*

He was about to step forward when he heard another sound, a sound he wasn't responsible for.

A choked growl, like water in the lungs of a drowning man.

A black, torpedo head of skin rounded the house followed by a massive shadow. An elephantine body slid above long, thin legs. Rust colored skin sagged against a withered frame, ravaged by frostbite, riddled with erupting pustules. A raw bullet hole sank above one shoulder.

The male.

Swathes of the polar bear's fur had fallen out, and it walked sideways as if it couldn't keep its balance. The eyes, though...

Paul stopped. The cold set to work on his skin.

The bear padded in front of the truck, between Paul and the stairs. Its nose twitched, black on black. It swung a heavy head side to side. Those white eyes rolled toward him.

Paul lunged for the driver's door, but the bear was faster. A paw knocked him aside, almost taking the door with him. He scuttled backward, awed by this mountain of decayed skin.

Didn't see this coming.

The bear reared up. It brought both front paws down on his head the way he'd seen them break the ice around seal holes. Instead of ice, his skull took the blow. He retained consciousness. Stunned and fascinated more than scared, he observed the massive beast. The bear took his boot in his teeth and tossed him across the ice. The hard ground knocked the wind out of him. *He's playing with me.*

He knew better than to play dead. He struggled to stand.

The bear shoved him down with his snout. It nipped at his neck. Paul felt the blood flow out into the snow.

He looked for a weapon of any kind.

A shovel lay in the snow under the house.

Paul lifted his bad arm and bent the stump at the elbow. The bear opened its mouth, but not wide enough to fit the whole arm. It paused a moment, mouth open, deciding where to bite.

Paul used his good arm to pull himself backward, closer to the house. He rolled onto his stomach, crawled, reaching out for the shovel. The bear placed a heavy paw on the square of his back and leaned, pinning him, crushing his pelvis.

I'm so close, he thought. *So close to everything I ever wanted.*

He clawed at the ice, his bare chest scraped raw. The bear started nipping at his neck again, then took a bite at the base of his skull.

He felt the tooth enter his neck, but it missed his spinal cord. When he moved again, it made a second attempt. This time it connected.

Paul couldn't see the bear anymore, but he watched in horror as the shack slid away. The bear latched onto his leg and pulled him toward the sea.

He fought for consciousness. Darkness and light. Every time his vision snapped back into focus, his house was farther away.

He screamed for help. He knew the remaining families would never hear him, tucked away in their warm homes, involved in their own grief. It was still early. They probably went back to bed.

He called out anyway. Again and again. It was his only hope. He needed them. He needed all of them.

I'm alone. The words recycled through his mind even as he continued to cry out.

I'm alone.

He had time for one more thought as the bear reared up on its hind legs for the killing blow.

This is what I wanted.

PEGASUS

This is what I wanted.

Buck stood on the deck of the Pegasus. Even though the movement of the ship and the arctic winds dipped the wind chill below 60, he couldn't get enough of the feel of the ship beneath his feet, the sound of it crashing through the waves, the knowledge that this was real. He did it. He set a goal, he made a plan, and he did it.

Plus, braving the deck, a place where no sane man should be, brought a rare moment of peace.

This was his idea, his dream, so that made him the go-to guy for some reason. Nobody asked him if he wanted to be in charge. They had the Captain and Mayor Fell, but no. The Mayor said he was only along for the ride, said he was the Mayor of Churchill, not the Mayor of Pegasus. And the Captain, without a professional crew on board, said it was his job to run the ship, not "keep tabs on civilization". Whatever that meant. The Captain named a few trained people for necessary tasks like the kitchen and the engine room, but otherwise he let the hierarchy grow organically. That meant, from Buck down.

Pranksters playing in the lower levels? Get Buck. Not enough water in the pipes? Get Buck. Vending machine isn't working? Get Buck. Disagreement over whose pillow belongs to whom? Too hot? Too cold? Too loud? Too spooky? You guessed it.

Two hundred people living on a ship built to house twenty left plenty of room for disputes, dysfunction, and confusion. And they looked to him to solve it. He was a non-stop maintenance manager, arbitrator, designator, administrator, and sometimes babysitter – for grown men.

By the second day, he delegated tasks out to various people, maintenance especially. He hated maintenance issues. They never ended.

Even then, he never got a moment's rest. He almost longed to be back in the forest, blazing a trail into the unknown. At least then he had four people to worry about. Not two hundred.

When a young runner told him the Captain asked for him, he almost drew the line. *Now I have to do the Captain's job?* But the Captain never called for him, preferring the bridge to the chaos below, so Buck went.

His peaceful refuge of the deck lasted just long enough to regain his sanity, and then it was back into the fray.

On the bridge, the Captain pointed toward the horizon. "Thought you might like to see this."

Buck didn't see anything. An endless expanse of black water spread under a featureless blue sky. Something shimmered at their meeting, a sliver of white among muted hues. "Tell me that's a mirage."

"Naw, that's ice."

Buck's knees went out from under him. He had to sit down. *Every time I have a dream, someone wakes me up.* "That's not possible. The papers said the channel was ice free for years. Why this year? Why now?"

"Chances are, it's seasonal ice. Not too thick and we can steam through it. But if it's multiyear ice, we have to drop to three knots. It won't stop us, we're built for it, but it'll slow us down."

"How far does it go?"

"Don't know. Could be a small section. Could be here to the Bering Strait. Don't have the satellites to tell us."

"What do we have?"

"I've got a drone on deck. Don't know if she works, but you can try. Fly it out over the ice and take a look."

"I'll get someone on it." This would be perfect for the Kid. "Give me the worst case scenario."

"Worst case, we waste a lot of time pushing through the ice, we don't make it to China in time for the cure."

"But we *will* make it through? How are we on fuel?"

"Again, depends how long it takes. If it takes two months to get to Barrow, we'll be dead in the water."

"And that's bad, right?"

"You ever hear of the Franklin Expedition?"

"I don't think I want to." *Try not to panic until you know how bad it is.* "We'll try the drone, hope for a short duration of seasonal ice, and go from there."

"You got it."

Wait, did I just make another decision?

He turned to go, but the Captain caught his arm. "Do me a favor. Don't mention this to anyone."

Buck understood. Even the Captain didn't want to turn back.

The steel steps echoed as he walked back down. Each step beat an emotional war drum in his chest. Anger and disappointment ganged up to shove a black ball of unfairness down his throat. It caught in a lump.

He stopped and sat on a grated step. 3000 miles of deception. He felt so stupid. This whole trip, all these lives, hung on an article he read once? At the time, it gave him the hope to live. Now that he'd involved so many others, it seemed a bit thin.

Let's hope the ice is, too.

He didn't want to go back down there and face those people, even if they didn't know. He wanted to spend the next three weeks right here in the stairwell. In the quiet. He wished he could skip forward through time and learn how it turned out. He didn't want to have to live it.

Words came back to him. *Now is the time to take stock of your situation, how little you've accomplished, and how little time you have left.* He didn't know where they came from.

He took a stroll on the open deck. The wind chill dropped even further, but he wanted to smell the fresh air. Ice formed on the ruff of his parka. The water rushed beneath the ship, hissing and crashing and heaving, ice free.

Tara and Fifty were already out there. He gravitated toward them, leaned against the starboard rail, close to Tara, but not touching. "Have you seen the Kid?"

"Probably with his girlfriend below decks."

"Far below," Buck insinuated.

"Not like you, always up here," Tara chided.

"I'm claustrophobic," he said.

Tara laughed and shook her head. A few strands of hair escaped her hood.

He watched the wind push the waves against each other. "I've actually never been on a ship before. I had no idea it was so... scary."

"Scary!?" She laughed again. "You fought Eaters for months, but a ship is scary."

"We're at the mercy of the ocean. Look at those waves! If something goes wrong, we're trapped. There's no place to run."

"You only run north anyway." She smiled.

"Ha ha."

"To me, a ship at sea feels almost... safe. It's nice, for once, to think about something other than survival. Unlike Fifty over there."

Not far off, Fifty leaned over the side, green. Seasickness had him in her grip since they left Churchill. Buck watched him weave with the motion of the ship then turned back to Tara. "Assuming things work out, the Chinese have the cure, the good guys win, the world goes back to normal, where do you picture yourself settling down?"

Tara squinted into the bright sunlight. "I don't know. I thought I had what I wanted. A little house, a family, time to myself away from the world, but that didn't really suit me."

Buck wasn't listening. "Me, I want a ranch somewhere. Lots of free land these days. Maybe head down to Argentina or Patagonia and raise me some beef."

"I want to move back to the city. Get a little apartment. Work hard. Catch dinner with friends. Live a small life in a big place."

"That's the problem with us." Buck hadn't meant to use the word "us". He wanted to stop after "problem", but he gave it away. He wondered if, under less gruesome circumstances, they might have had something together. He caught her looking at him. "Always going different directions even when we're going the same way."

She smiled "Yup. I run toward them while you run away."

He laughed. "You do that!" Bringing those creatures back, even as a joke.... "Why do you do it, though? You got a death wish? A vendetta? What is it with you and them? I mean, the rest of us, we fight for our lives, but you. For you it looks personal."

Tara didn't answer. The wind ruffled the fur on her hood. The lock of hair battered her face. He reached out to tuck it back in, but she beat him to it. "I blame them," she said, "for this. Without the Eaters, none of this would have happened. And until they're gone..." She rapped on Cuba's helmet, ever firm on her head.

"Six billion to go," he said without reading.

She held his gaze. It looked like something serious, but then she smiled. "Won't be less if you keep running away."

"I will keep running. And as I do, I'll show them a big, bright moon."

The ship's horn blew once. *Lunch time.*

The Kid appeared, bouncing across the deck. "Hungry?"

"Oh, decided to join us today. Got tired of that girl already?"

"Felicity? No, she's serving." He had a goofy smile when he said her name.

Buck punched him on the shoulder. "I got something for you to do after lunch."

The mess hall wasn't big enough to fit everyone on board, so they ate in shifts. Out of deference to the townsfolk, Buck and his team usually volunteered for the fourth and last. This was only the second.

"Should we go down now or wait for next call?" The Kid asked.

There it is. That look again. He was asking Buck for permission to go earlier than they usually did. Easy decision, right? Yes or no. Fifty/fifty.

So many decisions. So many little decisions.

What should we do, Buck? Tell us. Verbalize it. Make it your call so that later, when we're dead, you'll be wrong, and we'll laugh at you from heaven or hell, wherever you're least welcome.

"Buck? I asked you a question?"

Lead us, take the blame. Bear the weight of indecision for us. We could do it without you, but why? Why, when we can lay that weight on your shoulders?

When details get you killed, we give those decisions to you.

Even a decision this small, when to go to lunch, could be regretted later. Carry enough shotgun pellets in your belly and they start to weigh you down.

"What's wrong?" Tara asked.

"I'm tired. It's been a long trip."

"We're only three days from Churchill."

And with the ice, that may be as far as we get. He tried to think of something else. "The bluebells are coming out in Oklahoma."

Tara knew enough to leave his memories alone.

"I'm starving. Let's eat now." Tara headed toward the stairs leading to the mess hall.

Thank you, Tara, he thought. *This one is on you.*

Buck pulled Fifty from the rail. "Let's get something in you so you can spit it out later."

The ship was cold enough that no one took off their parkas, even inside. They rounded the corner to the mess hall. Buck didn't know what to expect, but he always got his hopes up. A menu scrawled in chalk on a painted board read:

> *Omnivores:*
> Chicken in a can
> Milk in a cup
>
> *Herbivores:*
> Beans in a can.
> Water in a cup.

"Felicity wrote that." The Kid smiled again.

Buck brightened up. "All right! Chicken!" He'd had it with beans. Some days it seemed like no one ate beans before the End. They were all anyone had in the cupboard. If he had to eat beans one more time...

"*Canned* chicken," the Kid said. "I'm so tired of canned food. Maybe she's got something special back there." He skipped over to talk to the girl.

Buck grumbled. "Nothing wrong with canned chicken. Kid doesn't know a good thing when he's got it."

Tara nudged Buck. "Hey, look who else is serving. It's your old friend."

"Wilson. That prick. Well, I'd rather have him wait on me than the other way around."

They were late. The line stretched out into the hallway. The faint smell of warm food drifted across them. "Mmm, I can taste that chicken from here." Buck's stomach rumbled in anticipation. "Feels like a family dinner. You and me and two hundred of our closest friends."

Some of Wilson's boys sat near the door, their loud voices echoing off the walls. Buck couldn't help but overhear the boisterous, crude chatter.

"*Better get used to chicken. You'll be eating General Tso's every day when we get to China.*"

"*I'd rather be eating his wife.*"

"*You know how to use chopsticks?*"

"*Sure he does. He's had a stick up his ass since birth.*"

"*I got your chopstick right here.*"

Buck frowned. "Listen to them, the progenitors of our species. Sad."

The Kid said, "They should invent a disease that only affects the stupid." No one laughed. "You're right. There'd be no one left."

When they reached the front of the line, Buck asked, "What's your special today?"

Wilson slid a can of beans and a cup of water across the counter.

"What's this?"

Wilson shrugged. "Oh, sorry. Ran out of chicken a minute ago. You can have beans, though. Got plenty of beans."

Buck pointed behind the man. "I can see the chicken right behind you!"

Wilson smiled. "You must be mistaken."

Buck lost it. He lunged across the counter and caught the man by the throat, crashing into the stack. Tins scattered in every direction. Buck landed a few blows before Fifty intervened, catching Buck's upraised arm, prying a can of beans from his fingers. Wilson got in a cheap shot to the chin.

Buck stood up, stepped back, rubbed his jaw. It hurt, but not as much as his pride. He flexed his shoulders and straightened his coat. He picked up a can of beans and glared at Wilson. "Almost made me break my only principle."

"Come back when you want some more." the man sneered, no concept of how close he came to the end of his existence.

Buck saw Fifty, Tara, and the Kid pick up cans of beans out of solidarity. Buck picked a table in the corner. He sat with his hands under the table until they stopped shaking. *Gotta get a grip on myself. I can't let them get to me like that.*

Everyone waited politely for Buck to speak first. The Kid held out a can opener, but Buck waved it away. He fished his knife out of a pocket and jammed it into the metal top. That felt good enough that he did the same for everyone, dropping the jagged lids on the table with aplomb.

Tara leaned in toward Buck. "Are you okay?"

"I fought through three months of hell to get here, and I didn't picture 200 tourists along for the ride. I feel like they stole my dream and shat on it."

"You're saving their lives."

"Maybe I'm killing them."

"What do you want, a medal?"

He gave a half smile. "Yeah. You got one?"

The Kid took Buck's knife and punched a hole in one of the can lids. He unthreaded the cord of his hood and laced it through the hole, tying it in a loop. This he held out ceremoniously. "To Buck! For bravery and leadership in the First Degree."

"Only a silver medal?" he teased.

The Kid flipped it over to where the treated interior of the lid almost looked gold. Buck bowed his head to accept it around his neck.

Tara took the knife next. "Kneel!" He went down on one knee. "I dub thee," she patted him on the head and shoulders with the flat of the blade, "Sir Buck, Knight of the Land of the Dead."

He beamed, caressing the rough disc. "I'll treasure this as long as I live. That's an easy promise to make these days."

They dug into their beans, spirits lifted.

Buck put down his fork. "You know, you're right. It's not everybody, just Wilson and his crew. I can live with that." He stood up. "Here's to beans!"

"To beans!" They toasted with cups of water.

"This calls for a good mooning!" He stood up.

"No! No," they said in earnest, pulling him back. "Geez, they hate us enough already."

By 'they', she meant the townsfolk. Hate was too strong a word, but resentment grew like a mushroom in the darkness below decks. Three days ago, these people were snug in their houses, comfortable and familiar. Now they lived like refugees, sleeping on cold steel, packed in close proximity to each other, awoken by the horrible, random noises of a ship at sea. Their sense of adventure faded by the second day. Discomfort needs a center of focus, and that center was Buck's little crew.

It took time for Buck to realize how much. When he passed in the halls, they stopped talking. He caught several sidelong glances. At first he thought it was the fact that he was an outsider, or that he took charge, but he soon realized they were talking about the rest of his crew, too.

Especially Tara. They didn't trust her at all. In their worst dreams, he knew, she came at them with a pool cue.

He couldn't do anything about that. She was a part of their collective trauma. *Sucks to be her.*

He raised the topic with her after lunch on their traditional postprandial walk. "I get it, you know? We took them out of their cozy little homes and put them on a ship to China. Many of them weren't ready to leave. They weren't hungry enough, weren't desperate enough. The people I'm used to collecting ran out of options." He smiled. "Their houses burned down and they had nowhere else to go."

"Maybe we should have burned Churchill to the ground." She said, serious.

"Oh, yeah, that'd make us popular." His voice softened. "All I'm saying is, watch your back. They don't like us. We're stuck together on a dangerous journey. Things are going to get worse, and when they do, the living are a lot uglier than the dead."

The Kid wandered up beside them., holding his stomach.

"You're supposed to be playing with the drone."

"I don't feel so good."

Buck felt another administrative nightmare coming on. "What's wrong?"

"My stomach. I think I'm gonna hurl."

"Are you seasick?"

"No."

"Was it the beans?"

"No, I, uh, I ate again in the third rotation." He looked sheepish. "Felicity gave me the chicken. I hope you don't mind…" He closed his eyes. "Oh, god, the chicken." He ran for the side. A wet splash followed. He wiped his mouth when he came back. "I'm going to go lie down."

Buck shouted after him, "After a can of beans it's a good idea for us to sleep as far away from each other as possible."

"Something's wrong," Tara said.

"Everything is wrong with beans."

"No. I mean, it doesn't look like the Kid is the only one sick."

She was right. The sour reek of regurgitation wafted past them on the breeze. More than one person sat on deck, sucking in cold fresh air, arms over stomachs. Some had the comfort of another to pat their head. Others leaned over the side. A minute ago Buck thought they were admiring the view, but now that he paid attention…

A chill far colder than the air passed through him.

Tara shivered, too. "Food poisoning," she said.

"If any of them die…." This was bad. There were so many of them and nowhere to go. "Go tell Fifty and the Kid to stay in their rooms. I'll warn the Captain."

Buck raced across the deck and pounded up the stairs.

The Captain assaulted him as soon as he arrived. "What did the drone see?"

"We've got bigger problems. Make an announcement to cancel the fourth lunch. They're serving bad chicken. No telling how many people ate it already."

"Bad chicken? We're about to hit sea ice, and you're talking about chicken?"

"Just do it!" He ran down below.

For the first time, the ship's speakers rang out with an announcement. The Captain's voice echoed off every metal wall. "All passengers are confined to quarters. Repeat. All passengers please report to your designated areas and remain in place. The fourth meal rotation has been temporarily delayed."

Shortly afterward the ship shuddered as it slowed. Everyone would take that as a bad sign.

Buck had an idea. He ran back up the stairs.

"Captain, will that ice hold the weight of a human?"

"It should."

"We need to get to that ice and stay there. We might have to evacuate the ship."

"And watch them stampede over each other in a panic? No thank you. I know you think I'm crazy, but when I'm standing here, on the bridge, I'm a real Captain. I have my moments of lucidity. If you want to make yourself useful, you'll go get the doctor instead of telling me how to do my job."

Buck backed out of the door with his hands up. "Ok, your honor. I'm on it."

At the bottom of the staircase, Buck cut across to a hatch when he saw Wilson talking to two men on the opposite side of the wheelhouse. He backed up a few steps, ducked behind a wall within earshot.

Someone said, "It doesn't seem right, heaving them overboard. They brought us out here."

"Exactly! They're a danger to us all." Buck recognized Wilson' voice. "You saw him attack me. He would have killed me! Over one can of food! What happens when supplies get short, when it's every man for himself? Who do you want to fight for the scraps? The big one? He'll crush you like a can. The girl? You saw what she did to Old Mike. Hell even the Kid is dangerous. I say we take them out now. One by one. We start with the Kid, tonight, when he's..."

Buck heard enough. He stepped out of the shadows. "Why don't you start with me?" He tried on his most cocky smile. It faded a little when he saw them. What he thought were a few conspirators turned out to be twenty men. They held blunt metal objects in their hands, ready to do damage. They shifted from foot to foot, nervous. He'd caught them in the act of planning something evil. They looked guilty as schoolboys.

It was not too late to avert a fight. They had doubts. If he pressed his advantage they might not attack. He ran through his options. Threaten them? Act polite? Make a fool of himself? Beg?

He targeted their leader, Wilson.

"You're not listening to this fool are you? He's just venting 'cause I kicked his ass."

He thought a little levity would lighten things up. He thought wrong. Wilson must have used his battle prowess as something to fear.

Wilson shouted. "Why are we being sent to quarters, Buck!? What happened? Did you bring the plague with you on the ship?"

"What? No. Food poisoning. Look, your friend Lane there has it." One of the men looked miserable, but he didn't let go of his pipe. "Listen, boys. It's going to be a long trip, and we have to make it together."

"We don't have to do it together," Wilson shouted. "We can do it without you."

Buck knew the other twenty men weren't looking for violence. They were being led into it. He needed to separate them from Wilson.

"Why don't two of you take Lane downstairs so he can throw up in peace? The rest of you better make sure your loved ones aren't down there suffering from food poisoning." He decided to stretch it a little, spread the blame. "It was Wilson handing out the chicken cans today."

"Yeah, but you took the beans. How did you know?"

Backfire. He shouldn't have gone there.

"I know you're scared, but this'll blow over in a day or so..."

The ship shuddered again and then jerked abruptly. The gang shifted sideways like bowling pins, many of them thrown off their feet. Buck smashed up against the steel wall of the wheelhouse.

Now the men were scared. There were cries of "What was that?"

Not good timing.

Buck picked himself up. "It's the ice. We hit a patch of sea ice. We're going through it."

Wilson sneered. "You said there wasn't any ice. That was the whole point of this trip. Boys, he won't get us to China in time for a cure. Everyone on this ship is infected, and he wants us all to die."

"Look at you! You're fine! I can tell you with authority that no one on this ship is infected. *No one* on this ship is infected."

The door flew open and three Eaters crashed into the group. One Eater took a man over the rails. Another fell on Lane. They punched through his stomach and started to pull out his entrails. One reached up to catch hold of another man, brought him down and went straight for the jugular.

"Shit," Buck said. *Not good timing!*

The Churchill men ran for Buck. *This is it.* He crouched, whipped out his knife. He'd take as many as he could. They spread out around him, then thundered right on by, running as fast and as far as they could go. Buck stood up.

Only Wilson remained, aside from the three snarling creatures feeding behind him.

Without his posse, Wilson was no threat. Buck focused on the Eaters. "Help me fight them off!" He ran toward the nearest Eater, but Wilson's pipe lashed out and struck him in the kidney. Buck hit the deck knee first, clutching his side, tears hot in the corner of his eye.

"It's feeding time," Wilson said. "Why don't you slow them down for me?"

He kicked Buck toward the nearest Eater. It looked up from feeding on Lane, clotted blood thick on its cheeks.

Buck took a swing, thrusting the knife into the Eater's eye, but not deep enough. It continued eating.

Buck rolled backward, still holding the knife, and came to rest against the side of the ship.

Wilson lunged on top of him. "Nothing personal," he said, fingers around Buck's neck. "Oh, wait, yes it is."

A knee to the wrist forced Buck to drop the knife. "Are you crazy? There are more important things..." An elbow to the sternum forced him to drop the sentence.

Someone stepped out on deck from the same door as the Eaters. It was the Kid, looking like someone woke him from a nap.

Buck tried to call him over, but nothing came out. He reached an arm over Wilson's head, kicked, and flipped sideways. This brought him on top. Wilson fought hard, but Buck stayed on top, pinioning his arms.

"Kid!" He managed to shout. "A little help!"

The Kid walked like he had all the time in the world. *What the hell? Is he scared? Is he too sick?*

He figured it out too late.

The kid reached out, twisting Buck by the ear. It hurt. Buck let go of Wilson to pry the Kid's grip. Wilson reached for the knife, caught it. Thinking he had the advantage, Wilson took a wild swing with the knife.

Buck lurched backward to avoid it. His ear tore free of the Kid's fingers. Twisting, Buck fell forward on his chest. The Kid lunged, missing Buck, falling full on Wilson. Wilson plunged the knife in the Kid's side, again and again, with no effect. Wilson screamed. The pitch rose and then cut off in a wet whistle as the Kid's teeth found his larynx.

Buck rolled backward and brought his feet up under him. The Kid turned to face him, Wilson's blood coating his shirt.

Buck ran down the hall, but the world looked all wrong, crooked.

Tara appeared at the other end.

"The Kid turned!" He shouted in warning, but she ran right for him.

"My god! Your neck! What happened?"

Buck reached for his neck. Warm, dark liquid coated his hands. His slick fingers found a foreign object lodged in his throat. The lid of the bean can, the Kid's final gift, still hanging from the lace, its ragged edges tucked between a muscle and his carotid. "I'm fine," he lied. "He's right behind me. Watch out."

The Kid turned the corner, eyes wide.

"Damn it," she said with compassion. Tara threw off her jacket. Holding it by the sleeves, she pushed it in front of her like a shield. When the Kid started to tear at the hood, she looped it over him. Pivoting on her heel, she wrapped the arms around him like a straightjacket. Back to back, she bent, lifting him, cocooned in the jacket, like a rucksack. He kicked his feet in the air, thrashing. She walked to the rail. "I'm so sorry, Kid." She turned and knelt, throwing the Kid over the rail like a slingshot.

Buck rushed to the side, leaned over. Crimson droplets fell down, down, down to stain the pristine white snow beside a crumpled body. *He's on the ice. The ice I promised him wouldn't be there.* The Kid stood up, one arm bent backward. Disoriented, he walked in a small circle. The Pegasus slid forward, crushing the flow, lifting up a great white slab under the Kid, flipping his limp body out across the barren surface. The violence of it would kill the living, but he stood up again. He wandered away from the ship in a zigzag pattern, as if in a daze, leaving a tumbleweed trail of dragging footprints in the snow.

Buck flashed on the Kid's future, wandering that immense space at the top of the world for as long as the ice supported him. Maybe longer. A monster, never a man. Forever alone.

Because I brought him here.

Tara fell against the rail, pulled at his coat. "Behind us," she said.

Buck turned. Four Eaters approached from the stern.

Tara pulled a pistol out of her jacket pocket and started unloading it on the nearest Eater. The short, hollow barks ricocheted across the top of the ship, blocking out, for a moment, what Buck realized was screaming everywhere else.

All four Eaters jerked and twisted as the bullets struck them. In seconds, they were down.

As Buck's hearing returned, the distant screaming continued.

"You didn't shoot the Kid," Buck said. "You must be getting soft."

"I couldn't do it. He looked like... himself."

Buck clutched his neck. "It's not your fault," he said, sliding back to the deck. "You did what you had to do. He's better off out there."

"Oh my god, look at you." She kneeled beside him. "We have to get you someplace safe." She helped him up, draped his arm around her neck.

She opened the door to the wheelhouse, listened for anyone nearby, then backed up, dragging Buck with her. She pulled him into a closet. It was narrow, barely big enough for the two of them, and filled with coveralls. They stank of fuel and sweat, an Eater magnet. Not the best place, but the only place.

"Cozy," he said.

Eaters from both directions followed them to the door. She shut it, but it stuck in the jamb. Hands pounded the metal as she pulled harder.

Buck reached out to help but he'd lost all his strength.

The door squeaked shut. Tara held onto the handle. "There's no lock!"

"I haven't seen one yet that can use a doorknob."

A strip of sunlight and cold air penetrated a crack in the door. Tara peered out. "There are six of them." They banged on the door like a tympani. "We're trapped in here." Tara held her pistol where she could see the chamber. She ejected the magazine. Empty. She peeled back the chamber, careful not to eject the last cartridge.

"One left."

Buck knew what she meant. "It's ok... to be selfish."

"Oh, I'm not using it on me." She closed the chamber and kept it pointed at the door.

"It's ok..." A violent cough brought up blood. He spit it out, grimaced in a whisper, "to share."

"You're not dying. We'll get you fixed up."

He knew that was a lie. Blood pumped out of his neck and down his arm. The tin had nicked the artery. Already the metal floor felt tacky.

She pulled all the coveralls off the hangers and threw them on the floor. She twisted one of the hangers to keep the door shut. Buck stood by, helpless and feeling worse. He kept a hand pressed to his throat.

"Let me help you with that." Tara tried to rip a suit into sections with her teeth. When that failed, she held it under her boot and pulled. The stitching separated at the sleeve. She tied the filthy sleeve around his neck. "Hold this in place." The waxed cotton surface did nothing to absorb the blood. She changed her mind and tried to undo it. "It's too dirty. It shouldn't touch your wound."

Buck put his hand over hers, holding the fabric in place. "There's only one infection I'm worried about."

The racket on the door abated. He could hear them shuffling about, moaning. They could smell his blood.

He didn't have much time left. He knew it. His thoughts drifted back to Oklahoma. "The bluebells are coming out."

"You said that already."

"Back home. It's spring. I always like it when the bluebells come out."

"Don't go delirious on me."

He closed his eyes and tried to swallow. "I had a girlfriend, before all this started."

"Crazy as you?"

"I was going to marry her. Probably. Eventually. No, definitely."

"No time for confessions. Live till you can find a priest."

"When I came home from work, I found her in the kitchen. Two of those monsters on top of her, eating. She was already dead."

"Buck, I don't want to hear it. You're going to live. I'm going to get you out of here."

The banging on the door resumed. The door shook like a hurricane.

Buck heard himself talking, but it was someone else telling the story. Someone he used to know, someone good and innocent, without blood on his hands. He missed that man. He watched the scenes as the man spun his tale. "I could have done something to protect her. Boarded up the house or stayed home from work. I knew what was happening. I'd seen the police shoot a few down, saw the news broadcast about how bad it was, but in my town we make do and move on. Like everyone else, I thought we'd survive. These things don't happen to us."

Tara put a hand on his head.

"I was half right. It didn't happen to me. But her.... I went back to the truck for a rifle. I shot them off, but it was too late. There was nothing I could do. She lay on the floor, covered in blood, her throat ravaged." *Her throat. Karma is fair if nothing.*

"Then she opened her eyes. They were fine. Beautiful. Serene. Lucid with purpose. The same eyes I fell in love with. I watched those eyes as she stood up. I watched them as she walked toward me. If she hadn't purred," he rolled his eyes toward the door, "I wouldn't have shut the glass door in time. She was a bloody mess from the neck down. She stood there, clawing at the glass. Her face went slack. But those eyes kept staring at me, wanting me. Needing me.

"I walked backward, got in the truck, and drove away. I... I left her. I didn't know what I could do. I still don't." He coughed again. He lifted his bloody hands in the light. "I still don't know what to do."

"It is not your turn." Tara said. She had tears in her eyes. "I won't let you, Buck, goddamn it. I won't let you."

He couldn't hear her. "I can't stop thinking about Hudson Bay, how they... protected their loved ones. Even after... They loved them. How could they love them? It never occurred to me to keep loving her. I was a coward. I was a coward."

His blood leaked out under the door. The beasts went wild, smashing their bodies against the metal.

"Those people, with their... compassion. They're good people. The kind that should inherit the earth. Not like us." He held his throat, weaker. "Not like me."

"You!" Tara was crying now. "I'm only alive because of you. You brought us here, to safety!"

He laughed, sniffed. "Safety."

"This was your idea. Go north! And it was the right one. We'll get to China. We'll find a cure."

"I did it. I reached my goal. The Pegasus. I never hoped, I never planned beyond that. I guess this is why." His hand closed around hers, pulled the pistol up to his chin. "Don't let me turn. I don't want a cure, even if there is one."

"No," she pulled the gun back down. "No."

He knew she wanted to say the right things: he would survive, they would get him to a doctor, he'd pull through, but those were bold lies. She knew it. He knew it. There was no one out here who could help him.

He watched her face, saw his own mortality in her reaction. "You have," he reached for her, "blood on your cheek." He pulled his hand back, remembering she didn't like to be touched. She caught it, pulled it to her face, nestled it, a tear in her eye.

She said nothing. She matched his gaze. She leaned forward and kissed him, in absolution. "You're a good... you're the *only* good man."

His lips had lost too much blood to feel her. *I'm so cold.* Particles of snow sparkled between them. "I've always been cold. There wasn't anything before... before I met you. Just snow. I should have... I should have stayed... " He laughed to himself. "Why didn't I go south?"

His eyes closed.

The beating on the door grew. No telling how many stood out there. In a moment, there'd be one in here, too. He felt slow, weak. His vision darkened into night.

He found the strength to whisper, "Don't kill him."

"What?" she sobbed. She must have thought he meant himself.

"The scientist. When you find him. Don't kill him." He halted, took a short breath. "I know... he's like us." His lungs wouldn't pull in air. "We didn't want to do... the things we've done."

She leaned forward and kissed him again, longer. His last breath was hers.

His eyeballs constricted. His mind found an autopilot setting and drifted. His limbs ached as if rubber bands willed them back into a fetal position, a marionette with a black hole for a heart.

That heart stopped beating. His brain shut down like a long panel of switches · first his memories, then his ego, his id, his sense of pain, his fear.

If he felt anything at all, it was a growing sense of hunger, as if he could eat whatever he'd lost, devour life and, in so doing, get it back. His nose collected particles of fuel and dead skin as Tara wrapped the pistol in a coat to suppress the blast. His ears sensed the silence as she hid his face in coveralls so she wouldn't see what she was about to do. The center of his forehead registered pressure against it, round and hard behind the stiff fabric. His ears perhaps even heard her as she stepped back as far as she could and shuddered "Goodbye, Buck." Despite his other senses, stronger than fear, lay an insatiable hunger that grew in the pit of his stomach. It sent forth an emissary, crawling up the throat, past the tonsils and the uvula, generating a low, rolling growl.

He didn't hear her pull the trigger.

INTERLUDE

THE BEGINNING

The beginning is undefined.

We think it starts where we came in. We think it ends where we are.

How narcissistic.

No one defines the beginning. The milestones we observe have no meaning beyond a celebration that a beginning, indeed, happened, though we can't pinpoint when.

The beginning is a long awakening, the part of the dream you hang on to, the one that shapes your day, your fears, your ambitions. It is the fragment your brain singled out, in lieu of all it forgot. It is the trip we take when we realize our bags our packed.

The beginning is the end of all that came before.

Tara began where she ended.

The door slammed. "What was that, Mommy?" A little voice whispered in her ear.

"Shush, bunny." Tara petted Chelsea's feather soft hair. "It's just Daddy coming upstairs." She could hear him thumping up the treads, straight to the bathroom. After his shower, he would want his coffee. She couldn't pretend to sleep. That's why he slammed the door, to wake her, to get his coffee.

Dawn peeped through the curtains like a voyeur. Her hand smoothed over his side of the bed, the blankets undisturbed. He spent the night in the basement again, drinking, reloading, and brooding. He hadn't been to town in a week. He grew restless. He resented the storm that kept him home last night. She knew this. He said the cartridges gave him a sense of security. He never forgot to buy gunpowder and alcohol, but he frequently forgot to buy eggs. Perishable goods were harder and harder to come by, but she didn't think he was trying to find them. Lord knew if they had any money left.

"Stay here, bun-bun." She dressed in a slip and hurried out. A light spread below the closed bathroom door. She avoided it and tiptoed downstairs to put the pot on.

The kitchen was cold. She knew they weren't out of propane because the stove turned on when she lit it. He'd turned off the heat to 'conserve resources'. She shivered as she looked out the window. What a storm! It must have snowed two feet. She could barely make out the lump of her car in the buried driveway.

She measured out the coffee and spread it on top of a cold pot of water. He liked it Turkish style. He never let her use a coffee machine.

Marriage is an unfinished argument. Trivial events unleash an army of bitter remarks, bait waiting for a bite. Those who strike first, and often, win. Those who prefer civility...

"Ta-RA!" Her husband's voice echoed through the house. "Get in here!"

She turned down the stove and ran back up the stairs. "Coming!" She stopped before the door, took a deep breath, and prepared herself before she turned the doorknob.

She found him half standing, half crouched, wavering next to the toilet, his pants unbuckled, drunk, again. His finger jabbed at the toilet paper roll hanging opposite the toilet. Several sheets unspooled from the back of the roll onto the floor. He cocked his head toward her and squinted. "Does this look right to you?"

Her face burned hot with shame as she reached to flip the roll.

He slapped her hand away. "Don't." She tried again. "Don't. No. How many..." He drew a deep breath, lips tight in frustration. "How many times have I shown you the correct way to install toilet paper? The loose sheet always faces the front! Like a hotel! How many times!?" The shower door rattled as he leaned against it, trying to pull his pants back on. The room smelled of soap and plastic and human waste. "Are you stupid or do you just ignore me?"

"I'm so sorry. I won't let it happen again."

"That's what you said the last time. *And* the time before that." He was working himself up.

She knew where this was headed. She hurried over to help him. "I won't forget this time. I won't. Please." He pushed her away.

"Please? Please! You don't have to ask me. Just do it, you know? Just do it." He zipped up his pants, but he pulled the belt out of the loops. "What you need is a reminder." He slapped the belt across her arm. His voice rose. "What this house needs... is discipline." The belt cracked again. He shouted. "Why am I the only one who cares around here? Don't you care about your family, about me?"

"Please, darling, she's still asleep."

He paused, thinking about their daughter in the next room. "Well maybe I ought to tell her to come in here and fix the toilet paper, since you don't care. Start 'em young."

"I do care." The belt hurt, but she tried not to show the tears. "I care about this family. I cared enough to come all the way out here..."

"Oh here we go again with the sad routine. Poor you. 'I was better off in New York. I sacrificed so much!' Bullshit! I built this house! For you! I filled it with nice things. For our daughter! And you don't have... the decency... to *listen* once in a while!"

He slapped her. Her head struck the wall. She buckled against the door and sat, trying not to touch her head, trying not to cry. "I know, Honey, I know. You've been so good to us. I know you're worried about what's going on out there. It's why you started drinking..."

"The same old argument. I'm a bad man. So I need a drink, now and then, to take my mind off your shitty housework. Any man would."

"I'm sorry. I'll try harder. I.."

"What are you doing on the floor? What's wrong with you? You're weak! The woman I married was strong. You were this big person. A Vice President! A real city girl! I fell in love with *that* woman. Where is she now? Who is this... mess!?"

The smoke detector shrieked through the house. The coffee! She'd left it on the stove!

He held his ears and shouted. "Ahhh! Damn it!" He pushed past her and stumbled down the stairs. She tried to beat him to the kitchen, but he held her back. "I have to do *everything*!" The alarm drowned him out.

Coffee grounds curled out of the pot and smoked in a black heap on the stovetop. In his haste, he snatched up the pot, splashing boiling water all over his hand. He tossed it in the sink where the black curd splattered. "God damn it!" He pushed past her, holding his hand, back up the stairs toward the bathroom and the medicine kit.

Tara stayed in the kitchen, unsure of what to do. Shaking, she mopped up the floor with a towel. It came away black. The sink needed cleaning as well. He left dishes from his night downstairs, a carving board for the sausages and cheese, a knife, a coffee cup, a tumbler with ice melting in it, all splattered with the coffee gunk. She had to take care of that first and give him a chance to calm down. The alarm blared on. It was hard to think.

She heard him shouting in the living room. He held a pink towel around his hand, dripping wet, as he jumped up toward the smoke detector. He jabbed at it with a broomstick leaving small, black holes in the sheetrock. She thrust her arms in the soapy water, sponging mechanically.

A crunching sound in the other room stopped the alarm. Her husband cried out in pain.

Jogging into the room she saw the remains of the alarm dangling from the ceiling. He stood with half a broken broom in his hand. The tip pierced his arm. Blood soaked the pink towel. She ran to help him but he pushed her down. He drew the broken wood out and threw the bloody stick at her. "Look what you did to me! You and your damn cooking!"

Chelsea appeared at the bottom of the stairs in her green bunny pajamas, crying, speechless. She knew better than to leave her room when Daddy was drunk, but the alarm frightened her. Seeing her mother on the floor, the smoke, his blood, she froze, tears squeezing out of her little eyes. She wet her pants on the carpet tread. Tara rushed to her side. "Mommy!" she bawled, burying her head in Tara's nightgown.

"Jesus Christ! The both of you!" he shouted, stunned. "Always 'Mommy!' What about me? I'm your father!" He held both hands out in supplication. She shrank back from the bloody hand he offered.

Offended, he slapped her, too. She stopped crying, and a look of surprise crossed his face. *This is the climax,* Tara thought. *Now begins the apologies.*

"I'm so sorry baby. I didn't mean to hurt you." He took a step toward them.

"Stay back," Tara shouted.

He stopped, perplexed. "Stay back? What, I can't comfort my own daughter?"

"Just go...sober up in the basement or something."

"You're saying this is all because I'm drunk? Yeah, that's right. It's all *my* fault." His voice grew louder. "I'm the one who left the pot on! I'm the one who set off the alarm, right? Because I'm drunk. That's what you're saying? I stabbed myself with a broom? Come here." He swung for her but missed. She shrank back.

"Get over here!" He shouted and lunged for them.

"Stay away from her!" She thrust her arm out to deflect him.

He paused. A shocked silence settled over him. His mouth dropped open. He looked down. His eyes rolled up toward her, questioning.

Three inches of a blade sank in the left side of his chest. Blood pumped through his t-shirt.

She looked at her hand, grasping the handle, as shocked as he was. She'd been washing the knife. She must have been holding it when she...

"Why?" He whispered, falling back.

She threw the knife across the room, but remained huddled with her daughter, covering her eyes.

He settled against the couch in a sitting position, as if in a stupor. It was not a superficial wound. He held out one hand. "Do something," he whispered.

She didn't know what to do. All the animosity and pain left her. She'd been through the violence so many times before, but this was new. She didn't know how to react. Someone rewrote the play but left the set the same. She didn't know her lines. This was all wrong. She sent Chelsea to sit with her husband. "Stay with Daddy," she said. "Hold his hand."

She ran into the kitchen. No ambulance would reach them in this snow. The county didn't even plow the roads this far out.

She dialed the emergency line. It rang and rang. No one answered. She hung up and tried again. "Come on!" She glanced in the living room. Her husband wasn't moving. The blood stopped pumping through the t-shirt. It soaked into the tan carpet, turning it black. Chelsea held his hand, her forehead wrinkled in concern.

She dialed again. Tears blurred her vision. The ringing continued. "Pick up!" The snow insulated the house, covering it in an unnatural silence. The ringing sounded cavernous, as infinite as space. Between each ring the silence came crashing down. She heard nothing. Not even in the other room.

And then she heard a low growl.

Chelsea screamed.

She dropped the phone and ran back to the living room.

Her husband sat up. He gripped Chelsea's hand even as she tried to pull free. His jaw cracked as he opened his mouth wide. He pulled her forward. Her little body couldn't resist. With a jerk, she fell on his bloody chest. His jaws clamped down on her bare shoulder, twisting his head, ripping through the green pajamas, tearing a chunk of muscle free.

Tara ran forward. She picked up the broken broom from the floor and swung it at his head. It cracked, but he didn't respond. She hit him again. His teeth angled for Chelsea's soft neck. She wriggled and screamed, punching him with her tiny fists, more like a wild animal than a child.

Tara battered him on the head. Ignoring the blows, he fastened his mouth on the girl's collarbone and bit again. Tara grasped a handful of hair, pulled his head back. One eye looked up at hers, full of hatred, and she pushed the broomstick through it.

His body fell backward, limp and silent. Chelsea backed against the wall, shrieking. Tara tried to hold her, but she fought back.

Tara held tighter. "Hang on baby. Mommy's taking you to the hospital."

Chelsea stared at the body of her dead father. Her tiny frame shook.

Tara pulled his body behind the couch. "Don't look at Daddy, baby. He didn't mean it. It's not his fault." She'd used those words so many times it was second nature. "He still loves you baby." She didn't believe them, even now.

Chelsea started hyperventilating. Dark red blood poured from her shoulder, drenching her green pajamas.

Tara petted her hair as she inspected the wound. "Calm down, now. Everything's going to be fine." The gash was deep and ragged. She knew it would take surgery to save her. She ran to the medicine cabinet for gauze pads.

The girl remained catatonic, her eyes distant, as Tara applied pad after pad. As each one filled, she reached for another. Her hands were slick with blood. She needed to get help from someone. Anyone.

"Mommy's going to get us ready to go. Just stay here, baby. Stay calm. I'll be right back."

She rushed downstairs where her husband kept a "to go" bag. She yanked one of his rifles off the wall, his favorite, the Savage, and stuffed a handful of cartridges in her pocket. Within minutes she had her parka and boots on. She wrapped Chelsea in a jacket and a down blanket and lifted her into her arms. The girl did not resist. She weighed nothing.

She threw open the door to the blinding light.

Tara stood outside Ochre River's single school wondering where everyone was. She couldn't remember how she got here. She didn't remember the hours spent carrying her daughter's limp body through knee deep snow, watching Chelsea's blood melt a dark red trail behind them. She remembered her husband saying they converted it to a hospital. She thought she would find a normal world when she arrived, filled with nurses and doctors and kind little old ladies who hold your hand in the waiting room while you cry and blame yourself. Even after she watched the news reports, when they lasted, even after her husband spent his nights in the basement preparing for the worst, even after he told her why he wouldn't let her go back into town, she refused to believe it. She hadn't seen it herself, hadn't seen beyond her own family drama. In isolation she could ignore the Event until it appeared in her own home, on her living room floor, biting her daughter.

Chelsea spoke with a calm, quiet voice. "Mommy, I'm cold."

"I know bunny, we're going inside."

An overturned ambulance blocked the driveway. The front fender smashed in the school's glass doors. Tara ducked through the opening. Snowdrifts gathered in the lobby.

She wandered the long halls, looking for someone to help her. The wind blew ghosts of snow over white vinyl tiles. Children's drawings taped to the walls rustled like dead leaves. Chelsea's body no longer gave off heat.

Tara pushed her way into a classroom. It used to be a classroom. Numbers and letters marched along the top of the walls. Finger painted animals hung from strings across the ceiling. Blue. Green. Red. Red. Red like the floor. The desks and chairs heaped in the corner, making way for makeshift beds. Mattresses on box springs lay directly on the vinyl tile beside yoga mats once used for naptime. Stained and soiled and ruined. The floor still slick with frozen blood and crayons and the litter of triage, discarded needles, empty IV bags, and something more, thick in spots, clotted with chunks of white.

She kicked over a mattress to the clean side, set Chelsea down, and collapsed on the floor beside her, never letting go of those little hands. Cold, cold hands.

Chelsea wasn't bleeding anymore. Her face relaxed, as if asleep, angelic and sweet, as if horror could never...

A rumble bubbled from the back of her throat, the sound of a purring kitten. No, not a kitten. The sound her husband made just before he...

Chelsea's eyes opened. She turned her head to look at Tara, opening her mouth as she did.

Tara couldn't look away. "No, bunny, no. Please. Not you, too." She backed out of the room and closed the door just as Chelsea rose from the bed.

Tara slid to the floor, back to the door, crying, wiping the tears with her wrists, shaking her head. "You're sick, baby bunny. You're sick, but you'll be fine."

A moan came from inside the room. Tiny fists beat on the metal door.

"We'll cure you, bunny. We'll find a cure. Stay here."

The light from the window at the end of the hall flickered as something dark moved across it. Someone in scrubs walked into the corridor. She laughed with joy, stood up. Before she could speak, she saw the horrible disfiguration in the sunlight, the absence of hair, or skin, the tattered bloody cloth.

She squinted as if stabbed. She couldn't leave her daughter here, but she dared not open the door.

Another creature entered the hallway behind the first.

She slid the rifle off her shoulder and leveled the Savage at the first creature. "Don't come down here!" It held its course. "Leave us alone!"

It reached within a few steps of her before she fired. She missed. The shot hit the window, shattering it. Shards crashed to the floor, skittering toward her. She fired again.

The creature's head exploded. The one behind it didn't even slow. It took three shots before it fell.

The thumping on the door behind her never stopped.

Tara could see at least six more outside, headed straight for the open window.

"Baby? Mommy has to go now. You stay in the room and don't open the door for anybody." The pounding intensified.

She slid to her feet, holding the rifle at her shoulder. "I'll be right back, Chelsea."

She touched her fingers to the door, whispering now, through the tears. "Mommy loves you. I'll be right back."

She never would go back.

She knew what waited for her.

She saw it every time she closed her eyes.

Chelsea still stood in that room, hunched beside the door, dormant. Hair and skin long gone. Tattered, bloodstained green pajamas covering a dark, frostbitten body.

Waiting for Mommy.

Forever.

Until the walls fall down around her.

Until the next ice age.

Until the sun dies.

Mommy should have killed her.

Mommy should have killed them both.

THE SOLUTION

Tomoko.

Can you read this?

Does this reach you, where you are?

It's so cold today. Like an icebox.

I miss you.

Did I tell you? I saw the aurora borealis.
I wish you were there.
You were supposed to be there.

We were supposed to have children and grow old together.

Now you will never be old.

Neither will I.

I think I will see you soon.

Tomoko. Can you hear me?

I love you.

The light of the phone illuminated her face. Her blue cheeks still smooth and young. Forever young. Frozen, but thawing from his body heat. A droplet of meltwater slid down one pale cheek.

Don't cry, Tomoko. I will see you soon.

His breath fogged the air, froze on her lashes. She looked ethereal, an ice princess, the Angel of the North Star.

He texted her again.

Tomoko.

I am afraid of your body.

I know you are gone
I know you no longer control it.
But if you can, tell it not to rise.

Tell it not to eat me.

Tell it to remain asleep.

Forever.

He slept. He woke. He slept again. His phone died.

He expected to die as well. Not out there with those undead creatures but here, hiding in the crate, with his wife.

He heard of people who gave up the will to live. They passed away in their sleep or in a comfortable chair or in a hospital bed. They willed it and made it so. Or old people who, upon the death of a spouse, followed them to the grave. They could not live as half a person.

So romantic.

Ando knew his wife for a few weeks, but he loved her enough for a lifetime. Why couldn't he die with her? Death took so many who wanted to live. Why not take someone who would welcome him?

Was hers the last peaceful death on earth?

He was surprised when he woke up.

Disappointed.

Ando waited several hours before he summoned the courage to raise the lid of the crate. He preferred the company of his dead wife to the undead comrades waiting outside, but even he recognized how impractical his hiding place was.

When they first appeared in the room, they made a terrible racket, clawing and pounding at the lid. After half an hour they gave up, but he could hear their clicking teeth. Four hours later, that stopped, too, leaving only the creaking of the ship.

They must be gone by now. He inched upward enough for one eye to peer out.

Three Eaters stood around the crate. Seeing movement, their nostrils flared, sucking up his scent. Their heads tilted in his direction. They lunged. He shut the lid and endured another half hour of pounding until he could no longer differentiate between their fists and his heart.

He remained in the crate, in the dark, alone with his dead wife. He traveled through his memories but always returned here. When he opened his eyes he saw the room outside, as if he had x-ray vision, and pictured them, waiting.

Once a day he grew impatient and lifted the lid. Once a day he found new patience.

A single bulb above the door told him two things. First, they were still there. Second, the ship still had power. So someone might be alive.

These daily surveys, though only seconds long, gave him unique insight into the nature of the dead, like a naturalist in a blind. They waited for him. They stopped moving, stopped growling, stopped everything but standing. Without lungs to contract, without a heart to pump, without a sense of fatigue, they stood as if frozen in time. After the first day, their skin blackened with frostbite. On the second, it cracked and began to leak. On the third the smell began. Their bodies bloated as their own organs rotted. Bacteria, like factories, transformed them from a solid to a gas, inside out.

He drifted in and out of consciousness. When his bladder begged, he urinated out of a gap between the boards. His aim improved over time. The pungent scent of urine drove them wild. They thrashed at the side of the crate in animal bliss, splashing until there was nothing left.

Later, he wished for it back.

He knew he would dehydrate if he remained, but he also saw death as inevitable. Better to die in the arms of his wife than the jaws of...

The door creaked open. A muffled voice called out. He held his breath in anticipation. They found him at last! Rescue was at hand! He heard the Eaters reanimate, heard them almost roar in delight. A scuffle ensued replete with panting and the impact of flesh on flesh. Something heavy crashed on the lid. He heard several crunching noises, the sound of bones beating on wood. A liquid penetrated the darkness to fall on his face. Whoever found him was now lunch.

The lid flew open. A dark form bent over him. He moaned, tried to rise, tried to run. His body failed him. Something hard smashed his skull, and he slipped into unconsciousness.

Ando's first sensation was one of warmth. Springtime. He smelled flowers, heard the wind rustle through a field, felt the sun touch his skin. If he opened his eyes, he would see Tomoko in a sky-blue dress amidst the bright yellow canola fields of Takikawa. He heard her. *Come.* She danced through the flowers, arm extended. *Come on.*

But it wasn't her voice. It wasn't Japanese. He frowned. His head hurt. His throat hurt more. *Come. Come on.*

"Come on," Tara said, annoyed. "Drink this." Hot water trickled over his lips. "Chamomile tea." He opened his eyes to the dull red glow of a heat lamp. Tara sat beside him, squeezing blood out of the towel into a bucket of water.

"Sorry about the bump on the head. You see someone coming out of a crate, covered in Eater gore..." she applied the dirty towel to a wound on his forehead, "you make certain assumptions."

His dry throat refused to answer.

"You're lucky I pulled my blow. I realized just in time."

"I don't feel lucky," he whispered.

This woman, whose crowbar downed three eaters and almost caved in his skull, now wiped his head with a wet cloth, tender as a mother.

"Have you been in there the whole time?"

He nodded.

He wrapped his hands around the ceramic mug, forced them to hold the hot surface. The smell of it revived him.

He sipped.

No one entered or left the room. They were alone. He didn't see anyone pass in the halls either.

She saw him looking around. "There aren't many left." She took the cup from him and filled it again.

He took it, drank, coughed, and spat it up.

She handed him a towel. "It took us three days to clear the ship."

He half listened as she told him what happened. "We'll never know who died first. Maybe someone cracked their head when the ship hit the ice. Maybe someone was too old to survive the journey. Once it started, it multiplied. The initial fighting lasted several hours. The food poisoning finished them off."

It took days to hunt down the remaining Eaters. Just as a cat hides when Death comes, those with mortal wounds or churning stomachs sought the dark, quiet spots to pass their final moments. When they turned, they lost the mental capacity to escape. The survivors found Eaters in the oddest places. The smokestack. The engine room. The lifeboats.

One hundred ninety six souls boarded the ship.

"Only twenty eight survived. Twenty nine, including you. We checked the manifest. You, and those three, were the only ones missing. In fact, we'd called off the search. Assumed you went over the side. I wanted to see what happened to Tomoko. Had to be sure."

"What about your friends, Buck? The young one? And the giant?"

"Fifty is with us." She said. She didn't say more.

"And the Captain?"

"He's alive. He locked the door to the bridge. It's like a fortress. No Eater could get inside."

"Good thing. He's the only one who knows the route."

"And how to run this ship. He's been giving us lessons, but we have a lot to do. The ship usually runs on a crew of twenty. He now has six."

"You said twenty-nine."

She squeezed more blood out of his rag. "You'll see." She applied a butterfly bandage to his skull. "Looks like you won't need stitches, but I'll have Fifty confirm that. He's taken on the role of ship's doctor. Seems to have some experience, though I don't know what that is."

He tried to sit up. His head took him to the left. Spots drifted across his eyes.

"I'm pretty sure you have a concussion. Don't move, but don't fall asleep either."

"I've slept enough," he said. "How is Tomoko?"

"The same."

Tara's fatiqued expression gave way to brief sadness, then, 'How did you two meet?"

"It was an arranged marriage."

"So you didn't know each other long?"

"We met once before the marriage. We knew each other a few weeks before..."

She winced, looked away. "Only a few weeks... How did she..."

"Yuki-Onna kissed her with her frozen lips."

"Yuki-Onna." Tara smiled like she believed in fairy tales.

She left it at that.

Fifty checked him out and corroborated Tara's opinion. They set him up with a bunk in the wheelhouse.

The next morning, Tara looked in on him.

"I feel fine. Should I see the Captain and get an assignment? I'm afraid my business school background won't be of much use on a ship, but I'm happy to learn."

Tara shook her head. "He's not taking visitors."

"What?"

"He won't open the door. We'll let him know you're alive. He'll be glad. Meanwhile, I need your help."

She led him back to Tomoko's room. Three bodies lay on the floor, fluids frozen in black pools. Tara took the feet of one. "Get the other end. We're taking them to the others."

He'd never carried a body before. Not even Tomoko. He didn't know what to do. The body she chose lay facedown, the hood of its parka covering the head. Liquid seeped through an indentation where the head ought to be.

"It's okay," she said, patient. "It won't bite. Reach under the shoulders and lift."

He tried not to look at it as he bent over, looped his hands under the stiff shoulders, and tugged. The bloody ice cracked, cakes of it coming up with the body, pancakes hanging down from the hood.

He followed as Tara waddled down the hall backwards. He didn't expect the body to be so heavy, but it remained stiff, making the job easier until they reached the stairs. With some effort, they finagled it around the corners, down two flights, and into a cargo bay.

Ando's head started to ache as Tara pushed through one more steel door, opening up into a dark cavern lit high above by a crack in the hold. Crystalline flakes sparkled down through the sunlight to settle on the rusty floor. Misshapen bundles of supplies lay on the floor, a light dusting of snow giving them a spectral aura. Around each lay personal belongings – boots, a stuffed animal, photo frames. Small candles in glass jars flickered over the scene. He wondered why they weren't placed inside the bundle.

There were over a hundred such packages, evenly spaced, taking up most of the floor of the cargo bay.

A lump caught in Ando's throat. He sensed a silence that should not be.

These people who were so kind to him, who fed him and Tomoko when money and transportation failed, who offered friendship to two lonely travelers, who treated Tomoko as the fever took hold, who consoled him when it won, who gave him a job and a warm place to stay when he had nowhere else to go. Now they lay on the cold, swaying deck of a freighter travelling further from home. Many of the faces lay uncovered, and he recognized them, if not by name then by kindness. They lay as tranquil as Tomoko, hibernating through the worst of times, waiting for whatever came next.

Then there were others, twisted, not whole, blankets covering appendages that refused to lay flat, empty spaces where heads should have been. These, too, had offerings. Innuit carvings, a pair of snowshoes, a video game, books and letters tied by wire fluttering in the sea wind as it reached deep into the space.

"Let him down here." Tara's voice was soft, hushed as in a temple. It disappeared in the vast emptiness. Ando knelt, glad to release the weight but certain he bore a new one he could never put down. Tara rolled the body over. The nose pressed sideways, one cheek flat. She found a blanket and covered it, tucking the edges underneath. "Someone will know who this is."

"You're not worried about contamination, about the Plague?" he asked.

"No." She walked away.

"Why didn't you throw them overboard?" He called after her.

Her words disappeared in the vast darkness. "Everyone is someone's family."

Ando became an everyman, helping others with odd jobs. He never stopped thinking about Tomoko. With such a small crew, the amount of work kept his mind off everything else – the journey, the others, the Eaters. He visited her each night, but he slept in his own bunk.

His tasks took him to every corner of the ship. The bitter cold chewed at him whenever his work took him above deck, but he hated even more being sent below. Those large spaces weren't meant for human habitation. Cargo didn't care about the tons of water slithering by on the other side of the hull. It didn't see things lurking behind pipes and doors. It didn't feel the chill of the wind that somehow found its way into even the most secure spaces. Most of all, cargo didn't fear the dead.

At first, he thought the ship was haunted. Hard surfaces reflected voices from the shadows, whispers swirling from nowhere, going nowhere. He caught glimpses of movement where no one should be. Dark forms watched from within even darker shadows. When he opened a door or came around a corner, he heard the scurry of feet ahead of him, on the edge of darkness, far too large for any rat. He found things in the strangest places, the bones of birds picked clean, a sock left hanging over a conduit, defecation beneath abandoned steel plates. He wondered if he was losing his mind, or if Tomoko was trying to tell him something.

Tomoko. What do I fear?

He refused to tell Tara or the others what he saw or heard, afraid of what it might mean. Was this how it began, the sickness? Were these hallucinations brought on by a fever? Did the strike to his head do more damage than he thought?

Meanwhile the small crew of six pushed on with their duties, too sad to speak when together, too tired to stay awake after the evening meal. He recognized it in himself first, the hollowed out emotions of survival, a consequence of losing almost everyone at once. Buried in his work, he didn't ask questions, didn't want to think, didn't want to feel. He tried not to wonder what happened to the rest of the living.

And then he saw one.

Ando stood near the bodies, sweeping snow away from the interior doors. Above him, blowing snow drifted through a gap in the cargo hatch. The Captain insisted on keeping it open a crack. He said it let the cold air in to preserve the bodies until he figured out what to do with them. Until then, the meager light that entered the chamber had the added benefit of reassuring the crew, even at night, that there were no resurrections.

He put down the broom, his fingers too stiff to hold it. He tore off his thin work gloves to ball them up, letting the palms warm his fingers. He sat on the floor, broom across his lap, pouring a cup of hot tea from a thermos, wrapping his fingers around the cup.

Whispers coiled around him like steam. His head snapped up, scanning the mass of bodies. Nothing moved, but one lump billowed higher than the others.

Then it stood up.

Scalding liquid sloshed over his hands as he scrambled to his feet. He cursed, gripping the broomstick and thrusting it ahead of him.

To his surprise, the figure did not approach, did not purr, did not reach out with stiff arms to crack the nut holding his brain.

It ran away.

He heard the soft pad of footsteps retreating into the deep dark and then silence. He was again alone.

That night over dinner, he asked what it could mean. No one spoke. Soft chewing and the scrape of steel utensils on plates did a poor job of filling the void, and he almost regretting having asked at all.

"They're shells," Tara said through a mouthful. "Leave them alone."

He pieced it together for himself.

No family remained intact. Most fell together, locked in a room or in close proximity to someone who turned. The horror of seeing loved ones attack each other, fighting back, tearing each other apart, feeding on the remains, was too much for the minds of kind people.

The survivors absconded from humanity. They hid away in remote areas, behind pressure locked doors, steel bolts, sturdy bulkheads, and barricades. They took their meals alone. They slept in hiding. When necessity forced them to cross paths, they watched each other for sickness like starved jackals.

He seldom came across them, but he recognized the signs. He knew what areas to avoid, territory staked out by the lone wolves. Septic remains warned him away long before his eyes did. When he kept his distance and waited, he sometimes caught a glimpse of them, watching, arms raised, mouths open, civilization forgotten.

Someone had been leaving them food and water. No longer afraid, he volunteered for that task. It was the least he could do for the few survivors he owed so much.

He listened, now, to the whispers, internalized them, tried to make sense of them. Snippets of tortured thoughts scraped free of parched throats, paranoid reflections on the Captain's wild theories, sobs and screams, entreaties of nightmares relived, again and again, sibilant speeches told to ghosts in the night.

I feel them, in my DNA.

Look! Look!

No! Please!

Let me tell you a bedtime story, the story my mother told me.

He thought they didn't communicate with each other, but he was wrong. The taps and sighs and whispers that he earlier mistook for normal ship sounds served as a complex pattern of communication. The survivors kept their distance, but placed their mouths close to pipes and vents and spoke for whoever might hear in what became a daily affirmation of sorts. Words coursed through the veins of the ship, bleeding out into the empty spaces, lapped up by the socially starved, empty of nutrients.

Dark words in the night rang hollow as a single human life in the history of time.

They feared the plague, mourned their losses, worried about survival and getting too close, yet one theme recurred, interlaced through multiple discourses, reinforced through repetition, the morpheme foundation of their sacred language.

Tara.

Her lightening dispatch of Old Mike, her battle prowess aboard ship, her sanity which remained strong even as theirs faltered, created in their mind a demi-god, one of swift vengeance, a dealer of last rights to those unfortunate enough to succumb, something to dread.

How do you feel today?

Not poor enough to seek Paija's Little Helper.

Paija's Little Helper. That was Tara, thanks to Old Mike's final words. Beautiful in deliverance, impenetrable as a whiteout, merciful as ice. They built her up, those whispers below decks, opinions gathering like dry leaves in a gulley, until she became more than human, more than something born of this plane. A wraith. A banshee. The angel of death.

Tara rarely went below decks, and the Captain never assigned her work there. The one time she did, the walls echoed with screams as if a lion had entered the monkey house.

Driven to madness on this journey, they would never be whole again.

They frightened him even more, these voices, now that he knew the source. Ghosts and superstition were something he could ignore. These were people, like him. Like thumbing through a travel catalog of Hell, they reminded him that people lived in places he might visit soon.

And sometimes, when he was alone, he heard himself whispering, too.

"We need a healing." The Captain's voice over the comm sounded tinny and distant. "It's time to give them a burial at sea."

He announced it at dinner. Ando, not knowing what was involved in a sea burial, assumed planning would begin in the morning. Instead, once decided, the ship came alive again. The crew collected up white sheets and ropes to bind the bodies, even tearing linens from their own bunks. It was a chance to do something for others, a distraction from the misery of survival. It made them feel alive again.

When they descended to the lower deck, almost every survivor was already there, puffing out the candles, clearing away the totems, and tidying up the dead. The Captain's words had reached them wherever they hid, and now they made ready to say their goodbyes.

After bringing the supplies down, Ando stood apart. Not knowing any of the dead personally, he felt awkward taking part in the rituals around him. Caught up in the emotion, he understood the powerful urge for closure.

Tomoko. Do you want me to let you go?

"I thought you wanted her cremated?" the Captain's voice asked. "You insisted on it. We had to restrain you. What gives?"

He didn't answer. Despite Japanese custom, he could not bring himself to burn his wife. He'd known her longer dead than alive, lain beside that perfect skin too many nights to see it harmed. He loved her too much.

Married to a dead girl, a funeral is a divorce.

The ceremony took place that night. The wind cooperated, itself dying, leaving a frigid, starlit night over a glassy black sea. The Captain even agreed to come down to officiate.

Though the rest of the bodies were wrapped and tied in cloth, for Tomoko they built a coffin. He couldn't let her slip into that dark, cold water. He sealed the seams as watertight as possible, adding foam sheets around the bottom like a protective boat. They painted the casket white and cut a hole in the lid, fitting a piece of glass over it. If she opened her eyes, she would see the sky.

Better to let her roam under the Northern Lights forever in the last pristine place on earth.

Tara helped carry her from her resting place.

She was as beautiful as ever.

They laid her in the coffin, head to the north. Beside her, he placed six coins.

"What are those for?" Tara asked.

"The Boatman."

"Like the Egyptians?"

"We have a similar belief in Japan. She will take one of three crossings to the underworld," he said. "By bridge, if she lived a good life. By ferry if she was average. If she sinned, she will wade through snake infested water."

The Captain said, "The Northwest Passage is sometimes known as the Arctic Sea Bridge."

"Good," Ando said.

He left his dead cell phone beside her where she could read his texts and know that he loved her.

They placed the lid on the casket, sealing the seams.

Ando did not feel grief. He felt love. He smiled, knowing he was sending her on a journey, one he could not take. Someday he would find her, and they would travel together.

With a brush and black paint, he spelled out an elaborate name on the lid, despite her young age. He explained to Tara, "We rename the dead so they will not return when we call them."

"That's a long name."

"It's best to be certain."

He never practiced Buddhism. He attended the funeral of his grandparents, where the Buddhist rituals prevailed, but he didn't know the proper sutra. He said his own goodbye, silent as a prayer.

Tomoko. You have been a good wife to me. I have loved you, and I will continue to love you until we are reunited. I will stay in this world, but it is a hard world, and I am glad you are spared its hardship. Please wait for me where you are going. I will carry your memory with me in this one. It won't be long. Eternity waits for our happiness.

They say the sound of soil striking a coffin provides a measure of closure, and when Ando heard the coffin strike the water, he felt that chapter of his life close. It disappeared before reemerging and righting itself on the surface.

Concentric circles rippled outward, disturbing a congregation of stars. Tomoko floated in the center of the universe. No earth or sun or moon. Just a ship and her casket, pure as an iceberg, floating in a celestial sphere.

The Captain produced a prayer book and read from it as he paced behind the mourners.

> *Corinthians 15: For since by man*
> *came death, by man came also the*
> *resurrection of the dead...*

The murmurs of the survivors almost drowned out his voice, as one mourner wept. They watched, incredulous, the mystic ties of their world shattered.

Tara broke down, fell to her knees beside Buck's body, one hand on the sheet, the other gripping Fifty's massive arm. She wept for more than one man. She wept, Ando realized, for the lost. This funeral honored more than the bodies on deck. It honored those who lay forgotten, those whose circumstance prevented a proper burial, those left behind on the cold ground, even those who still wandered.

She, the Angel of Death, Paija's Little Helper, wept for them all. In the eyes of those below decks, she became a mortal.

The healing could begin.

> *Behold, I shew you a mystery; We*
> *shall not all sleep, but we shall all be*
> *changed, in a moment, in the*
> *twinkling of an eye, at the last trump:*
> *for the trumpet shall sound, and the*
> *dead shall be raised incorruptible, and*
> *we shall be changed...*

One by one, the bodies tilted up and over the side, dropping like rice through the night into the darkness below.

> *...So when this corruptible shall have put on incorruption, and this mortal shall have put on immortality, then shall be brought to pass the saying that is written:*
> *Death is swallowed up in victory.*

Long after the last body fell, after the tears froze on the wind, after the others went below, Ando stood on the deck with his eyes to the north. He could still make her out, drifting away on a slate black sea, the purity of ice in an iceless ocean, a white braille period at the end of the world.

He recalled his last words before the Captain retreated to his fortress in the sky. "Do me a favor. Rename the ship."

Two weeks later, on April 3rd, the Tomoko arrived in Shanghai.

They had long since shed their parkas. Even in April, the air grew hot.

The harbor filled with sloops and transports of every kind. Tankers and cruise liners anchored beside sailboats and trawlers. Even a seaplane found solace in the smooth, toxic mouth of the Yangtze River. There were small islands of barrels tied together with survivors lashed atop them. Shipping containers buoyed by inflatable tires. An old masted ship. Anything that could remain afloat long enough to reach Shanghai, had. So many ships crowded the bay, one could walk across them to reach dry land. Many did.

Tara shaded her eyes. "I guess we weren't the only ones who got the message."

The noise was terrific. Chains and halyards, hulls and doors, shouts and cries, gulls and waves. It sounded like a pot menders convention. A sinkhole opening up beneath a Turkish bazaar would not have echoed more. "It's enough to wake the dead!" Tara said. No one laughed. "Har har har."

Many refugees entreated to be brought on board, especially from the more rickety boats. They ran along the lines of "you have such a big ship, with so few people." These the Captain denied, and no one argued with him. Fortunately, the air of anticipation kept everyone civil. Rebuffs were met with smiles and waves. No attempts were made to scale the hull or invade the ship. Better times were days away. No one felt like fighting.

The air filled with the odor of cooking from every continent and the chatter of a hundred languages.

Shanghai glistened in the sunlight. Any damage the Plague might have caused wasn't visible from out here. Ando laughed. "The last time I was in Shanghai, the smog was so thick you couldn't see the next block. Four months without factory smoke and look how beautiful the city is. I guess some good has come of it."

Even after arriving, the people below decks never came out to see the sun. If anything, the noise outside made them more nervous. The survivors became, essentially, a crew of eight. Tara, Fifty, Ando, the Captain, and four others.

The boat people gossiped freely. They had their own interpretations of the cure, what it was, who made it, how it would be delivered. The stories varied so wildly, conflicted so heavily, that it was impossible to believe any single theory. The only factor they had in common was the core information. Come to Shanghai on April 5th. In a world with so little concrete information, this message alone drew crowds.

The myriad theories disturbed Ando. He interpreted the Chinese broadcast one way. Chinese, being a language filled with metaphor, homilies, and ancient meanings, could be interpreted many ways. He spoke Chinese, but not as a native. The theories he heard from native speakers were vastly different from his own. Would the Captain have been so interested in China if he'd heard these interpretations instead? Would Buck have encouraged the whole village to go? Ando's poor interpretation initiated this trip, or at least ignited the schemes of dreamers. Had he translated it wrong? Was his poor translation responsible for the death of Churchill?

The Captain, for his part, embraced all theories as having a modicum of truth, and he decided for himself which parts were true. He even made up a few of his own, and prided himself when the gossips came back with one he started. He was in his element here.

There were rumors that the city of New Pudong rose on the ashes of the old one. A certain Mr. X ruled there, keeping a civilized society behind walls of barbed wire. Mr. X broadcast an open invitation to the boat people to come ashore to live in New Pudong, to build a new China.

Tara wanted to know why no one went ashore now. The gossips reassured her, Shanghai wasn't safe. Still overrun by millions of Eaters, or Jianxi as the Chinese called them, entering the city meant certain death. With a strong scope, one could see them wandering the streets in hordes, congregating around buildings hiding survivors.

Tara made it clear she didn't want to wait. She wanted to get in there, start the killing, maybe even make a few rescues.

She didn't have to wait long. Today was the Clear Brightness Festival. Whatever that brought, it would happen soon.

An adjacent group of boat people from Northern China beckoned to be brought onboard. The Captain agreed, and lowered the crane.

They were tall, and friendly. They brought baskets of food – sweet green rice balls, peach blossom porridge, crispy cakes, snails, and eggs. One who spoke English told them the tradition. "As prescribed by Chong'er, Duke Wen of Jin, you must eat this food cold."

They ate the food together on the monstrous deck overlooking the harbor. It was a singular view, boats as far as the eye could see, the skyscrapers of Shanghai beyond. They were quite an international crowd. Chinese, Canadian, Dene, Japanese, American, all chatting in English, every one of them in a good mood.

Tara leaned over to Aldo. "It reminds me of the 4th of July in the States. One big cookout while everyone waits for the fireworks."

Ando liked the food, but something about the conversation disturbed him. "Chong'er," he said aloud. "Now I remember the whole story."

"What story?"

"I've been thinking about the Chinese broadcast. It's strange that they used the term Clear Brightness Festival and not Tomb Sweeping Day."

"You have a theory of your own?"

"Qingming is Tomb Sweeping Day, the time to remember and care for the dead. But Clear Brightness Festival is much older. Later on, it merged with Qingming."

"What are you saying?"

"Over two thousand years ago, Prince Chong'er was forced into exile after multiple assassination attempts. He wandered for 19 years with only his servant, and the servant remained faithful to his lord. When they were short on food and near starvation, the servant made his lord a broth with a piece of meat carved from his own thigh."

"Ew."

"When the Prince returned and became Duke, he wanted to repay the servant, but he couldn't locate him. The servant had disappeared into a forest. An advisor told the Duke, 'Set fire to the forest, and the servant will be smoked out.'

"The Emperor set fire to the forest, but the servant did not come out."

"What happened?"

"The servant burned alive in the fire."

No one spoke. The party paused, fingers raised to their mouths, minds grasping at straws.

Tara put down her rice ball. She looked out at Shanghai for a moment, as if seeing it for the first time. "You mean..."

"Maybe it isn't a cure. Maybe it's..."

"...an extermination." Tara leapt to her feet. "Captain! Get this boat up and running! We need to put in some distance!"

The Captain chewed on a rice ball. "We're hemmed in by dozens of ships. The only way out is over them. We're not going anywhere."

"This isn't a cure, it's an annihilation. The Eaters in the city... they're going to be wiped out."

"Isn't that what we're here for?"

Ando pointed to the sky. "Too late."

Tara looked up. "Fireworks."

Three cylindrical objects approached the city from three directions, leaving boiling contrails in their wake. Too fast for commercial airliners, it took only a moment to recognize what they were. As they converged over Pudong, Ando said again, "Not the cure. The solution."

Fifty tackled Tara, pushing her back into the wheelhouse and closing the door just as three nuclear suns bloomed over the glass towers of Shanghai.

Ando stared at them, rooted to the spot, happy to die. Whatever waited for him in the afterlife, he wanted to see it, eyes wide open.

I'm coming, Tomoko. We can be together.

The blast cloud spread down and out, like the bottom of a bowl, settling over the city and then expanding out toward the bay. The shockwave rolled over the ship, shoving it against the others. Fragile crafts overturned or broke apart under the pressure. Rust chips and paint blew like shrapnel.

Ando couldn't see a thing. A white light hovered in front of him, fading at the edges, as darkness fought its way in.

The hollow pounding as steel ships collided competed with the crackling splinter of fiberglass boats caught in between. Screams and shouting rose over the splash of a sudden surf. The deck vibrated as feet ran past him.

His body stabilized, no longer rocking with the ship. The wind died. White light surrounded him, warmed him. He smelled ozone, like the scent of the first spring rains on a country road.

Is this what heaven smells like?

Tara's voice filtered through to his ears. "Ando, what did you see?"

The white image faded, dancing away, smaller and smaller until eternal darkness remained.

Tears mixed with blood streamed from around his white orbs.

"Nothing," he said, wiping his open eyes with the dirty back of his hand. "I saw nothing."

He waited for sight to return. He turned toward the sound of her voice, heard her gasp. "Your eyes!"

He stood still, like a statue waiting to be carved. He wondered who she was talking to.

All the world was darkness, yet he was still alive.

Disappointment hollowed him out. He expected, desired, death. Blind and cursed with life, he wondered what he could possibly hope for.

Then he blinked.

THE END

For all that was
But is no more
Requiem
If we start again
Let it be in
Love not defiance
Joy not revenge
Grace not anger
Relief not fatigue
Grateful

Acknowledgements

A book is a journey, and I've traveled with some wonderful people. A special thank you goes out to all of you who helped with the making of Dust Eaters.

Dust Eaters Trailer
Judy Golden, Keith Chernin, Chad Rupnarine, Preston Vismala

Dust Eaters Video Game
Jill Calouro and J.L. Calouro of Crazy Robot Games

Kickstarter Dust Eaters Video Game Backers
Carol Guthe Straughn, Frank Schlesinger, Juan S. Lopez, Charles Pastor, CDSAfghan, Phillip Ada, Rickman, Judy Golden, Pegasus Organs, Mark Hurst, Zeb Leatherman, Scott Bock, Shiouwan Ho, Remy Stieglitz, Arman Bostani, Vivian Chu, Jesse Munning, Rebecca So, Myung Eun Jung, Andrey Kustarnikov, Sumita Rao, Hong Jin, Jan Colbert, Kyle Wooten, Dennis Barrios

Essential Supporters
Fellow authors Mary Fan and Emma Larkins, Youn Jung Kim and everyone at the Asian American Film Lab, Liling Tan and Ira Spitzer with CCTV, Don Conway, Michael Sargent, Jim Harris at G&H Soho for printing, and finally Sam and Marc-Andre for making Churchill real.

"Bronzed Compass Rose with Shadow" on cover by Deviantartist prettywitchery

Thank you for reading Dust Eaters!

Please leave a quick review wherever you bought
Dust Eaters. I read them. I live for them.
And let me know! I always respond to personal
emails. Write to: **ronancray@gmail.com**

If this book had a soundtrack, it might sound like
the **Dust Eaters Playlist** on my Youtube channel.
Don't forget to Subscribe!

Find me on Social Media:
Instagram: **@ronancray**
Twitter: **@ronancray**
Facebook: **RonanCray**
Youtube: **RonanCray**
Pinterest: **ronancray**

On Pinterest, you'll find photos that inspired and
informed the locations found in my books.

See all this and more at my website:
www.ronancray.com

Stay tuned for **DUST EATERS EAST**, due out 2017.
Meanwhile, read **RED SAND**. Again.

Cheers!
Ronan Cray

ABRASAX

CPSIA information can be obtained
at www.ICGtesting.com
Printed in the USA
LVOW12s0210291116
514785LV00001B/308/P